# GIFT OF HONOR
### Knights Of Honor
### Book Eight

## Alexa Aston

Copyright © 2018 by Alexa Aston
Print Edition

Published by Dragonblade Publishing, an imprint of Kathryn Le Veque Novels, Inc

All rights reserved. No part of this book may be used or reproduced in any manner whatsoever without written permission, except in the case of brief quotations embodied in critical articles or reviews.

## Books from Dragonblade Publishing

*Dangerous Lords Series* by Maggi Andersen
The Baron's Betrothal

*Also from Maggi Andersen*
The Marquess Meets His Match

*Knights of Honor Series* by Alexa Aston
Word of Honor
Marked by Honor
Code of Honor
Journey to Honor
Heart of Honor
Bold in Honor
Love and Honor
Gift of Honor

*Legends of Love Series* by Avril Borthiry
The Wishing Well
Isolated Hearts
Sentinel

*The Lost Lords Series* by Chasity Bowlin
The Lost Lord of Castle Black
The Vanishing of Lord Vale
The Missing Marquess of Althorn

By Elizabeth Ellen Carter
Captive of the Corsairs, *Heart of the Corsairs Series*
Revenge of the Corsairs, *Heart of the Corsairs Series*
Shadow of the Corsairs, *Heart of the Corsairs Series*
Dark Heart

*Knight Everlasting Series* by Cassidy Cayman
Endearing
Enchanted
Evermore

*Midnight Meetings Series* by Gina Conkle
Meet a Rogue at Midnight, book 4

*Second Chance Series* by Jessica Jefferson
Second Chance Marquess

*Imperial Season Series* by Mary Lancaster
Vienna Waltz
Vienna Woods
Vienna Dawn

*Blackhaven Brides Series* by Mary Lancaster
The Wicked Baron
The Wicked Lady
The Wicked Rebel
The Wicked Husband
The Wicked Marquis
The Wicked Governess

*Highland Loves Series* by Melissa Limoges
My Reckless Love
My Steadfast Love

*Clash of the Tartans Series* by Anna Markland
Kilty Secrets
Kilted at the Altar
Kilty Pleasures

*Queen of Thieves Series* by Andy Peloquin
Child of the Night Guild
Thief of the Night Guild
Queen of the Night Guild

*Dark Gardens Series* by Meara Platt
Garden of Shadows
Garden of Light
Garden of Dragons
Garden of Destiny

*Rulers of the Sky Series* by Paula Quinn
Scorched
Ember
White Hot

*Highlands Forever Series* by Violetta Rand
Unbreakable

*Viking's Fury Series* by Violetta Rand
Love's Fury
Desire's Fury
Passion's Fury

*Also from Violetta Rand*
Viking Hearts

*The Sons of Scotland Series* by Victoria Vane
Virtue
Valor

*Dry Bayou Brides Series* by Lynn Winchester
The Shepherd's Daughter
The Seamstress
The Widow

# Table of Contents

Prologue .................................................................... 1
Chapter 1 .................................................................. 7
Chapter 2 ................................................................ 14
Chapter 3 ................................................................ 22
Chapter 4 ................................................................ 33
Chapter 5 ................................................................ 43
Chapter 6 ................................................................ 51
Chapter 7 ................................................................ 58
Chapter 8 ................................................................ 66
Chapter 9 ................................................................ 73
Chapter 10 .............................................................. 84
Chapter 11 .............................................................. 95
Chapter 12 ............................................................ 104
Chapter 13 ............................................................ 111
Chapter 14 ............................................................ 120
Chapter 15 ............................................................ 129
Chapter 16 ............................................................ 136
Chapter 17 ............................................................ 146
Chapter 18 ............................................................ 154
Chapter 19 ............................................................ 166
Chapter 20 ............................................................ 175
Chapter 21 ............................................................ 184
Chapter 22 ............................................................ 193
Chapter 23 ............................................................ 204
Chapter 24 ............................................................ 213
Chapter 25 ............................................................ 222
Epilogue ................................................................ 228
About the Author ................................................. 234

# PROLOGUE

*Whitley Castle—1371*

ELINOR SWAN OPENED her eyes, not sure where she was. She glanced around the darkened chamber and remembered that Eunice had lifted her from her bed last night when the bedclothes around her were wet and cold. The servant told Elinor to stay here and sleep while her mother birthed the new babe.

But no one had come to wake her this morning. Had her mother already given birth?

Elinor wished she understood more about birth but she was only six. Eunice told Elinor when she grew older, her mother would explain everything to her and it would make perfect sense.

Twice before, her mother had grown large, her belly swelling, along with her face and feet. She'd promised Elinor both times that soon she would have a new brother or sister to watch over. Yet, Elinor heard the servants whispering about the babe being stillborn. If a babe still wanted to be born, why didn't it show up? Elinor could tell that it wasn't hiding in her mother's belly any longer until it was safe to come out. Maybe that's what made her mother weep so much.

Last year, Elinor overheard Eunice telling someone that the baroness had lost another babe—but how could a small babe be lost? Where did it go? Was it lost inside and couldn't find its way out? Her mother's belly hadn't even grown large that time. Elinor wondered if her mother might be broken inside because no babe ever appeared.

It was so confusing and no one explained anything to her. Ever. They patted her on the head and sent her on her way, shushing her when she asked a question. She'd learned to keep quiet around their servants because she wouldn't learn anything from them.

Elinor wished she could ask her father. He knew everything. He was smart. Handsome. Powerful. Elinor couldn't help but be afraid of him, though. Any time she found herself in his presence, she tried to make herself small and not bring any attention her way. Yet, she longed for him to notice her. Talk to her. Pull her onto his lap. Tell her stories. Tickle her. She craved attention and never received any.

She thought her mother might have loved her when she was tiny. But each time no babe came, her mother grew weaker and saw her daughter less than before. It was as if the baroness had lost interest in Elinor as time passed. And Father was always with his soldiers—training, talking, drinking—never bothering to glance her way. She couldn't remember him ever speaking to her or calling her by name. It was as if she didn't exist for him.

In that moment, Elinor realized how lonely she was. One parent was too sick for her while the other one ignored her. She had no siblings. No one to play with. She angrily brushed away a falling tear and got out of bed. She was a big girl. She could make herself useful. That might gain her some attention. Then her parents might decide they loved her.

More than anything in world, Elinor wanted to be loved.

She realized she could start by helping her mother birth this new babe. She would make sure it didn't get lost or misplaced this time. Everyone would think she was so clever and praise her for helping the babe to come live with them at Whitley. Excited by this idea, she dressed quickly and left the bedchamber. Creeping down the hallway, she stopped in front of the door to the chamber where she slept with her mother each night.

The door was closed. For some reason, fear filled her. She raised her hand to open the door but lost the courage to do so. Her hand fell back to her side.

"I can do this," she told herself, determined to help her mother and gain a brother or sister in the process. Standing tall, she nudged open the door and peered inside as a guttural moan began. It sounded like a wounded animal that had been caught in a trap for many hours. Then the groaning increased in intensity and turned into a full-blown, bloodcurdling scream. The sound bounced off the stone walls and continued to echo in Elinor's head even after it died down.

It came from her mother.

The baroness was lying in the bed they shared, surrounded by several women who fussed over her. Her mother's hair was plastered to her head and her face was unnaturally white. Sweat soaked her bed gown. She thrashed around, moaning again, before her scream pierced the air once more. This time when it ended, she collapsed against the pillows, sobbing.

From listening to the servants, Elinor had learned her mother needed to provide Whitley with a son and heir. But it pained her to watch her mother in this effort. She caught the uneasy glances the women surrounding the bed gave one another. Elinor's chest tightened. Panic set in.

Wordlessly, she closed the door and leaned against the wall, her breath coming in spurts. Her heart pounded viciously, each beat driving the fear that threatened to swallow her whole. She couldn't get the awful image out of her mind, seeing her mother helpless and in agony, with no one able to relieve her pain.

Elinor never wanted to have a babe if it meant doing what she had just seen. In that moment, she understood she would never be able to marry. Wives had children—and Elinor wanted nothing to do with that.

Instead, she fled downstairs to the great hall where people were breaking their fast. She sneaked toward the dais and took a seat on the end. Her father sat in the center, chewing thoughtfully on a piece of bread he tore from a loaf placed before him. She wondered if he even knew his child was being born upstairs and how much his wife suffered.

Elinor only hoped this child didn't get lost like the others. She wanted to help with the babe. She couldn't feed it. But she could bathe it. Play with it. Spend time with it. Even love it. If she took care of it and showed what a good girl she was, then her parents would be proud of her. They would want to love her.

No one brought her anything to eat or drink since the meal was almost over, so she sat and watched the others present, not daring to glance at her father. Looking across the filled room, she saw the serfs who worked the land at Whitley. The servants who kept the keep running smoothly and efficiently. The soldiers who guarded the estate and were sworn to protect the Baron of Nelham and the entire Swan family.

Movement near the doorway caught her eye. Elinor saw Eunice and another servant hovering in it, standing close together. One held a bundle in her arms. Eagerly, she sat tall. Was it the babe? Did they bring it to show her father? Mayhap, she could also hold it and wash it and dress it.

Disappointment filled her as the servant scurried away with the bundle, leaving Eunice to enter the great hall. Reluctantly, the old woman made her way to the dais. Elinor held her breath.

"My lord?"

"What?" her father snapped as the servant approached.

Eunice flinched. Swallowed hard. Elinor saw her red eyes and thought Eunice might have been crying. She bit her lip, not wanting to hear what the servant would share.

"My lord, I am here to tell you that—"

He held up his hand to silence her. "Let me guess. My wife failed—again—to give me a son. To give me, the Baron of Nelham, an heir."

The large room grew quiet at his raised voice. Elinor already winced at his harsh tone.

Eunice sighed. "It was a boy, my lord. He was stillborn."

The baron glared at the servant but she bravely continued. "And my lord, she . . . the baroness . . . she is gone."

"Gone?"

Elinor heard surprise in his voice even as tears filled her eyes, for she understood exactly what Eunice meant.

Her mother was dead. She would never come back. Ever.

"Gone?" he echoed.

"Aye, my lord," Eunice confirmed and bowed her head a moment.

Her father slammed his hands down on the oak table in front of him. A thick silence clung in the air.

"So, she is dead. She and the boy. My son."

Eunice nodded. "Shall I send for the priest?" she asked.

His lips curled in distaste. "I don't care what you do. I wash my hands of her, a worthless wife who gave me a lone girl child. What good is a girl?" he shouted. "No good at all. I have no need of her."

Tears stung Elinor's eyes. *She* was the girl child he spoke of so callously. The one he couldn't bring himself to even name. The one he had ignored ever since her birth.

She was nothing to him. Nothing.

He rose and looked across the great hall at those gathered. "You people can bury my wife and this lifeless babe. I have no use for the dead."

"And what of Lady Elinor?" asked Eunice boldly. "The poor girl just lost her mother."

"Well, she lost me, as well," her father replied. "I have no need to parent a female brat. I don't care if I ever see her again."

Elinor began to shake. She felt all the eyes in the room turn to gaze on her in pity.

"She's your daughter, my lord," Eunice insisted. "You must do right by her."

The baron rested his hands on the table and leaned toward the servant. "I have no son. Therefore, I have no child," he said, his voice low and deadly. "Do something with her. I never want to see her inside my keep again. Do you hear me?"

Elinor knew everyone present had heard. She froze as her father strode from the great hall without a backward glance. Immediately, voices broke out, buzzing in her head as a group of bees. Then her trembling grew out of control. Elinor shook so badly she feared she might pitch from her seat and embarrass herself. Pushing against the table, she stood on wobbly legs as she gripped it tightly for support.

Her mother was dead. She would never see her again. And that last terrible image of her trying to give birth kept rolling through her mind.

"Eunice?"

Elinor turned and saw a man standing in front of the dais, next to Eunice. Something passed between them. Eunice nodded as if in agreement before facing Elinor.

"Lady Elinor? Come here." The servant motioned her over.

Elinor was reluctant to release her grasp on the table. She forced her fingers to relax before she took the few steps to the edge of the dais.

The man stepped to meet her. Pale blue eyes in a tanned face the color of leather looked her over. His brown hair had bits of gold in it, as if he spent a lot of his time outdoors. He wasn't very tall and looked lean and wiry, so unlike her father and all of his soldiers.

"My lady," he said softly, "I live here at Whitley. I lost my wife and son years ago." He gave her a smile. "I've always wanted a daughter."

She looked at him, not sure why he told her this. Finally, she said, "I'm sorry you lost your family."

"I am sorry, too, for what has happened to you," he replied. "I could use a hand with my falcons. Would you like to come live with me and help me with my birds? I could teach you to be a falconer."

Elinor didn't know what a falconer was. She only saw the same sadness she felt inside reflected in this man's eyes. He said he needed help and she wanted to make herself useful.

Especially since her father never wanted to see her again.

Elinor nodded.

The man took another step toward her. "I am Jasper."

"I am Elinor."

He lightly grasped her waist and lowered her to the ground before taking her hand. As her hand rested in his, she drew comfort—and strength—from their contact.

Looking down at her, Jasper said, "You'll make a fine falconer, Elinor. Fine, indeed."

# CHAPTER 1

*The Midlands, England—17 November 1387*

HAL DE MONTFORT wished he was back at the royal court in London guarding the queen and her ladies-in-waiting instead of sitting at a camp in the Midlands. Waiting. All they seemed to do was wait, as they had for months now. He itched to do something. Go somewhere. Fight someone.

"Your turn, Hal."

He took the dice from another soldier and tossed them. Cheers broke out when they rolled to a stop.

"You won again, de Montfort," growled one of the Cheshire bowmen, a member of the king's royal guard, as Hal himself was. "If I didn't know you better, I would say you cheated us with your run of good luck."

"But everyone knows I am a de Montfort," Hal proclaimed smoothly, "and true to my oath of knighthood. I would never resort to loaded dice in order to win."

The soldiers gathered around the campfire nodded to themselves. Hal had his father to thank for his good name. Geoffrey de Montfort had been known throughout England as one of King Edward's foremost knights in the wars against France. A man known for his fighting skills as much as his word of honor, Geoffrey had passed along what he most valued to his three sons. Hal absorbed many lessons at his father's knee and had become a trusted knight in King Richard's court, guarding the monarch as had his brothers, Ancel and Edward.

But both brothers now led vastly different lives from Hal. Ancel, the eldest of the three boys, had married Margery Ormond six years ago and become the Earl of Mauntell. They lived at Bexley with their young children, Cyrus and Miranda. Ancel would one day inherit the de Montfort home, Kinwick Castle, and become its earl. Edward, knighted on the battlefield near Scotland, had been invited to join the royal guard and remained in it until he'd married Rosalyne Parry two years ago. Thanks to his thorough work on a secret mission for King Richard in Canterbury, the monarch allowed Edward to vacate his court assignment and return with Rosalyne to Kinwick. Upon the death of Rosalyne's uncle, Benedict Bowyar, Edward would be named Baron of Shallowheart. For now, the couple raised their young son and child-to-be at Kinwick.

Hal knew Rosalyne would have had the babe by now. She'd been due to deliver sometime in August. Hal had been on the road with the king's troops since early summer, though, and no missive had reached him with the news. He missed his family dreadfully even with the life he'd led in the various royal palaces, with a bevy of court beauties to charm and amuse him.

Life had grown dull once the king withdrew from London, angered first by the removal of his favorite, Chancellor Michael de la Pole, followed by Parliament appointing fourteen Commissioners to oversee the Crown's expenditures. Richard had dragged his army through the Midlands in order to rally supporters loyal to him. They had stopped at both Shrewsbury and Nottingham, where the royal courts at each place had given a resounding reaffirmation of the king's rights.

"Another round, Hal?"

He started to reach for the dice again when a man stepped in front of him. Hal raised his eyes and recognized one of the Cheshire bowmen.

"The king wishes to see you, de Montfort."

Hal collected his winnings and rose to his feet, handing the pair of dice to the nearest soldier. He was eager to see what the monarch might want. The group of bowmen from Cheshire had continued to act as the king's personal guards once they'd left the safety of the Palace of Westminster. Hal and the other knights who had been assigned to the queen's service and ordered to march with the royal army from London had not been involved with the king in any way. His curiosity grew as he followed the Cheshireman through the encampment. They weaved their way through men and horses until they reached the massive royal tent.

"You may enter." The bowman gave him a curt nod and retreated.

Hal pushed aside the flap of the tent and stepped inside. The luxurious surroundings made him think he might be back at court. Thick, Turkish rugs lay spread against the dirt of the ground. A large table of fine oak sat in the middle, with benches on both sides. He caught a whiff of roasted pheasant from the gold platter sitting on the table. Silver goblets inlaid with jewels rested next to it.

The king looked up from where he sat, a quill in hand and parchment before him. "One moment, Sir Hal." He dipped the quill in ink and went back to writing as Hal stood patiently.

He thought the royal tent would be filled to the brim with advisors. It always had been when Hal and Edward accompanied their father when the royal army fought the Scots. Geoffrey de Montfort had been one of the king's military advisors and he had insisted that his two sons be allowed to witness the strategy sessions as they unfolded. Hal became used to seeing a multitude of men crammed inside the royal tent, as well as several servants scurrying around. Tonight, only one servant sat in a corner, a needle in hand as he mended an item of clothing sitting in his lap.

Looking back, Hal watched the king lightly sprinkle fine sand across what he'd written before he rolled up the parchment after a moment. Placing warm wax along the fold, Richard affixed his personal seal and then set the missive aside.

The king looked weary. Dark circles under his eyes aged him well beyond his twenty years. Hal thought Richard might be missing his wife. The monarch and Queen Anne's great love for one another was hardly a secret. Hal surmised he had been summoned to discuss bringing the queen north after the couple's separation of several months. The queen favored Hal among the men who guarded her and the king would know that—and trust Hal to bring his wife safely from London.

The monarch stood and moved away from the desk. Hal bowed to the younger man and was told to rise.

"Sit," Richard commanded. He motioned to the lone servant, who sprang up and poured them both generous cups of wine, handing one to the king and then to Hal before retreating from the tent altogether.

"Do you know why I've asked you here?"

"No, sire." Hal waited while the king swirled his wine and sipped it thoughtfully.

"Ah. At least the French have learned how to do one thing right." He took a deep swallow and then continued. "I remembered how your brother did me a great service regarding the wall being built at Canterbury."

"Aye, your highness. Edward was pleased that he was able to serve you in that matter."

"The incident unveiled how the Crown was being cheated," the king said before dabbing his mouth with a cloth. "And Sir Edward negotiated for the wall to continue construction for another dozen years without it costing my royal treasury a single pence."

Richard dropped the cloth on the table and steepled his fingers, studying Hal. "Both your brothers have served me well. My early years as king were difficult ones because of my youth but Sir Ancel advised me without telling me how I must act. In doing so, he helped me mature and find my own way. Ancel had me use my mind as much as my heart and gut in making decisions."

He lowered his hands to the table. "And Sir Edward not only was clever enough to save my leaking treasury, he also brought Lady Rosalyne to court to paint my portrait and the queen's. When one of us eventually passes on, the other will have a precious piece that will allow us to always remember our loved one, thanks to Lady Rosalyne's ability to bring us both to life."

The king sighed. "Since your brothers—and your father—have been good friends to the Crown, I'd hoped you would be the same."

"Name anything you need done, your majesty," Hal told him. "I will see it happen."

"Good. 'Tis exactly what I wanted to hear from you." He paused. "What you hear now is for your ears alone. 'Tis why no one else is present at the moment." Richard rose and brought two rolled parchments back to the table and seated himself again.

Hal recognized one as the one the king labored over when he first arrived. He hadn't seen the other. Anticipation rippled through him as he waited for what the monarch would reveal to him.

"You know how the Lords Appellant rid me of my chancellor, waiting until my uncle, the Duke of Lancaster, left the country. They are angry they have fallen from royal favor and that I have appointed new, younger men to help me rule my kingdom."

Hal was certainly aware of the demands the Lords Appellant had made for the king to remove many of his councilors, claiming since Richard was still a minor by law that they, as a Council of Government, would rule in his stead until he came of age. It was the very reason the monarch fled their presence months ago, turning to the courts to assert his right to rule England as he saw fit.

"They are frightened by the opinions the judges rendered in my favor," the king continued. "Because of it, I received word that they have brought an *accusatio* against my allies and demand arrest of members of my royal court—those closest to me."

Hal had enjoyed his lessons in Latin and knew the king spoke of a formal appeal. And he knew that could mean only one thing between the king and the Lords Appellant.

*War.*

The sovereign's gaze remained steady as he met Hal's eyes. "Before the accusation, I had already sent word to two men, men who are my allies and would lay down their lives for me without question. My closest friend, Robert de Vere, secretly gathers troops for me, as does Sir Thomas Molineux de Cuerdale, the Constable of Chester. You know most of my royal guard comes from Cheshire and I look to Molineux and his enormous influence in the area to collect additional soldiers who will show their loyalty to me and the Crown in the weeks ahead."

Hal steeled himself. "Then what do you need of me, sire?"

"I need all the men they have assembled to join me in haste, Sir Hal. I have learned that my uncle, the Duke of Gloucester, has convinced the other four members of the Lords Appellant to mobilize their forces against me."

That would be a formidable group to face on the battlefield. Besides Gloucester, that meant that men under the command of the Earls of Warwick, Arundel, Nottingham, and Derby would combine their armies to march against the king. Richard had brought a small force with him from London but de Vere and Molineux would have to persuade many more men to join the king's side for the numbers to come close to being equal. Even then, Hal doubted those volunteering to fight for the king would be half as well trained as the soldiers marching under the banners of the Lords Appellant.

Richard handed him both parchments. "These are for de Vere and Molineux." He told Hal the general areas both men would be located near. "De Vere will need to march swiftly and join forces with Molineux before they meet up with my army. Together, I am confident we can defeat these usurpers."

The king gave Hal a grim smile. "Hide the missives and set out immediately."

Hal slipped both of the small scrolls up his left sleeve as both men rose. Richard put a hand on Hal's shoulder. "I am counting on you and your loyalty, Sir Hal."

"I will not disappoint you, sire," he told the monarch, his face brimming with confidence.

Leaving the tent, Hal's smile faded as he made his way through the camp to where his horse stood. The king was a fool if he thought his small army and whatever volunteers his friends could rouse would be able to defeat the soldiers brought to the fight by the Lords Appellant.

Each of the five noblemen were superb soldiers in their own right and well respected throughout England, while Richard was counting on his friend de Vere, who had no battle experience and had been accused of treason, to miraculously save him and his throne.

As he mounted his horse and set off to deliver the missives, Hal remembered how only an hour earlier he had been bored by the inactivity and lack of action these past few months. Now, his mission would bring about certain battle.

And he was almost guaranteed to be on the losing side.

Hal sped off into the night, wondering if his days on earth were numbered.

# CHAPTER 2

*Radcot Bridge—20 December 1387*

HAL GLANCED OVER at the Earl of Oxford as they road south to reunite with King Richard. De Vere had gathered an army of fifteen thousand, which marched behind them. As always, the earl sported a neatly trimmed beard and mustache and was meticulously dressed in midnight blue and gold under his armor. Tall and lean, he rode well in the saddle and had an air of excitement about him. But Hal knew the nobleman hadn't a clue how to manage a force this large and lead it into battle, much less get along with Sir Thomas Molineux, the other man Hal had visited in secret when he delivered the first of the king's two missives.

It alarmed him that while Molineux had taken the king's orders to raise an army to heart and enthusiastically gathered soldiers throughout the area, the five thousand troops Molineux provided for this effort had not all come along on this crusade willingly. After Hal found de Vere's location and Oxford assembled his army to march and link up with that of Molineux's, Hal learned that those not immediately agreeing to join in the fight on the side of the king had been forced into service by Sir Thomas.

And men who had no loyalty and were not invested in a cause?

*Those men could not be counted upon when swords began swinging and blood was spilled.*

Hal discovered there was little leadership and even less experience among the combined armies of men who headed toward Radcot Bridge, the only route available since their scouts had informed them that Earl of Arundel had blocked the most direct course. They would need to cross the bridge in order to rendezvous with the king and his men. Knowing that a good portion of these twenty thousand soldiers might bolt once they engaged in battle, Hal could only hope that he would come out of any upcoming conflict alive. To think that being on the king's side had suddenly become the wrong side was disheartening. Yet, he'd made a commitment to Richard and would serve him until the bitter end.

He couldn't help but wonder when that end might occur. After more than three hundred years of Plantagenet rule, the strong possibility existed that Richard could die in battle against the armies of the five Lords Appellant. If the king fell, he had no direct heir to take his place since Queen Anne had yet to provide any children in the course of their marriage. Hal imagined chaos ensuing, with a bloody, desperate fight for the throne.

A rider appeared on the horizon, galloping at breakneck speed. As he drew near, Hal recognized him as the last of the scouts sent out days ago.

"'Tis Renfred," he told de Vere, who looked frightened as the soldier approached. Sir Thomas merely grunted, his lips pursed.

De Vere held a hand up to halt the forward progress of their force. Moments later, the scout reached them, pulling his horse up in front of de Vere's.

"The Duke of Gloucester has changed direction," the man panted from exertion. "He's on the move, headed south, and made Derby his deputy."

Hal's gut clenched. This was the worst news possible. Henry Bolingbroke was the Earl of Derby and nephew to the Duke of Gloucester. At only twenty, Derby was cunning and capable. Hal would almost rather fight Gloucester than his daring, reckless, young nephew. It also didn't help that de Vere had recently repudiated his wife—who happened to be a cousin to Derby. The young earl would be out for blood, both de Vere's and any man who accompanied him.

Renfred drew in another breath and continued. "Derby and Nottingham have blocked off all routes crossing the Thames, my lord. They are camped between the twin bridges near Faringdon. When I left the area a few minutes ago, I overheard that Pidnell Bridge has already been demolished."

"And what of Radcot Bridge?" Hal asked when de Vere simply stared openmouthed at the scout.

The soldier shook his head. "Derby's men have Radcot Bridge under guard and were beginning to dismantle parts of it to prevent our troops from using it."

"What are we to do?" whispered de Vere, his body sagging in disbelief.

Hal seethed as he watched de Vere crumbling before his eyes. He glanced behind him and saw the hordes of soldiers listening in, watching Oxford's courage wilt. A low grumbling began to rise as the closest men to the front began spreading word of the situation to those behind them. Within minutes, Hal was certain that refusal to advance—if not outright desertion—would set in.

Wanting to fight but knowing failure would result upon contact, he leaned close to the commander. "My lord, we can find a different route to King Richard. We haven't nearly enough men to take on Derby and Nottingham, and those present are mostly ill-trained as soldiers. I advise you to turn now, while we still have time, else a slaughter will occur."

"But how will *I* reach my dearest Richard?" de Vere wondered aloud, not seeming to care what happened to the gathered mass of soldiers behind him.

Sir Thomas glared at the earl through narrowed eyes but kept silent.

Before Hal could intervene further, de Vere straightened his shoulders, determination filling him as he came to a decision. "Give the command to storm the crossing," he ordered.

Knowing the move to be a dreadful mistake, Hal reluctantly issued the order, listening as it was passed along the ranks. Hoping to encourage those around him, he made ready to charge ahead but halted when a loud roar came from his left. Turning, he saw Derby's colors flying in the wind, as a large group of reinforcements from the north now surrounded the fledging army. The men in front assembled quickly in close pike formation and surged toward the royalist group.

Before the action even began, de Vere and Molineux's men broke ranks. Some rushed toward the marsh that they had just marched around. Others fled in the direction of the river, thinking to swim it. The remainder froze, ready to surrender without a blow being struck. De Vere turned his horse in circles, panic written across his face. He gave a shout and took off in the direction of Pidnell Bridge.

Hal didn't bother to follow. Even if he could convince the young earl to return to his troops, the cobbled together royal army had decided not to stand with the king's representative. He glanced at Sir Thomas, who looked determined to fight despite the circumstances. Yet moments later, Molineux also took off like a bird in flight, racing toward the Thames.

Screams filled the air as those who'd run for the marsh began sinking in its mire. Men called out in terror as they began to be sucked under and drowned. Hal knew they were lost, as did those who had remained behind, not engaging with Derby's men.

Those left now faced Derby's army without a leader. Hal spied Henry Bolingbroke riding in his direction and realized it would be up to him to surrender in shame to the earl.

As Derby approached, Hal rode out toward the youngest of the Lords Appellant. They met halfway and halted their horses.

"My lord." Hal bowed his head in submission.

"De Montfort." Derby studied him. "So you were the king's errand boy, sent to gather this rabble." The handsome earl's smug words cut Hal to the quick. The nobleman was wholly in control of the situation and arrogant enough to be enjoying it.

"I don't suppose you would allow us to retreat," Hal ventured. "There are few of us left. We would pose no threat to you and your men."

"Nay, my lord," Derby responded. "You are canny enough to still find a way to lead these men to my cousin and unite with the royal army. I think not."

Hal thought the earl looked bored—and disappointed that no bloodshed had occurred.

"What would you have us do?" he asked, staring down the newest member of the Lords Appellant.

Derby met his eyes for a long moment then looked at the line of troops still standing there. "Lay down your arms, all of you that are left. Strip away any armor that you wear." The nobleman's voice carried across the cold, windless day.

At that command, Hal noted every man immediately responded to the authority and leadership before them. All forms of weaponry and armor began being tossed to the ground, the thud of steel and metal hitting the hard ground sounding like thunder rumbling in the distance.

When it finally grew quiet, Derby addressed the group again, shouting, "Return to your homes. I order you never to take up arms again in the king's name."

Disgust filled Hal. Without a single blow, the new army dissipated as men turned their backs and shuffled away from the scene.

Hal asked the nobleman, "And what should I do, my lord? You are aware that I am a member of the royal guard. I must return to see to the king's safety—even if he is to be locked away inside the Tower of London."

It surprised him when the earl dismounted and indicated for him to do the same. Hal threw a leg over and landed on the ground. He took a few steps toward Derby, who pulled his helm from his head. Hal followed suit. Up close now, he could see the nobleman's high cheekbones and calm brown eyes. Though he wore a beard, Hal still saw traces of the skin disease that disfigured a portion of Derby's face.

With an almost fatherly look, the earl said, "Nay, I cannot allow you to return to the king."

"What?" Hal had sworn an oath. Just because he had acted as the king's messenger, it was imperative for him to return to his duty.

"I have great respect for you, Sir Hal. The de Montfort name stands for loyalty. Bravery. The best of what England has to offer." A frown creased his brow. "I will confide in you that 'twill get ugly in the weeks ahead for my former playmate. I will do all I can to see that Richard keeps his head, for I have a deep and abiding love for my cousin. We spent a great deal of our childhood together since our fathers were brothers. I feel as close to Richard as a brother could, especially since we were admitted together to the Order of the Garter. Our bond is one which is unbreakable.

"But charges of treason will be issued by my uncle, Gloucester, and the other Lords Appellant. Executions and exile will occur for those closest to our king. You are a good man from what I know. I wouldn't wish to see you caught up in the nastiness of court politics."

"Are you saying there's to be a new king?" Hal demanded, wondering if the Lords Appellant would have the audacity to depose Richard. If they did, Henry Bolingbroke, the Earl of Derby, would be a strong contender to become that new ruler. Young, yet seasoned. Intelligent. Fearless. First cousin to the present king. If so, 'twould mean a new royal house and a new day for England.

Hal had always thought Richard foolish to play favorites and alienate the old guard at court. He wondered if it would come to the monarch losing not only his throne—but possibly his life.

"Let me protect you," Derby continued. "You—and my cousin—as best I can."

"You would do what?" Hal boldly asked, not wanting any favors from this enemy.

The young nobleman gave him a sad but determined look. "I will ask you, too, to lay down your weapons and not fight your way back to the king. As of this moment, you are no longer a member of the royal guard, Sir Hal. You have escaped that fate as your two brothers did before you."

When Hal failed to move, Derby said firmly, "Strip off your armor. Leave your weapons and even your horse. Go home, Hal. Go home."

Anger mixed with humiliation filled Hal as he proceeded to do as commanded, thousands of Derby's soldiers watching him silently from afar. He had dreamed of the very day he could leave the king's service but never thought it would happen in shame and disgrace. Defiance filled him as he told Derby, "I swore an oath to protect the king," and slammed his cuirass to the dirt.

"I tell you that time has passed. *I* will be the one to keep Richard safe from the other Lords Appellant."

"You would challenge your own uncle who leads this pack of wolves?" Hal shook his head. "Gloucester is more than twice your age, with plenty of courtiers in his corner."

"True," Derby admitted, "but above all, you must remember—I am my father's son. And not only the king's cousin," he said softly, "but also his friend."

Derby gave him a long look. "Despite what you believe, I ask that you trust me, de Montfort. Let the Lords Appellant draw their blood. Rid themselves of Richard's favorites, whom they consider their enemies. I will see my cousin is kept safe from harm." He paused and added, "I have already sent word abroad so that my father will return and help remedy this situation. You know in all these years since the old king's death, the Duke of Lancaster has stood by his nephew, the king. I promise you Father plans to do so again. And no matter what you think, I, too, still stand by Richard's side, despite having joined the Lords Appellant."

Hal considered Derby's words. Lancaster had never tried to usurp the throne during the ten years Richard had ruled as king. He had remained loyal while keeping the king's critics at bay. From what Hal knew of Derby, the young nobleman was also a man of his word, as his father, Lancaster, had always been.

Still, Hal chafed as he removed the last bit of armor and dropped it at his feet. He glanced at his sword lying forlornly on the ground, hating that he must give up the elegant steel that had been presented to him during his Oath of Knighthood Ceremony.

He bent and handed the sword to the man before him as his final concession.

"I pledge to return this to you one day, Sir Hal. For now, go home to your parents. When the time is right and our king returns to court, I will tell him to send for you. Your sword will await you, though I cannot guarantee that your place in the royal guard will."

"May I keep the baselard that rests within my boot? I am loath to undertake a long journey by foot with no protection from highwaymen."

Derby nodded. "You may." He placed a hand on Hal's shoulder. "I admire your courage and conviction. Please give my regards to Lord Geoffrey and Lady Merryn."

With that, the earl replaced his helm and remounted his horse. He reached for the reins of Hal's mount and rode toward the cheering troops. Hal stood and watched as orders were issued and the army turned from him and marched away. Though he longed to rush to the king's side, he had given his word to the earl. Above all, his own father had taught Hal that a man's word of honor must always take priority. His heart heavy, Hal turned south. Toward Kinwick.

*Toward home.*

# CHAPTER 3

*Whitley Castle*

EMPTINESS FILLED ELINOR as Jasper's words from yesterday echoed in her mind.

*"Your father is dead. The Baron of Nelham no longer can hurt you. You might finally be able to go home, Elinor."*

Numbly, she stirred the fire as she thought of the look of hope on Jasper's face when he broke the news to her. News that had meant nothing.

She barely remembered what her father looked like. A tall, vague shadow flitted through her mind but she could no longer see the face that went along with it. Elinor remembered he was large and loud and seemed magnificent whenever he entered a room yet she couldn't have told anyone what color his hair or eyes were or what his voice sounded like.

Too many years had passed since he'd banished her from the keep.

Each year on this very day, she would take the blade that Jasper had given her and carve a small notch into the trunk of a tree that stood near their cottage. It signified that she turned another year older. She could remember the date of her birth since it had happened two days after Christmas, which had recently passed. Now, her father had died the day after that holy day.

Elinor felt a deep void inside her at the news. She stood and retrieved her dagger from her boot. Not bothering to drape her extra tunic over her for warmth, she slipped from the cottage and went to the large oak tree, running her fingers over the notches from the previous years, counting aloud as she touched each one. Then she carved the latest into the trunk and stood back.

Ten and six notches in all. Ten and six years since she had been ordered from her home. That meant she had turned two and twenty.

Jasper did not know she kept track of the passing years in this manner. If it didn't concern his beloved raptors, he cared very little—except for Elinor. He'd taken responsibility for her long ago. She'd never been lavished with love by Jasper but at least he'd proven himself trustworthy to her, unlike her parents, who'd given her life and gone on with their own, her mother desperately trying to birth a boy while her father ignored both of them.

She said a prayer of thanksgiving to the Virgin for Jasper's care of her. Jasper felt it important that she continue to pray even though she had never attended mass in all the years since her exile. When she first came to him, he had said prayers with her each night before she fell asleep. Elinor had kept to the habit and found herself speaking to the Virgin occasionally, almost as if the Holy Mother watched over her.

That would change today. Jasper had insisted that they go to the funeral mass that would be said for the Baron of Nelham this morning in Whitley's chapel. For the first time in years, Elinor would be in the midst of others.

The thought frightened her.

She had sometimes seen other serfs and servants from afar but had never drawn close in order to speak to any of them. A few times, she had traipsed through the woods, trying to catch a glimpse of Jasper and their falcons when a hunt occurred. She'd caught glimpses of various nobles riding by so swiftly that their images blurred together. Even if they'd come to a halt, she doubted she would have recognized the man who sired her.

Elinor touched her fingers to the notches in the tree again, wondering if she would be here with Jasper this time next year. Or would she finally be allowed to return to the keep after all this time now that her father was dead?

She knew her father had never remarried because Jasper kept her informed of what he heard and saw when he went to the castle. Vaguely, Elinor remembered a cousin, a boy a few years older than she was, who had visited Whitley a few times. She supposed he would be the one to inherit the title and estate. It saddened her that she could not even remember his name.

The only person she still recalled clearly was Eunice. The woman had been a servant in the keep, someone Elinor's mother trusted. She recalled Eunice's face as she broke the news to the baron about the baroness' death and how there would be no heir. That was what had set off her father's rage.

Thank the Living Christ that Jasper had stepped forward to claim her, for if he hadn't? Elinor had no idea what would have become of her.

Shivering, she returned to the cottage and went to stand beside the fire. She shoved her hands close to the flickering flames, willing the warmth to fill her.

Jasper coughed and stirred from his pallet in the corner of the room. He sat up, sleepily rubbing his eyes, his sparse hair sticking out in several directions. Elinor stifled the laugh that threatened to bubble up from her as the falconer tossed aside his blanket and nodded at her. He left the cottage to relieve himself and greet their pair of falcons, Cleo and Horus.

While he was gone, she readied some bread and set the crock of raspberry jam on the small table. Lifting their two mugs from the hook on the wall, she poured each of them some ale so they might break their fast. Something deep in her memory told her it was wrong to do this before they went to mass but her grumbling belly assured her she acted in the proper manner.

Jasper joined her and they ate in silence. Elinor wondered if any other memories might surface once she entered the bailey and saw others up close.

"Once we finish, we'll need to be off," Jasper said gruffly.

When she'd first come to live with him, his brusque manner took some getting used to. She had rarely been around men other than briefly in the great hall during meals and had never spoken to any of them. Her day had been spent with her mother and the women servants in the keep. But she quickly adapted to Jasper's ways, instinct telling her that this man cared for her when no one else had.

Elinor took the last bite of bread and wiped her mouth with the sleeve of her tunic. Rising, she took their empty cups and rinsed them in the small tub of water Jasper had brought in last night.

Sensing his eyes on her, she asked, "Is something wrong?"

The falconer frowned. "I hadn't thought about your clothing. The way you dress."

Elinor glanced down at the wool tunic of brown and dark pants. Every now and then, Jasper returned with something new for her to wear. She had no idea how to sew and never asked him where the clothing came from. Looking back at him, she said, "I don't understand."

He sighed. "I've dressed you as a boy all these years, Elinor. 'Twas easier for you to learn how to be around the falcons."

She looked again at the clothing she wore. A flash from long ago reminded her that she used to wear something very different when she was a child of the nobility. Something she couldn't even recall the name of since it had been so long since she had dressed in it.

"It doesn't matter," she reassured him. "I go to the chapel merely to pay my respects to the baron." She didn't add that she had no respect for the man who'd turned her out from her home. The only reason she would accompany Jasper today was because he insisted she go and she didn't want to disappoint him.

Giving him a pitying glance since she believed she saw shame in his eyes. Elinor said, "You will not be judged by what I wear."

"But you will be," he said, sorrow crossing his face. He placed his hands on her shoulders. "I have always tried to do my best by you, my girl. I have taught you everything I know about birds. It troubles me that I am letting you down."

"I appreciate how you took me in and made me understand falcons. I know them better than I do people," she admitted. "As for what others might think of me, it matters not, Jasper." She kissed his leathery cheek. "Come, 'tis time to leave for Whitley Castle."

Elinor pulled a larger, heavier tunic over her in order to ward off the biting winter wind. They stepped outside the cottage and started for the castle, which rose in the distance. As she looked at the clouds in the sky, she thought snow would dust the ground by the end of the day.

Walking in companionable silence, they arrived at the open gates of the castle three-quarters of an hour later and walked through. A prickling teased her neck and hairline. The outer bailey had an air of familiarity about it. The prickling increased as they entered the inner bailey. They passed the blacksmith shed. The stables. The training yard.

Then the keep appeared. Elinor felt as if someone had punched her hard in the belly, causing all the air to rush from her. She found it difficult to breathe. She stopped in her tracks and then pulled cold air deeply into her lungs, forcing it in and out until she calmed.

Everyone in sight had their heads down in protection from the wind as they hurried to the stone chapel that stood next to the keep. She and Jasper followed the crowd and enter the holy structure. She imitated his gesture as he dipped his hand into water and made the Sign of the Cross, remembering doing this many years ago. The cold penetrated the chapel and people huddled together, no one speaking.

Until a buzz that sounded like a bee tickling her ear began to hum low throughout the place.

Elinor realized that many eyes were on her. Her skin heated with embarrassment as she skirted a group standing near her and she slipped into the corner, away from the others who had gathered for the mass. She dropped her eyes to the floor, uncomfortable by the silence that now blanketed the room.

She had told Jasper that she didn't care what others thought of her—and had believed the words when she spoke them. Yet, being in the midst of those who lived and worked at Whitley, she suddenly felt very different.

Jasper joined her, putting an arm about her. She huddled next to him for warmth and reassurance.

The atmosphere inside the chapel changed, causing Elinor to glance up surreptitiously. She watched a man and woman enter, both dressed in rich furs. The man held his head high with pride, while the woman glanced about haughtily. The couple strolled to the front of the chapel.

"'Tis your cousin, Sir Nigel Swan," Jasper said quietly. "And his wife, Lady Rohesia."

Elinor could not fault her cousin for being proud. He was the new Baron of Nelham, probably something he'd always longed for. Nigel would have known for several years that he would assume the title upon his uncle's death since no male child had been born. Something about Lady Rohesia bothered Elinor, though. She had looked out at the people of Whitley as if they were not worthy to even be present at the former baron's funeral mass.

Elinor didn't know any people and certainly had never despised anyone—other than her father.

Until now.

The priest appeared and began the mass, chanting in Latin that she could barely hear, much less understand. Elinor found herself growing sleepy despite her shivers. Finally, he quit speaking. Moving around, he fussed with objects on the altar and then raised something in his hands and began murmuring again in Latin.

"The priest offers the host," Jasper whispered to her. "For all those who have confessed and been forgiven of their sins."

She had no idea what that meant. Eager to move after being in one place for so long, she wanted to do what everyone else did when she saw them lining up and told Jasper so. He looked exasperated but nodded in agreement.

As Elinor joined the line and filed forward, she heard the whispers spreading and knew they were about her. When she reached the priest, his eyes widened. He offered her what looked like a small bit of bread, so she reached out and took it, popping it into her mouth since she was hungry again. The priest gaped at her, horror spreading across his face, as gasps echoed throughout the chapel. Not knowing what sin she had committed by eating what he offered her, Elinor turned away and hurried to her place in the back.

She couldn't help but notice that Nigel Swan observed her as she passed, as did his wife. While her cousin looked slightly perplexed, Lady Rohesia didn't bother to disguise her anger. Elinor ignored them both and walked to the rear of the chapel. Instead of returning to her seat, she made her way to the doors and pushed them open, welcoming the blast of cold that slammed into her.

Quickly, she exited the chapel, wanting to be away from the bold stares and murmuring. She had not wanted to come today and wished now that she hadn't.

"Elinor. Wait!"

She paused so Jasper could catch up. As he hurried toward her, he began coughing again. The cough had lingered from last spring into the summer and through the fall. It worried her that it clung to him in winter and only seemed to grow deeper and harsher as time passed.

If she lost Jasper, Elinor didn't know if she could survive.

He reached her and continued to cough, bending from the waist. She pounded him on the back as he spit out thick, dark mucus. That seemed to help. He stood up, his eyes watery.

"The baron. Your cousin. He wishes to speak with you. In the keep." Jasper swallowed, trying to catch his breath.

*Inside the keep?*

It had been hard enough to come through the gates and enter the chapel. Elinor couldn't imagine walking into what had been her former home. It was something she had longed to do for years after she left. She'd even begun to fantasize that the new baron might come to her at their cottage and apologize for the years she'd been ostracized. But now that speaking with him was a reality, she seemed frozen to the spot.

"He told me to bring you to the steward's office," Jasper revealed.

Elinor looked over his shoulder and saw people beginning to

stream from the chapel. She did not want to speak to any of them.

"Then we shouldn't tarry. Come, Jasper." She took his arm and propelled him toward the keep.

As they drew closer, her heart began pounding fiercely, as if she were an animal being hunted by one of her raptors. Elinor raced up the stairs, practically dragging Jasper along. She stopped at the door.

Should she enter?

Glancing over her shoulder, she saw others making their way up the stone steps, curiosity written on their faces as they openly stared at her. That helped her decide. She pushed open the door but had no idea where to go.

"This way," Jasper indicated, pointing to his left.

Elinor went the direction he indicated. Jasper led her to a small room lined with shelves. Huge volumes rested on them. They must be books. She had learned her letters and could spell a few words before her banishment but she doubted now that she would be able to read anything.

Closing the door to keep prying eyes away, they stood in silence for some minutes before the door swung open. In came Nigel Swan looking as regal as a king might.

"Greetings, Cousin."

Elinor responded in kind, while Jasper bowed next to her. She wondered if she should do the same now that Nigel was the new Baron of Nelham, so she bent at the waist and lowered her head. Raising her eyes, she saw the bewildered look upon his face. Knowing she had done something wrong again, she thought she better apologize.

"I am sorry. I have offended you in some way."

"You . . . I suppose . . . you do not know any better, Cousin," he sputtered. "Come and sit." Nigel indicated a chair in front of a large desk. He looked at Jasper. "You may wait outside."

Jasper looked as if he wished to protest but clamped his lips together and left the room, closing the door behind him.

Nigel went behind the desk and seated himself in a large chair. He rested his elbows on the desk and steepled his fingers. As he studied her, Elinor grew uncomfortable under his scrutiny.

"What do you want of me?" she blurted out. Again, by the look on his face, she realized she should have waited until he spoke to her. She kept making mistakes today and had no idea how to correct them.

"You have no concept of the rules of conduct, do you?" He paused. "How . . . how long . . . have you been gone from the keep?"

Before Elinor could answer, the door swung open. Lady Rohesia floated in, a picture of elegance in cream and burgundy. She slammed the door shut and confronted Elinor.

"Why are you dressed in such a despicable manner?" the noblewoman demanded. "You appear from the woods like some wild thing, wearing rags, looking like a filthy boy who's never even washed. What did you do that was so terrible to make your father abandon you?"

Elinor shot to her feet. "I did nothing, my lady." Her palms began to sweat and she chewed nervously on her bottom lip as the couple looked at each other and back to her.

"Our steward says the former baron banned you from the keep." Lady Rohesia's eyes roamed up and down Elinor, her lips curling in disgust. "Not only are you dressed as a boy but you look like a serf. No one would ever guess you were from the nobility."

"I am a falconer," Elinor said, proud of the work she did.

"A . . . *falconer?*" The noblewoman appeared baffled, so Elinor thought she would explain.

"Aye. I train the Swan family's falcons from the time they are young. I teach them how to hunt in the woods. We—Jasper and I—use them in hunting to provide food for Whitley. Jasper and our raptors also accompany the men when they choose to hunt in the forest." Elinor paused, casting her eyes downward. "I am not allowed to join in. Jasper was fearful my . . . the baron . . . might object to my presence."

"So, you live away from Whitley. In a cottage?" her cousin asked. He gave her an encouraging smile before one look from his wife wiped it from his face.

"I do. I share a cottage with Jasper. Cleo and Horus, our falcons, also live there under our care."

Lady Rohesia shook her head. "The entire matter baffles me. But then again, you won't be involved in our lives."

The small hope that Elinor had hidden deeply inside when Jasper told her she might actually be going home withered and died.

"I won't?" she asked softly.

"Nay," Lady Rohesia proclaimed with authority. "Why would I want some vile, unmannered creature who lives with *birds* to grace the great hall of Whitley, much less mingle with our children and guests? She would be nothing but an embarrassment and reflect poorly on us. We have a son and a daughter, Dumphey and Helewyse. I would never expose them to someone as odd and awkward as *you*." She looked to her husband. "Nigel, darling, you agree with me, don't you?" Her pointed look spoke louder than any words could. "Exposing Dumphey and Helewyse to this cousin of yours would be most unacceptable. Helewyse would never understand a female dressing and acting in such an uncouth manner and Dumphey is such a sensitive boy. He would feel sorry for this creature. You know he needs to mature. He doesn't need a distraction such as this."

The noblewoman lay a hand on her husband's forearm, giving him a tender smile. "I know you have a kind heart, dearest, but even you must see what a mistake it would be to allow this ill-bred woman into our lives. Think of our children and what a horrible influence she would be on Dumphey and Helewyse." She paused. "You do want what's best for our family, don't you, my love?"

Nigel squirmed uncomfortably behind the desk. "Do you enjoy falconry, Cousin?" he finally asked.

Elinor smiled. "I do. I enjoy being with my birds more than people."

"See, Nigel?" Lady Rohesia said. "She would rather live in her cottage and help the estate in this way. There is no need for her to give up such valuable work and return to live at the keep. We have no need of her here. Ever."

Lady Rohesia was cut from the same cloth as Elinor's father had been. Elinor wouldn't live under the same roof as this woman no matter how Cousin Nigel might try to entice her. Though this noblewoman did not even know her, she had already rejected Elinor.

She would not go where she was unwanted. She resolved never to set foot inside the keep again. This time because it was her decision, no one else's.

"I don't know what your plans might have been for me, Cousin Nigel, but I would prefer to continue living as I have the past six and ten years. Away from Whitley. Caring for my raptors."

He rose, sadness in his eyes. "Only if you insist, Cousin."

Elinor lifted her chin a notch. "I do."

"Then it is settled," Lady Rohesia declared, relief evident as her body visibly relaxed.

Elinor nodded curtly to the pair. Taking measured steps, she left the room. Jasper stood outside, wringing his hands.

He looked at her expectantly. "Will you come back to live as you should?"

She swallowed. "Nay. I will remain with you." Elinor quickly walked down the hallway and threw open the door to escape the oppressive keep, blinking back tears as she hurried along.

Only when she reached the bottom of the stone steps did she realized that, as her father had, neither her cousin nor his wife had called her by name.

It was as if Lady Elinor Swan had ceased to exist.

# CHAPTER 4

A SWISH OF hay woke Hal. His head pounded fiercely and his mouth was bone dry as he tried to remember where he was. A curved shape moving stealthily next to him reminded him of the tavern wench he'd bedded down with after drinking too much.

The one who now seemed to be robbing him of what little coin he had left.

His hand darted out, catching her wrist as she tried to slip his small coin purse inside her kirtle.

"You shouldn't take what isn't yours," he chided softly, his tone warning her.

He twisted her wrist, his fingers brushing against the breast he'd caressed a short time ago, and yanked her arm toward him. Retrieving the leather purse with his other hand, he released her.

She leaned toward him, a sliver of light catching her face, which wore a sour look. Hal held up a hand to block her from leaning into him. His palm met her chest, now heaving in anger for having been caught in the act. Without warning, the woman slapped him and darted away, muttering under her breath.

His face stinging, Hal quickly slipped into his clothes again, secreting the purse beneath the rust-colored gypon his mother had sewn for him. The serving wench had been all too willing to flirt with him openly last night, even following him out to the barn where he had arranged to sleep. The owner took a pence from him in exchange and Hal and the unnamed woman had romped half the night in pleasure, the jug of wine she'd brought along quenching their thirsts between bouts. Still, he didn't know where she went now or whom she might call. He wasn't in any position to keep trouble at bay. Best he move along before he found himself in a difficult situation that might be hard to extricate himself from.

Dawn had already broken as he left the barn, wishing he could saddle one of the horses within it and ride the rest of the way to Kinwick. He had never walked so much in his life—and he still had a ways to go before he reached home. Ignoring his belly gurgling in hunger, he hurried down the road before anyone appeared, his arms swinging briskly to ward off the penetrating cold. After several minutes and seeing that no one followed him, he stopped to relieve himself and then returned to the road, alone in the still, damp morning.

As he walked, Hal realized what a charmed life he'd lived. He came from a loving family, with two brothers, three sisters, and parents who cherished them all. He'd fostered at the estate next to Kinwick with the Earl of Winterbourne, a family friend and trusted confidant of Geoffrey de Montfort. Lord Hardwin had taught Hal almost as much as his own father had about how to be a good knight and better man. His years as a page and then squire at Winterbourne had flown by until he underwent his Oath of Knighthood Ceremony and achieved knighthood.

On the battlefield, he'd proven his valor and accepted the request to enter the select few who made up the king's royal guard. Though he despised the political nature of court, Hal enjoyed his time serving in the queen's household. Women had flocked to him in droves. He treated each lady well without committing to any of them, charming the lot with his boyish appeal and lazy smile, which proved hard for any female to resist. He made it clear that he wasn't interested in marriage and was a roamer at heart. Because of that, no woman ever pressed him for more, simply beseeching him to recite them more poetry—or if alone, begging him for more kisses.

As much as Hal enjoyed the company of women and appreciated them for who they were, he also proved popular with his fellow knights and other men at court. A natural leader, he liked nothing more than to swap tales or toss dice in their company. More importantly, his lightheartedness vanished whenever he took the field. As a knight, he lived to train and engage his fellow soldiers in combat exercises. He displayed a cool head no matter what danger occurred and could strategize and defeat an opponent with his quick mind as much as his sword arm.

But everything had changed a week ago at Radcot Bridge when Henry Bolingbroke stripped him of his pride as much as his armor and horse. Although Hal remained a knight of the realm, he had disappointed himself and his king when he'd been forced to yield to the brash, young Lord Appellant. As he now trudged home to Kinwick, uncertainty filled his future. Everything in life had come easily to him and had always gone his way.

Till now.

Bitterness threatened to swallow him up but Hal fought it, afraid he might give in to it. He would return home and seek his parents' advice. They would know what to do. Countless people across England, from the old king upon high to those who tilled the land at Kinwick, asked for guidance from Lord Geoffrey and Lady Merryn de Montfort. He could trust in their word. They would take the broken man he had become overnight and set him back on a course straight and true.

As he journeyed along the road, he kept alert as a light snow began to fall. Trouble filled the highways and byways throughout England. Cousin Raynor had met his future wife, Beatrice, when he helped rescue her from highwaymen who attacked. Even his brother-in-law, Kit Emory, one of the most capable knights Hal knew, had been accosted by a band of roaming cutthroats when alone on the road. Robbed, beaten, and left for dead, Kit was alive today thanks to the healing hands of Hal's sister, Alys, who'd become Kit's wife and mother to their three children.

So Hal knew to keep watch as he traveled, for trouble could spring up when travelers least expected it. Though he no longer possessed his sword, at least he was armed with a baselard. The dagger might be small but it could prove deadly if needed. Not that he had much to fight over if a thief tried to rob him. The coin purse he wore under his clothing had not held much to begin with. Since Hal had traveled with the king's army as one of his elite guardsmen, his need of food was provided to him. He required nothing else.

On the road on his own, however, no one cared who he had been. They only saw him as he was now—a man without a mount, with only the clothes on his back and a dwindling set of coins. To save on expenses, Hal had slept in the woods several nights and traded a coin or two to sleep in a stable other times when the cold proved unbearable. He couldn't afford to stay at an inn. He stopped at a few along the way and purchased a hot meal when his belly groaned from hunger pangs but the rest of the time he'd bought a simple loaf of bread in a village he passed and made due with it. Even then, he knew he would run out of money before he arrived home.

Would he sink to stealing food in order to survive? It went against every part of his knightly code of honor.

He looked to the heavens, as if God would have an answer for him. All he saw were gray clouds being pushed along by the brisk winter wind that blew at his back. At least he wasn't walking into the north wind as he wound in a southerly route toward Kinwick, though he wished desperately that he had a cloak to wrap about him to ward off winter's chill.

A pair of birds racing across the sky caught his attention. Hal saw they were falcons, the fastest birds known to man. The two began a series of dives and spins, much like the acrobats he'd witnessed entertaining at court, except this pair had taken their antics to the air. Up, down, across they went, in precise spirals and steep dives. Hal stopped to watch the show they put on, a sense of wonder overwhelming him as he watched them in flight. They looked almost like lovers who danced for one another, attracting each other's attention in order to come together.

He determined that this must be their mating process. These birds performed a courtship ritual as they showed off for one another. He'd never seen anything like it before and wondered if his younger sister, Nan, had ever witnessed it. She was always tramping through the woods, talking to and observing animals even as she hunted some of them. Hal smiled, fondly remembering how he had been the one to teach her how to use a bow and arrow. Before long, the student surpassed the teacher. Though a female, Nan was more talented than any bowman from Cheshire. She had taught many a soldier under her father how to use them. Her skill amazed visitors to Kinwick, who constantly challenged her to contests—and inevitably lost.

One bird went into a dive so swift, it blurred as it dropped from the sky. The other began circling, soaring gracefully. Curious, Hal waited to see what might occur next. Moments later, the first bird shot from the earth through the air. He saw it had something in its talons, most likely a field mouse. Suddenly, the circling bird flipped upside-down as it flew across the sky. The two birds met in mid-air, with the first one handing off the captured food to the other. Then both birds gracefully floated away. Hal hoped they would share in the meal. He decided the male bird had been the one who awarded his catch to the female and hoped the gift had worked in the male's favor.

He started up again and as he rounded a curve in the road, spied a man, his eyes raised to the sky as he watched the pair of birds fly away. Hal grew wary as he closed the distance between them. The stranger did not appear to be a threat, though. An older man, balding, on the lean side, with his hands full of something that he clutched to his chest. Still, he would be on alert until they had passed one another.

Then it happened suddenly. Two men came crashing from the woods, tackling the traveler in front of him. The bundle that he held flew from his arms. One thief leaped up to claim it. The other robber began brutally beating the man with his fists.

His sworn code of chivalry included aiding the weak and defenseless. Though he had no sword or mace to fight with, Hal ran toward the highwaymen, determined to protect their victim from a savage beating and return his property to him intact. Hal planned to subdue both men and escort them to where they would meet justice. It would help if the older traveler would give witness to what happened to him at the hands of these men.

Reaching the trio, he grasped the first attacker by the tunic with one hand. With his other, he captured the man's arm as he lifted it to deliver another blow with an already bloodied fist. Yanking back hard on it, Hal heard the loud snap. A howl followed as the robber pulled the broken limb close. He jerked the man to his feet and spun him around, delivering two quick, punishing blows before the thief collapsed to the ground.

Sensing danger behind him, Hal quickly dodged to his left and twirled as the second highwayman's hand cut through thin air, missing him. Startled, he gaped at Hal a moment, which gave Hal time to slam his fist into the man's nose. A crunch, followed by a shriek, rang out in the morning quiet as blood spurted from the broken nose.

But the injury only angered the man. He shook off the pain, murder in his eyes, and came at Hal again, swinging. Each man landed a few blows. Then experience told Hal to turn. As he did, the robber with the broken arm pounced at him. A sudden stinging turned to white-hot agony. Hal shoved the man back as hard as he could. As the robber fell, Hal saw the bloody blade in his hand. Then the thief hit the ground hard, his head cracking against a rock. No movement occurred.

Glancing down, Hal saw blood stained his gypon. The wound throbbed as if molten lead had been poured inside him. At least he'd sensed the thief's approach and taken the blade in his side. If stabbed from the back, Hal doubted he would have survived. He pressed his hand to his side, blood leaking between his fingers as dizziness was overcoming him.

Knowing the other attacker was still nearby, Hal tried to turn to fend him off but he swayed unsteadily. Then sharp pain rippled through his leg. As he fell, he caught sight of the thief standing next to him with a log in his hands. The man must have run with it and swung it, making contact with Hal's leg. He crashed to the ground awkwardly, hearing a cracking noise. Blinding pain engulfed him. Somehow, he reached for his baselard, fumbling as the highwayman drew near, the log held high above his head. Hal knew he couldn't defend himself from the oncoming death blow.

As the man approached, Hal rolled to his side, sucking in a quick breath at the flash of pain that sparked through him. His arm shot out and swiped his blade across the man's calf. The highwayman screamed, dropping the log, and fell to the ground next to Hal.

Committing to his next action, Hal slammed the knife against the side of the man's head, embedding it to the hilt in his temple. The thief froze, surprise on his face, then collapsed wordlessly.

Hal yanked the blade out, gripping it tightly. Then, as the darkness swallowed him, he caught sight of a woman approaching.

ELINOR DECIDED SHE would surprise Jasper and meet him. He'd gone to Long Bellbridge, the closest village to them, promising to bring back a few needed supplies. Once, long ago, she had gone to that same village with her mother, standing close as pretty ribbons and cloth were fingered and purchased. Sometimes, Eunice would take Elinor with her when she needed to buy things for the keep. She recalled holding the servant's hand as she skipped along, excited to be away from the castle, greeting people, petting animals, and smelling fresh bread baking.

She supposed she could accompany Jasper to Long Bellbridge on his infrequent trips. Just because her father had forbidden her from entering the castle grounds did not mean she could never go anywhere else. Yet in the beginning, Jasper had kept her home anytime he went to the village, wanting to keep her safe. That became their routine and, consequently, Elinor never ventured anywhere. She didn't regret her time with Jasper but after having been at Whitley recently, she longed to get out and mingle with others. Not those at the castle. They had been far too judgmental of her. Mayhap the people at Long Bellbridge wouldn't look at her as odd, though. Elinor determined the next time Jasper decided to go to the village, she would accompany him.

Cutting through the woods, she caught glimpses of Cleo and Horus at play. It was mating season and the two birds, coupled for life as falcons always did, still went through their ritual, as if the game were new to them each time.

That thought brought her to a halt. Elinor closed her eyes and saw her mother in childbed, her rounded belly swollen and distorted. She could hear the screams echoing in her head as her mother moaned and twisted on the bed, begging for it to end. As lonely as she was, Elinor never wanted a man to touch her so that her belly would grow huge. Not that it would ever occur. The chance of her speaking to a man, much less getting with child by him, caused her to laugh aloud.

She saw something scurry in front of her. Before she could react, Horus had plunged from the air and snatched it up, soaring high again in order to bring his offering to Cleo. She laughed. At least her falcons were happy. Cleo never seemed to be in the pain Elinor's mother was when she laid her eggs. And both Cleo and Horus shared the task of warming the eggs as they waited for them to hatch. She thought it sweet that Horus participated in bringing his fledglings into the world.

The road was now visible through the trees. Elinor spied Jasper, who stood looking up. He must be watching Horus give his present to Cleo. As the falconer glanced back down, something moved from the far side of the road. Two men emerged, running full speed, slamming into Jasper. Elinor ran toward them as Jasper fell to the ground, dropping what he carried. One man punched Jasper while the other went to retrieve the bundle of goods from the village. She reached the edge of the forest and then stopped.

She had only a small knife in her boot and these two large men were dangerous thieves. How was she to protect Jasper, much less herself, from them? Elinor realized they could easily overpower her. Hurt her.

*Kill her.*

But Jasper needed her. That overrode all other instincts to run as she reached and pulled the knife from her boot.

Suddenly, another man appeared. He assaulted the robber that attacked Jasper. Elinor was close enough to hear the man's bone break when wrenched behind him. Then the stranger fought with the second thief, smashing his nose, blood streaming from it.

Before she could cry out a warning, the first robber came at the stranger, who must have heard him approach, for he wheeled about just as the man jabbed him. Elinor saw the knife come away, blood on it, and knew the man who'd come to Jasper's aid had been stabbed. Still, he shoved his attacker with such force that the man sailed backward and landed on the ground with a thud. He didn't move. Elinor didn't know if the highwayman was unconscious—or dead.

The stranger gripped his side, his face scrunched up in agony. Without warning, the other thief swung a large piece of wood, striking the man from behind. He fell awkwardly. Elinor feared his leg broke with the sickening sound she heard. Somehow, the stranger struck his attacker, who fell. Then in an action as swift as one of her raptors, he drove a dagger into the side of the man's head and quickly jerked it out.

She ran over to them. Blood was scattered everywhere, bright against the snow that continued to fall. Neither highwayman moved as she approached, her dagger in hand. They must be dead. Elinor saw the man who'd come to Jasper's aid turn his head in her direction before his eyelids fluttered several times and then closed. She wanted to help him but Jasper needed her first.

Hurrying to him, she knelt and lifted his head, cradling it in her lap. Only then did she see the lifeless eyes staring past her. Bile rose in her throat. Her protector had died in a senseless attack. Elinor felt as if her own heart had been stabbed. Life without Jasper was unthinkable. She eased his head back to the ground and bent, tenderly kissing his brow and brushing her hand against his eyelids until they closed. Tears welled in her eyes.

*Wait.*

She needed to help the man who had come to aid Jasper. Elinor rushed to him and placed her fingers against his throat. The beating under her fingertips let her know he still lived. She might not have been able to save Jasper but she owed it to this stranger to do everything she could to keep him alive.

# CHAPTER 5

Stopping the blood flowing from the wound in his side was her first thought. Elinor looked around wildly for something to use. She ran to one of the prone bodies and yanked the dead highwayman's tunic over his head and then did the same with the other thief's. Rushing back to the stranger, she knelt and tore the cloth of one into long strips since neither highwayman wore a belt at his waist. Then she folded the undamaged tunic and placed it against the wound, pressing down. From there, she wound the strips around his body several times, tying them so they would hold the cloth into place and absorb the blood. The entire time, his eyes remained closed. He grimaced twice as she moved him about but never regained consciousness.

How could she get him to the cottage? He was much larger than any man she'd ever seen, tall, long-limbed, and broad through his shoulders and chest. Elinor could never drag someone his size that far a distance. Even if she could, it could tear open the gash even more, not to mention his broken leg being jostled about.

She ought to address that now that she'd stanched the flow of blood from the tear in his side. Biting her lip, she rotated and straightened the leg to its normal position. The man whimpered softly, pain flickering across his face before he stilled again. She worried about the cold. Already, his face grew pale and his lips seemed to be turning blue. He didn't wear a cloak and needed to be warmed.

Rising, Elinor went back to Jasper. Though he'd always been brusque and never minced words, he was a generous soul. He would want her to do everything in her power to save the life of the man who'd tried to rescue him. Though it pained her, she stripped both garments from his upper body. One tunic he wore every day and the other, a larger one, he wore over the first when the weather grew chilled. Bringing them back to the stranger, she didn't attempt to place them over his head. They would prove far too small for him to wear. Instead, she draped both over him and tucked them around his body, hoping that would help ward off some of the cold.

Next, Elinor hunted in the nearby woods for a couple of broken tree limbs that would be long enough to strap to the man's leg on each side. After a quick search, she found two almost the same length and both about as round as the size of one of her fists. Hurrying back, she placed them on either side of his damaged leg. Using his belt and Jasper's, she secured the splints to his limb as best she could, adding a few of the strips that she hadn't used when binding his stab wound.

Working with birds that had broken a wing, she knew how important it was to stabilize and then immobilize the man's leg so it would have a chance to heal properly and not cause him to limp. Fortunately, she had experience not only with injured birds but people, too, since Jasper had suffered a broken leg many years ago. Elinor planned to follow the instructions the falconer had given her and do for this stranger what she'd done for her adopted father. Once she had this man back at the cottage, she would need to clean both the injury to his side and that of his leg but, for now, this was the best she could do.

"The wheelbarrow!" she cried aloud.

Jasper hadn't used it in ages but Elinor knew exactly where the handcart sat. If she could manage to somehow get the man into it, she would be able to wheel him back to the cottage. A few bumps along the way would be better than taking the better part of the day to drag him home.

She brushed the hair back from the man's forehead, only now realizing how handsome he was. Elinor hadn't really looked at him before since she'd been so worried about trying to save him.

His hair was black as night, thick and plentiful. Cheekbones as sharp as knives stood out, as did his sensual lips. A tingling rippled through her as she studied him, an unfamiliar feeling that made her uncomfortable and excited at the same time.

Elinor pushed back his hair again and said softly, "I must go but I will come back for you. I promise," not knowing whether he could hear her or not. Still, she wanted to reassure him that she didn't abandon him. At least he still gripped his blade in his hand, the one he'd used to kill the thief. If he awoke before she returned, it might comfort him that he had the weapon for protection.

Rising, she retrieved the small bundle that had cost Jasper his life. It was too valuable to leave behind for any passerby to take it. Inside contained precious items that she hadn't the coin to replace, including grain for bread, as well as leather to make anklets, jesses, and hoods for their raptors. Though the Baron of Nelham had always supplied the monies to buy the leather and other equipment for the birds, Elinor did not want to explain to her cousin why she needed more so soon after Jasper had requested the funds.

She glanced at the stranger one last time before racing through the woods. She wondered how Lord Nigel would react to the news about Jasper's death. Would he sympathize with her—or send her away and replace Jasper with another falconer who was a male? Nigel was so new to the title and seemed under the thumb of his vicious, domineering wife. Elinor didn't want to supply the baroness with any reason to be rid of her.

That meant keeping Jasper's death a secret—for now.

Elinor dropped the bundle of goods inside the cottage and located the wheelbarrow. Thankfully, the wheels turned easily as she ran behind it through the forest. She would have to bring the stranger back first and shelter him in the cottage before she returned for Jasper's body. It would be impossible for her to bury her friend with the ground as hard and cold as it was. She could keep the body behind the cottage, out of sight, and put him in the ground once spring arrived. Something told her that would be wrong. That Jasper needed to be mourned by those who'd known him and have a funeral mass as her father had. Mayhap later, she would reveal that the falconer had passed and a mass could be said for his soul. He had coughed enough over the past year. Since he visited the castle grounds every now and then, people would know Jasper had been ill for some time, especially when they did not see him for a while. She could tell them he'd passed away in his sleep.

That would give her time to prove to her cousin how valuable she was. How he needed her as Whitley's falconer. That it would be unwise to send her away when the people in the keep depended upon the falcons she trained to provide game to eat.

It would also allow the stranger time to heal and be on his way.

Elinor arrived back at the road. The snow came down hard enough now that the two highwaymen had started to disappear. Sometimes, the baron sent soldiers to patrol the roads near the castle. She didn't know how frequently that occurred but, more than likely, they would be the ones to discover these bodies. If they happened by while she returned the stranger to the cottage, they would also discover Jasper's body.

Setting down the wheelbarrow, she hurried to Jasper and grabbed hold of his ankles so she could drag him from the road and into the forest. He was light enough that she accomplished it without much effort. Elinor placed him next to a fallen log, which partially hid him. His body was far enough from the road that she doubted anyone would spot it, especially with the snow falling.

Returning to the cart, she wheeled it over to the man who had almost given his life for Jasper, worried that he might still lose it because of the injuries he'd suffered. She was no healer. She could only do the best she could to try to save him.

Wincing, Elinor grabbed under his arms and lifted his upper body from the ground, knowing how much it would hurt him if he awakened.

"God's teeth!" the man roared.

She promptly dropped him.

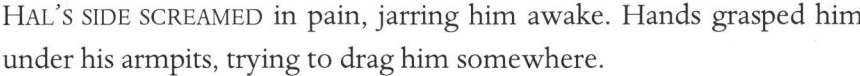

HAL'S SIDE SCREAMED in pain, jarring him awake. Hands grasped him under his armpits, trying to drag him somewhere.

"God's teeth!"

His hand tightened on his baselard as he glanced down and saw two branches lashed to his leg with a couple of belts and strips of cloth. The leg throbbed dully, while the place where the highwayman stabbed him burned white-hot. Then his head hit the ground. Whoever tried to move him had released him. Looking up, he saw the face of an angel leaning over him.

*Had he died?*

Surely not. He'd asked Father Dannet once if people felt pain after death. The priest assured him that pain did not exist in Heaven. That Hal would get a new body from the Christ and spend his days glorifying the Father, Son, and Holy Spirit.

Unless he'd gone to Hell. Now that was a place where pain would be constant. But not like this. Hell was supposed to be a lake of burning fire, utter agony with souls constantly screaming for relief. As far as he knew, he was lying in the snow. And the pain was manageable. Not nearly what he would expect from hellfire and damnation.

He studied the face hovering above him. The woman was no angel, for she had no wings of pure white. Still, she was a welcomed sight with her warm brown eyes and heart-shaped face.

"I am so sorry," she apologized. "I was trying to move you to the wheelbarrow. It's just that you are . . . so . . . heavy. So large."

Hal noted she was of medium height and slender and dressed as a boy, just as his sister, Nan, often was. He pushed himself up on one elbow, the one opposite the knife wound in his right side, biting back the foul words that came to mind.

"Are you the one who straightened my leg?"

"Aye. And bound your side. I will do better for you once I can get you back to the cottage."

"I doubt I can walk anywhere at the moment." He paused. "And I'd rather not be dragged through the woods if it's all the same to you."

She brightened. "I won't need to drag you. As I said, I've brought a wheelbarrow. If I can get you into it, you can ride in comfort."

A dimple flashed in her left cheek for a moment. Hal's heart skipped a beat. He looked about and spied the cart only a few feet behind him.

"Help me to my feet," he said. "I can stagger the few steps to it if I'm standing."

The woman lifted material that rested on top of him and set it aside. He still held his baselard.

"May I take this?" she asked, indicated the dagger.

He hesitated a moment and then handed the weapon to her. Elinor put it in the wheelbarrow then knelt and gripped his upper arm tightly. She might be slender but her fingers were strong. Using his right leg to push off, somehow the two of them manage to bring him to his feet. He didn't think he could hop on the good leg because he didn't want the bleeding that had subsided to start up again.

"Stay," she ordered.

Hal swayed when she released him but managed to remain upright as she rolled the wheelbarrow behind him and lowered it flat again.

"Lean on me," she instructed.

He slipped his left arm around her waist, his weight remaining on his right leg. The broken left one now throbbed angrily. His right side also pulsated, protesting the movement. The woman lowered him until he sat.

"Push back some," she instructed him. "Move as far as you can. Then you can lean back and most of your leg will be able to be out straight in front of you."

Following her suggestion, he eased back. The snow that had collected in the cart sank into his pants but at least he wouldn't have to walk to her cottage.

Retrieving what he recognized now were tunics, she laid them on top of him. He looked over at two dead bodies resting in the snow and realized she'd stripped them in order to bind his wounds and keep the cold away. His savior had proved to be not only beautiful but intelligent. Hal wanted to laugh, thinking how his brother, Edward, would tease him unmercifully for noticing a woman's beauty in the midst of a crisis. He knew better, though, and bit back any laughter, afraid it would aggravate the wound in his side.

His rescuer definitely proved to be strong. It couldn't have been easy to push his weight as she did but she kept a steady pace as she transported him through the woods. They hit a few bumps and he bit his tongue to keep from cursing, knowing she did her best—and then some.

They arrived in a clearing. Hal spotted a small cottage in the center, with a coop for hens nearby. A large group of cages sat next to the cottage but he didn't see anything inside them although a door was swung open to one of them.

"What are those for?" he asked, pointing to the wire structure.

"Those are mews," she replied. "For our falcons."

"Your husband is a falconer?"

"Nay." She paused. "I am the only falconer—now that Jasper is dead."

Rolling him to the cottage's door, she rested the wheelbarrow on the ground and opened the door.

"The doorway isn't wide enough to push you inside. Let me help you."

She helped Hal stand. Leaning heavily against her, he hobbled inside, wondering who Jasper was.

*Hoping he hadn't been the man on the road.*

No, he couldn't have been. The balding, lean man was much too old for this woman to have been her husband. Yet, Hal knew oftentimes women married men decades older than they were, be they serfs or nobility, merely to have a man's protection.

Helping him to a corner of the room, it took several awkward moves before she was able to lower him to the straw pallet. He shivered, his wet pants and gypon now soaked through.

"Let me build the fire up again." She stirred the embers and fed in twigs until the flame began to grow.

He saw in the corner that one wall of the cottage had the same type of cages he had seen in the clearing.

"Do your falcons sleep inside?"

"Only in the coldest of weather. And when they are waiting for their eggs to hatch. We take the best of care of them."

Hal knew the Kinwick falconer treated his birds as if they were his own children. Though he'd never spent much time with Joseph, he knew the falconer played an essential role at Kinwick.

The woman stood. "While I am gone, you need to loosen the splints I attached to your leg so that you can remove your wet clothing. Keep your leg as still as possible." As she spoke, she retrieved a large blanket and handed it to him. "You can wrap in this."

"Where will you be?" He wanted to point out that the wound in his side needed to be tended to immediately, washed and doused in healing herbs. Hal had played an invalid many times for his sister, Alys, who had grown up to have a great knowledge of the healing arts, as did their mother. Alys would already have started water to boil to cleanse the wound.

The woman studied him a moment, uncertainty in her eyes.

"I will help you once I fetch Jasper."

*So she had known the man on the road.*

"Who was Jasper? Besides being a falconer?"

Her eyes filled with tears. "He was my . . . father."

With that, she turned and swiftly left the cottage.

## CHAPTER 6

ELINOR ONLY WENT a few steps before she realized she could not abandon the injured man. Jasper was dead. He wasn't coming back. She'd already moved him away from the road and doubted in this weather that if anyone stumbled across the bodies of the highwaymen, they would scour the nearby woods for more. Jasper should be safe where he was. She could return later and bring him back.

But the man inside the cottage needed her now. Elinor knew any type of wound which bled could bring serious problems. Infection might set in. Fever could take hold. It was foolish to walk away and leave him to suffer after all she had already done to help him survive. She would push aside her grief for the man who took her in and do everything in her power to save this stranger.

Going to their well, she lowered the bucket and brought it up, pouring the water into a pail sitting beside the well. She filled all four empty pails since the snow showed no sign of easing up. She'd rather have the water on hand than to find the well had frozen by morning. That meant walking to the stream to retrieve water, something she wished to avoid.

Elinor lifted a pail in each hand and brought them back to the cottage. Setting them down, she opened the door.

And gasped.

The stranger had done exactly what she suggested and stripped his clothing away. He sat naked as a newborn babe on the straw pallet as he inspected the slash in his side with his large hands, a frown on his face. It wasn't the wound her eyes went to.

It was everywhere else.

Her breath caught in her throat as she gazed upon his physical beauty. She'd never thought of a man as beautiful. She'd seen Jasper numerous times over the years, stripped to his waist in the hot summer.

This man looked nothing like that.

His shoulders seemed broader than the wall he leaned against. Thick, powerful muscles corded his arms and chest. A fine mat of dark hair covered his chest, tapering down below his waist. Elinor couldn't see where it went because he had one foot propped flat on the floor, revealing a bronzed leg that she longed to stroke.

He looked up in surprise. "You came back."

"Aye."

Thankful that her pails hadn't crashed to the ground as she gazed upon his splendor, Elinor brought them close to the fire. Without another word, she left again and returned with the remaining buckets and closed the door, slipping the bar into place. She busied herself setting water on to boil, avoiding looking in his direction since she felt the heat warming her cheeks.

At least she tried to keep her eyes off him—and proved unsuccessful. She stole a few glances when his head bent, examining where the blade had pierced his skin. Finally, he moved away from the wall and returned to a prone position, pulling the blanket she'd provided over him.

Elinor went to him and deliberately stared at his face, avoiding the rest of him, which the blanket barely covered, thanks to his great size.

"I've put water on to boil so that I can cleanse your wound. I also want to wash your leg and wrap it tightly in clean linen before you dress again. Then I can stabilize it once more with the wood but, this time, I'll tie it more firmly with jesses—leather strips. 'Twill hold better that way."

She picked up his clothing and draped it atop the wire strung near the fire, spreading it out so it would dry move quickly.

"Where's my baselard?" he asked.

"I'll fetch it."

She unbolted the door and stepped outside. The wheelbarrow stood next to the door. The blade still rested in it. She picked it up, her fingers grasping the hilt as she stared at the blade, traces of blood lingering on it. Elinor shivered, knowing only a short time ago the weapon had been used to take a life.

Shutting and bolting the door again, she brought the knife to him. As she held it out for him to take, he shook his head.

"Drop it in the hot water," he ordered. "It will need to be boiled before we heat the steel."

Elinor wondered what he meant for her to do and then realized what he asked. "You want to *burn* your skin with it?"

"Aye, once you've cleansed my wound, that is. My mother and sister are both healers. They would be the first to tell you that the wound must be sealed so nothing harmful can enter. Fire will purify it. I cannot leave it alone to become putrid. That would mean certain death. As it is, there's a good chance infection has already set in."

She did as he requested and placed the knife in the water, wondering if she had the courage to hold the hot steel against his flesh. Elinor busied herself by gathering clean linen and strips of leather to use on his leg.

As she worked, he said, "The thief's knife entered just below my waist. He didn't strike anything but flesh and it didn't go as deep as it could have. I suppose you could say I was lucky."

By the time she had the needed supplies, the water had boiled. She let it bubble some before removing it from the fire, thinking the wound was much deeper than he let on and that he tried to reassure her. Ladling out some into two wooden bowls, she would let the water cool slightly before applying it to him. She also retrieved the dagger and rested it atop a clean bit of linen, dreading what she would do to him with it.

Elinor brought everything to her patient and rested it on the ground beside him. She pulled the blanket away from his chest, lowering and folding it back until she had access to his pierced side.

*Why was it so hard to breathe?*

Because, despite the ugly slice marring his skin, he was perfection.

Anticipation rippled through her, knowing her hands would now touch him. It caused her heart to race. A strange, unknown fluttering filled her, confusing her.

She shook it off and dipped a cloth into the water. Focusing on the task at hand, she thoroughly cleansed the area of blood and dirt, trying not to aggravate it so that the bleeding started up again.

The man studied the area. "You did well. Now wrap the hilt of my baselard in cloth and hold the blade in the flame of the fire. Be careful not to burn yourself."

Reluctantly, Elinor left his side and did as requested. "How long do I rest it here?" she asked over her shoulder.

"I'll tell you when to remove it." He paused. "You don't have to do it if you're squeamish. I can seal it myself."

"I'm not squeamish," she insisted. "I merely have never done anything like this before. I don't want to hurt you."

"You will if you don't cauterize my wound. A burn can heal. I've had this done before." He pushed the blanket away from where it rested on his upper thigh and indicated an area on the side. "An arrow pierced me here. Once it was removed, I had to sear the flesh. If I could survive that, which was much deeper, I will manage this."

Elinor fought from reaching out to stroke the marred flesh. She had never had any inclination to touch a man. Then again, the only man she had ever encountered for years was Jasper.

But this man—this brave stranger—made her feel things she'd never experienced.

Keeping her fingers to herself, she heard him say, "You can remove the blade from the fire now."

Elinor did as he said and walked steadily toward him. Kneeling, she steeled herself for the moment she dreaded. Her eyes met his blue ones, which had darkened and were now a darker shade than before.

"We will do it together," he reassured her and placed his hands atop hers.

A jolt of lightning seemed to strike her as his hands guided the blade to him. Elinor stiffened.

"Look at me," he commanded.

She did as he asked.

"Keep your eyes closed. I'll guide our hands."

Elinor swallowed and nodded, doing as she was told. Their joined hands moved. Then she heard a sizzle and smelled his flesh burning as the dagger branded him. She tried to rip the blade away but he held fast. She squeezed her eyes tightly as she heard his gasp of pain.

Then the pressure eased and he lifted their hands away. She opened her eyes, seeing agony on his features as he expelled a long breath.

"That's the worst of it," he said, trying to smile and failing as his eyes clouded over.

"What can I do?" she asked, feeling small and helpless.

"You can tell me your name," he whispered.

Her lips parted to do so but his eyes closed. His hands fell away from hers and dropped to his sides.

Elinor rose and put more water on to boil before returning to his bedside. She needed to immobilize his leg once more so that he wouldn't damage it further moving about in his sleep. But to do that, it must first be cleansed. Her hands reached out tentatively and folded the blanket back, revealing his broken leg. Dipping her cloth into the warm water and rubbing it against soap, she washed his leg carefully so as not to jar him from the rest he needed.

The odd tingling started up again as she bathed the long limb. She determined the only broken bone was in his lower leg. That meant she could saw off the wood and only be concerned with the area between his knee and ankle. That would be easier to confine than the entire length of the leg. After cleaning the whole limb, she dried it and wrapped the lower part tightly in linen before restraining it with the splints she sawed off to match.

She recovered him with the blanket and then brought another one from her pallet. She worried about fever developing and decided to sit by his side and watch him closely. Sure enough, within the hour, he had started to tremble from chills. Another hour passed and he threw off the blankets in his sleep. Elinor touched his brow and found it scalding.

Glad she had brought in a large amount of water from the well, she set aside the blankets and began bathing him, trying to cool down his body. Constantly, she dipped the cloth into the water and drizzled it across him, wiping and kneading his burning flesh. At times, his manhood began to stir. She tried to push it back down at first but her touch only sparked it to grow in size. Elinor had never seen anything quite like this and became fascinated by it. She longed to grasp the rod and decided that would be too personal.

"I need to leave you a moment to check on my raptors," she said quietly, touching his shoulder lightly.

She had spoken to him the entire time she bathed him, needing the sound of her own voice to calm her sudden bout of nerves, something she rarely experienced. She brushed away the dark hair that had a tendency to fall across his brow, again drawn in by his handsome looks. Elinor began to spin tales in her mind about him and why he had been coming down the road when he did. She only hoped the fever could be controlled and then evaporate, for only then she might learn who he truly was.

Leaving the cottage, she crossed the yard to the mews. Horus sat inside the cage he favored while Cleo flew down from a branch and began circling the open area. When she refused to land, Elinor knew it to be a sign that the falcon was ready to lay her eggs. She motioned for Horus to follow. He hopped from the cage and flew to the door just as she opened it. Cleo swept in, followed by her mate. Both birds flew to the smaller version of the mews located inside the cottage, each landing in a separate cage.

Knowing the time drew near, Elinor had helped in feathering the nest where Cleo would lay her brown, speckled eggs. If nature took its course now, within a couple of days, Cleo would have laid all of her eggs. Usually, a fertile peregrine falcon produced three or four but since Cleo was three and ten and nearing the end of her reproductive years, Elinor would be happy with one or two eggs. It would give her new falcons to train. Horus was two years older than his mate and would soon need to give up the hunt. Though he still soared with an unmatched beauty through the skies, it was time he and Cleo made way for a new generation of falcons at Whitley.

Elinor closed the cage door of each falcon and returned to the stranger's side. As she sat beside him, his head began to twist back and forth. Then his entire body started moving. She knew he thrashed about due to the fever and feared he would do further damage to his leg or break open the knife wound. Not knowing what else to do, she lay down next to him, throwing a leg over his body and using both hands to pin his shoulders to the pallet as her shoulder trapped one flailing arm.

"You are fine," she reassured him, her voice soft yet insistent. "Be still. I am here. I am with you. I will not leave you." It was the same tone she used with her raptors, firm but quiet.

Gradually, he calmed but Elinor was afraid to release him. She tested it by removing her hands from his shoulders but left her leg across him in case he grew violent again. He murmured something and then his arm came around her, drawing her near. His body radiated heat from the fever, almost singeing her.

Yet, Elinor chose not to move away. Instead, she eased her head against his shoulder and wrapped her arm about his waist. Immediately, the stranger relaxed. His breathing evened out. A peace descended over him. She couldn't stay this way forever. Only for a few minutes. Just to make sure he would rest easily.

Her eyelids grew heavy. The day had been so long and not only physically but emotionally exhausting. She was so very tired. She decided to rest her eyes for a few moments and then retreat to her own pallet. Even as she thought to do that, the man's warmth drew her in. His arm held her to him. Need for the touch of another human caused her to remain by his side.

For the first time in years, Elinor felt secure as sleep enveloped her.

# CHAPTER 7

A DELICIOUS WARMTH enveloped Elinor as she stirred. She opened her eyes and found fingers lighting stroking her arm. A shiver ran along her spine. She realized she'd fallen asleep next to the stranger. His body heat blazed hotter than any fire she'd sat beside.

Elinor tried to ease away from him but his hand shot out and held fast to her arm. She glanced up and saw that he still slept, though a frown creased his brow.

"You will be better soon," she promised in soothing tones. "Infection usually brings a fever but it will pass. Lie still now."

His fingers relaxed but did not turn her loose. Not wanting to disturb him further, she remained by his side, her cheek resting against his beating heart.

How long had it been since she'd felt the touch of another?

Elinor couldn't say. When she came to stay with Jasper all those years ago, he never helped her dress or combed her hair. She did it herself and her independent streak had only grown over the years. In all honesty, she hadn't missed the interaction with others. Seeing them. Hearing them. Speaking with them. The falcons had been sufficient in filling the void within her. Training new birds always proved to be a challenge and all her conversation had been saved for this purpose. Once Jasper taught Elinor what do, they had spoken very little to one another. Her years with him had been ones spent in quiet, save for any noise the birds made and the few times they addressed each other.

One of her favorite things was to stroke her birds. They didn't allow a caress very often but it had always given her great comfort. Now, Elinor realized that although she'd done without others in her life, she had missed being touched. Having her hair stroked. Being given a hug of reassurance. All those things from her past now came crashing back, bringing about a fierce longing that made her heart ache.

Gradually, she moved her palm up the stranger's bare chest, craving to touch as much as being touched. The ridges of hardened muscles seemed foreign. Her fingers brushed against his throat and rose higher. She cupped his face, her thumb stroking his cheek. New sensations trickled through her, causing her to be more daring. Elinor pushed herself up and brought her face close to his. She allowed her fingertips to explore his brow, rubbing away the crease in it as he sighed and relaxed. She smoothed his eyebrows. Slid fingers softly down his nose. Then lightly traced the outline of his full, sensual lips and skated back down his throat.

He murmured something in his sleep. She pushed his hair back and studied him carefully. Never having been this close to a man, she wondered at how different he seemed from her. How he seemed different from any other man she'd encountered.

And then the urge to kiss him overwhelmed her.

It came out of nowhere. Elinor barely remembered what a kiss was and had certainly never kissed anything other than her mother's cheek but, suddenly, her lips twitched and then began to ache in need. She wanted to place her mouth on his.

If she didn't, she might die.

Raising up, she eased his fingers from her arm and placed his hand back by his side. Before she lost her nerve, she straddled him, hovering above him while she kept her weight off so as not to further injure him. Flattening her palms on both sides of his head, Elinor leaned closer, her lips drawn to his like a magnet as she slowly lowered them to his.

She rested her mouth against his for a moment, then instinct took over as she softly brushed her lips against his. The most delightful tremor ran through her at the contact. She continued and then ran her lips to his cheek. Up to his eyelid. Kissed her way down his nose and arrived back at his mouth. For a moment, she pressed her lips to his in yearning, not understanding what she did or why she had such great need to do this. Then she realized she needed to stop. He had not invited her to kiss him. She took advantage of him while he lay unconscious. If the positions were reversed, she would not wish for someone to assault her while she slept.

Reluctantly, Elinor pulled away. Her mouth hovered just above his, longing to touch it again. She wouldn't do it. No matter how much she wanted to, she would refuse to act on these mad impulses.

Then the man below her came to life. His massive arms enfolded her, forcing her to collapse against his fever-hot chest. Pinned to him, Elinor could not move. Though his eyes did not open, his lips twitched irresistibly, causing her to lick her own in anticipation. Then one of his hands slid up her back sensually, taking its time to arrive at the nape of her neck. When it got there, strong fingers massaged it—then pushed her head down toward him.

Elinor's lips met his. Another shiver ran through her at the touch as something sparked between them. Before she could protest, his tongue shot out and languidly traced the outline of her mouth. The sparks erupted into fire, shooting through her like a blaze out of control. She opened her mouth to him, knowing it would lead to something dark and dangerous and wonderful.

*It did.*

His arm tightened around her. A hand pushed into her hair. And his tongue slipped inside her mouth, tasting her, stroking her, teasing her. Elinor had no idea this happened between a man and a woman. All thought—all reason—left her. She became the stranger's instrument as he took and gave. Desire shot through her limbs and then puddled low in her belly, even lower, bringing with it need and want. Her hands latched on to his shoulders, digging into the bare, heated flesh, kneading them like a cat.

Still, he kissed her and Elinor returned the kiss, boldly beginning to imitate his movements. Jasper always said she'd been a quick learner when it came to the raptors and this was no different. No, it was different. She innately understood what to do, as if her body held a history of what women did and wanted, all those who came before her now whispering in her ear, telling her exactly what to do.

Elinor kissed the stranger with everything in her heart, willing him to awaken from her kisses, fearing he might and stop this madness. They kissed long and deep, tasting everything the other had to offer. Then his hands melted away from her, falling back to his sides. His tongue stilled, as did his lips. She broke the contact between them and gazed upon him.

He slept again.

She rose unsteadily, unsure of what had just occurred between them, her body humming with vibrations that called out for more. Much more. Yet, his chest rose and fell, as he sank back into oblivion. Elinor's fingertips grazed her lips in wonder of all that happened.

And she still did not know his name.

---

HAL SENSED THE warm woman lying against him and drew her closer. One arm tightened possessively around her. The other reached out and found the sweet curve of her hip. He caressed it, his hand sliding up and down several times, causing his loins to tighten. He moved it up to her waist and beyond, to where his fingers brushed the swell of her breast. He sighed contentedly.

Then his eyes flew open.

He had no idea where he was. Nothing looked familiar to him. Hal's eyes dropped to the woman cuddled next to him. Rich, brown hair fell in waves, draping over him. Her heart-shaped face betrayed a rare beauty. Pink lips, begging to be kissed, were slightly parted. Something told him he knew those lips. Knew them well.

Yet how?

He did not recognize the fully-clothed woman lying next to him. Moreover, he didn't have a stitch on, while she was not only completely dressed—but dressed as a young boy. Yet no one would be able to mistake her curves for that of a male. Hal closed his eyes, willing some memory of this lovely creature to return to him.

The itch in his side reminded him of everything all at once. As did his left leg, stiff and unmoving, straight out before him.

Everything flooded back, images quickly appearing and disappearing. Walking in the cold. Watching the falcons fly. Seeing the man in the road. Then the highwaymen attacking. Hal frowned and remembered being stabbed by one. That was what the damnable itch was about. His side had been pierced.

And the woman beside him had helped to seal the wound.

He recalled killing the thief who slammed something into him. Whether that broke the bone in his leg or if he injured it falling, he might never remember. Hal only knew he had gained his revenge and killed the man before the robber could slay him.

This woman had come to his aid, just as he had the traveler on the road. Wait, she had called the man her father. Said he was a falconer. That *she* was a falconer. Hal had never heard of a woman holding that position in a castle but he supposed it was possible. Mayhap the man had no son and decided to pass along his knowledge to this daughter.

He looked at her again, her lips slightly parted, her breath slow and steady in sleep. Why did he feel he knew her? He had no name for this woman yet Hal believed something intimate had passed between them. A deep hunger for her filled him, like none he had ever known. It baffled him. Hal de Montfort did not yearn for any female. He charmed them. Kissed them. Coupled with them.

But he never needed them—or any one of them, in particular.

He did this one, though. Whoever she was, something about her called out to him. Stirred his blood. Had they coupled? Surely, he would remember if they had. He hadn't been in any shape to perform those kinds of duties. Not with his leg broken and what he assumed was a raging fever, caused by the infection in the wound that he'd told her wasn't serious, when he knew it was. He'd had a fever before and when it broke, it felt as he did now. Weak. Tired. Ravenous.

The woman stirred in his arms. She would awaken at any moment. More than anything, he wanted to take his fill of her. He hungered not only for food—but for the taste of her.

Hal brushed his lips against the top of her head, drawing in her scent. She smelled of the wood fire and outside. As if she'd come in from the cold, the wind still in her hair, and nestled against him for warmth. He longed to kiss more of her but two things stopped him. The first was he would have to move a good ways to reach her luscious mouth. With his leg and her position, it was all but impossible.

The second?

She seemed so innocent as she slept. Not only had he never taken advantage of a virgin but he had never tried to make love to a woman while she slept.

Especially when he didn't know her name.

The haze of the fever and the long sleep dissipated as Hal became more and more aware of her—and how much he wanted to touch her. His manhood threatened to rise to the occasion. He refused to let her awaken to his member pressing urgently against her. Reluctantly, he began moving around in order to make sure she came to before he lost the little self-control he held on to by a thread. He sighed loudly and stretched his free arm above his head.

She burrowed further into his chest.

Would the maid ever awaken?

Hal had two choices—either give in and kiss her senseless—or cough.

He chose the latter. Grudgingly.

Forcing a loud cough to erupt, he hacked away until she stiffened and pushed away from him. By that time, his act had turned into a true cough and he kept on, not able to catch his breath.

She scrambled to her feet and dashed to retrieve something for him to drink. Helping him to sit up, she pounded him on the back as hard as any fellow soldier would before holding the cup to his lips and tilting it. Hal drank in the ale, realizing as it went down his throat how parched he was. Draining the cup, he handed it to her.

"More," he got out, regretting that her warm hand left his back to do so.

The woman refilled it and brought it to him. This time, Hal drank more slowly, savoring the ale as it went down. He lowered the cup.

"How long . . . have I slept?" His voice sounded rusty from disuse.

"The fever took you and held you in its grip for eight days," she replied. "Your wound was more serious than you revealed to me." Then a blush rose on her cheeks.

Hal realized she must be embarrassed that he found her lying next to him.

"I must thank you for caring for me."

"You are most welcome. I owed it to you."

"Because I came to your father's aid?" He shrugged. "I am only sorry that I could not save him from those criminals."

Sadness blanketed her, making him want to cradle her in his arms. "Jasper would have appreciated what you did for him. It was the least I could do to try and help you recover from your injuries."

He wondered why she called her father by his Christian name but did not press her.

"Did I speak nonsense during the fever?"

She looked surprised. "Aye, you did. The first day, you went from chills to burning up. You thrashed about so much I had to hold you down to keep you from hurting yourself. The only thing that kept you still was if I lay beside you and talked to you. But you did chatter away after that first day. Mostly nonsense. Nothing that I could understand."

He nodded. "Then that is why your voice seems so familiar to me, I suppose." It was low and melodic. "I have had an infection before."

"Like the one from the arrow that pierced your thigh?" she asked.

"You know about that?" He supposed she had seen the marred flesh while bathing him to cool the fever.

"You showed it to me. Just before you . . . we . . . cauterized your stab wound."

"I did?" He remembered nothing about that. Hal touched his side and saw the burnt flesh now recovering. "Do you have any honey?" he asked.

"Nay. I am afraid you are being cared for in a very poor household. Why?"

"My mother and sister are healers. They have used honey in the past, smearing it on a burn to help it heal."

She bit her lip. "I am sorry that I cannot obtain any for you."

He shook his head. "Don't worry. It looks as if I'll live," he teased.

"I hope so," she said earnestly. "I have done my best to care for you, day and night."

"I do appreciate how you have cared for me." He paused. "But to thank you properly, I need to know something."

He stared deep into her eyes. "What is your name?"

# CHAPTER 8

"Elinor."

She fought to keep her eyes focused on his face when all she wanted to do was drop them to his torso. He was naked from the waist up and Elinor longed to brush her palms against the fine matting of hair and feel the muscles bunch under her hands. She swallowed and stared into his eyes. He looked at her as if he knew her.

As she knew him.

Oh, she had been wicked this past week. Every day and night she had lain next to this stranger, talking to him, telling him stories, placating him when he grew restless. She washed his scorching body often, trying to rinse away any sign of fever. Or that was her excuse. True, the fever did plague him and she would have needed to bathe him with cool water to bring it down.

But did she have to enjoy it so much?

She certainly had. At this point, Elinor knew every line of this man's body because she had touched it. Lovingly. Reverently. It didn't take her long to realize just how magnificent he was.

And she had kissed him as he slept. She tried not to but any restraint she attempted to exercise had failed miserably. Elinor had kissed his fingers. His forearms. His shoulders. Her lips had brushed against every part of his face and chest. She'd even found his knees wildly attractive and nibbled on them.

He never responded as he had that first time when he'd kissed her with passion. She understood that had been the fever speaking for him. A man such as this would have nothing to do with her. She didn't even dress as other females did. She dressed as a falconer would.

But Elinor believed her kisses had been just as much a part of the healing process as anything else. She had bathed him to bring the fever down. Fed him bits of broth, which he'd thirstily sucked down. She made sure movement was kept to a minimum so that his side and leg could mend properly.

"That's a lovely name."

His gaze warmed her as his eyes wandered over her. He searched as if he looked for some answer that she could provide.

"Might I also ask your name?" she asked in return.

He startled, as if being drawn from a reverie. "Hal," he said absently. Then, "My name is Hal," came more firmly from him.

"I am pleased to make your acquaintance, Hal." Elinor paused. "Where were you headed on your journey? Will you be missed?"

His lips tightened. Instinctively, she knew something unpleasant had happened to him. She doubted he would divulge it to her. After all, they were mere strangers.

*Though she knew every contour of his body well.*

"No one will miss me," he said quietly. "I have been absent from home for a long while. I was returning there but no one knew to expect me."

"Then I suppose you will have to stay here as you heal."

"Aye. If you'll have me."

Cleo shifted in her cage, drawing his attention.

"You keep birds inside? I know some farmers keep their animals in their cottages during the coldest of winter but I have never witnessed someone who lived with birds."

Elinor went to the mews to open the wire door. "Oh, these aren't just any birds, Hal. You may not remember but I told you that I am a falconer. Jasper always insisted that once Cleo and Horus had mated, her eggs should be laid indoors. He wanted the pair's offspring protected from any type of danger, at least until they hatched. I will return them to the outside mews after they are a few weeks old so they won't become too tame. They will need to learn to fend for themselves."

"I think I observed your falcons as I journeyed in this direction. Seeing them in flight was mesmerizing, like a dance without music."

"They are quite beautiful when in the air. Hopefully, I'll have little eyases soon and introduce you to them."

"Eyases? Are those their chicks?"

Elinor nodded as she opened the cage's door. "Cleo has laid two eggs. I had hoped for more but she's getting up in age." She looked at the raptor, whose eyes were alert. "Are you ready to hunt?"

Walking to the door, she unbolted it and made a motion with her hand. Cleo flew from her mews, only to be replaced by Horus entering the cottage. The bird glided into the cage and settled atop the eggs his mate had left behind.

Astonishment filled Hal's face. "Is he sitting on her eggs?"

Elinor laughed. "He is. A falcon who is to become a father will do his part and warm the eggs for short periods of time each day although it is the mother who spends a majority of her time nesting with them. One parent always stays with the eggs while the other hunts. Since females are the better hunters where falcons are concerned, 'tis usually Cleo who provides for both of them."

"How long until your little eyases appear?"

She noted the curiosity on his face and approved of it. "Less than a month. Cleo's eggs have hatched as early as twenty-nine days and gone for as long as thirty-three before the eyases have made their appearance."

Elinor reached under Horus and rotated both eggs. "I turn each egg daily to help them develop properly. I have to take great care not to break an egg because if I do, one of the parents will eat whatever is inside." She closed the door of the cage and stepped back as Horus resettled himself.

"May I see them?" he asked hesitantly.

"Of course. But you may want to dress first before I help you rise from your pallet."

Hal glanced down at the blanket draped across him. Before he could ask, she gathered his clothes and brought them to him. She had washed and scrubbed them, getting out most of the bloodstains, and then dried both pieces by the fire.

"I tried to mend the gash in your tunic from where the highwayman's blade tore through it. I am sorry such a fine garment was damaged and that my repair is obvious."

He took the clothing from her. A smile played about his lips as he fondly stroked the gypon. "My mother made this for me. She is an excellent seamstress."

She frowned. "You told me your mother is a healer."

"Aye. That, too. Mother can do anything she puts her mind to. Why, she could probably learn falconry if she had a tutor such as you."

Elinor wondered again if once she revealed to the baron that Jasper had died, whether or not her cousin would provide someone new to help her with the raptors. Not only would she be caring for Cleo and Horus, but if both eggs hatched, she would have two little ones to train. It would mean that she needed help, for she couldn't do all of it on her own.

"I need to fetch more water from the well. I will leave you to dress."

Elinor left the warmth of the cottage and took her buckets to the well. She drew the water slowly, allowing Hal time to clothe himself before she returned. Cold still pierced the air, causing her breath to appear in puffs, but no more snow had fallen in the past week. She decided it was time to retrieve Jasper and bring him home.

As she headed for the doorway, Cleo returned to the clearing, a duck captured in her talons.

"Eat your fill and I will send Horus out to you," Elinor told the falcon, knowing the raptor understood her after so many years together.

She entered the cottage again and rested the buckets next to the fire. Glancing at Hal, she saw he now wore his clothes. Elinor doubted she would ever see him any other way again. Disappointment flooded her. She shook it off, hoping he never learned of her wanton ways with him.

"Are you ready to try and stand?"

"More than you know," he replied. "Although my limbs feel weak, I'm also restless. I'm not a man to stay still."

Elinor looped his arm around her neck and realized he was still hot. The back of her hand immediately went to his brow but it surprised her when it merely felt warm to the touch and not burning.

"Hmm. I thought you still had fever," she told him.

"Nay, it's done and gone," he assured her.

"But you are still quite warm. Your arm and your hand both."

He laughed. "I'm always this way."

She smiled. "And I am forever cold. Even on a hot summer's day, I can feel a chill unexpectedly race up my spine."

He brought his arm about her shoulders again and she wrapped hers around his waist. After several efforts, Elinor got him to his feet.

"Try not to put any weight on your broken leg," she warned.

"I can hobble with the best of them," Hal told her. "I just need to move before I lose my mind."

They crossed the room to the small mews where Horus sat, diligently warming his offspring, his eyes studying the stranger as they approached.

"This is Horus. He is a peregrine falcon, as is Cleo. Falcons are known as raptors, or birds of prey," she told him.

Hal studied the male in his cage. "It surprises me that while his back is dark brown, his wings look almost blue-gray."

"Aye, that is the coloring of a peregrine. Horus is also a buff color underneath."

Hal leaned closer. "I can see. Are those spots on his belly?"

"Aye. Dark brown flecks run throughout the buff."

"His face is identical on both sides." Hal pointed. "That black stripe on his cheek matches the other side to perfection. He is beautiful, even with that hooked beak of his."

"Beware of his beak. And his talons," Elinor warned. "Don't go putting your finger inside his cage, especially as he guards his young.

He would tear you apart in seconds."

"I don't plan to." Hal thought a moment. "Are they named from *peregrinus*?"

"You know that word—what it means?" she asked, surprised because it was Latin. Only priests and educated noblemen knew that language from old. Jasper had taught the word to her the first day she came back with him. It was the only Latin she knew.

Hal shrugged. "I am curious by nature. I pick up new words, here and there."

"You are right. The peregrine falcon is named from *peregrinus*. That is a foreign word that means *to wander*. Jasper always told me of all the many types of falcons, peregrines are the fastest flying birds in the world."

"I would believe that after I saw Horus plunge through the sky and then rise just as fast. He gifted something to Cleo. In mid-air, I might add. I was fascinated."

Elinor laughed. "'Tis his way to seduce her. Unlike an English noblewoman, she doesn't need fine jewels or beautiful clothes. Cleo is a hungry, greedy girl who enjoys food as a gift."

"What do they eat?"

"Other birds, usually. Cleo is in her mews outside now eating a duck she brought back. Sometimes, she'll return with songbirds. Pheasants or pigeons. Even bats if she's hunting at night for herself. She stalks and catches her prey mid-air, thanks to her speed."

"I don't think it was a bird Horus brought to her when I saw them together. He dived to the ground and then soared back up with something in his talons."

"My guess would be he brought Cleo a field mouse or rat. At times, they'll hunt hares or squirrels. Rarely do they seek mammals, unless it's on a planned hunt for the baron and his guests or when Jasper and I take them out to provide food for the castle's inhabitants."

"Where am I?" Hal asked suddenly.

"You are on lands owned by the Baron of Nelham. He lives at Whitley Castle and all the estate's lands are also known as Whitley."

Hal nodded thoughtfully. Elinor sensed him beginning to sway.

"You need to return to your pallet," she told him. "You've been on your feet long enough."

"I'd rather sit up if I could. I am tired of lying abed."

"As you wish."

He leaned on her heavily as she escorted him to the bench next to their table.

"Turn so you can rest your leg outright while I am gone."

"You are leaving?" His blue eyes searched hers. Elinor found it hard to look away but she did, moving to stir the simmering porridge in the pot.

"I must go back for Jasper's body."

"Surely, someone will have discovered it by now."

"Nay, I dragged it a ways into the forest. The baron's patrol may have discovered the dead highwaymen on the road but they would have come here and told me if they'd also found Jasper."

Elinor slipped on her extra tunic as protection against the cold. "I will bring him here, using the wheelbarrow, as I did for you."

"Is Whitley Castle too far for you to take him?" Hal asked.

"The keep lies about three-quarters of an hour from this cottage. But I don't plan on taking Jasper there. Not until I've begun training the eyases and the ground will allow his grave to be dug."

"But shouldn't you at least inform the baron—"

Elinor cut him off. "'Tis not your concern, Hal. I will do what I feel is best." She smoothed her tunic down, hating the hurt she'd seen in his eyes in reaction to her harsh tone. "You won't be alone for long. I will return as soon as I can. I'll even have Cleo bring us something to add to the pot for our meal."

She opened the wire door and signaled for Horus to come out. He did as she opened the door and, moments later, Cleo had traded places with her mate and rested atop the eggs again. Elinor shut the door and left the cottage without another look at the man she now knew as Hal.

# CHAPTER 9

Hal sat on the bench, his home for the last few weeks as his leg mended. He stared across the room at Cleo sitting contentedly on her eggs. Today would most likely be the day the chicks appeared. Two nights ago, he'd heard a small noise several times. It had kept him awake for hours, anticipation in finally seeing the tiny eyases building within him.

When morning came and he told Elinor about the sounds, she explained to him that the chick's head, which had been tucked under its wing, had a muscle contract in its neck when the time to enter the world drew near. It caused the head to snap up, making the egg tooth, a hard-pointed knob on top of the beak, crack the eggshell from the inside. She called the cracks spreading across the eggshell pipping and promised him within a day, the chick would start to move about inside its shell. The movement would scrape the egg tooth against the shell and cut a ring through it, freeing the chick to break out of its confined space.

Hal reflected on the time he'd spent with Elinor, just the two of them in the cottage. Certainly, it was not the way of the knight he had been. This life was quiet. Simple. In fact, he had seen no one since his arrival. Yet, he hadn't been lonely in the least bit. He thought of court and how far removed he was from its trappings deep in the countryside, with one woman and a pair of falcons for company. If anyone had told him he would have enjoyed living in such pure isolation, he would have laughed in his face. He, Hal de Montfort, a teller of tales and a man fond of women, wine, and training would be the last person to take to life in a one-room cottage.

And he had. Oh, he missed the daily training exercises with the other knights and mayhap the camaraderie that accompanied it, but he hadn't needed the company of the many women at court.

Not when he had Elinor to speak with.

He laughed aloud. Elinor didn't converse as other women of his acquaintance. She had never been exposed to the extravagant living at court or life of the noble class. Her world revolved around her falcons. She had never seen, much less longed for, pretty baubles and elaborate cotehardies of silk in every color of the rainbow. Frankly, Hal found it refreshing to be around her.

She didn't start conversation often but was happy to engage in it with him. She made no demands on him. In fact, she knew next to nothing about him. Elinor did not know he was a disgraced knight, a former member of the king's royal guard who had been forced to abandon his position in humiliation. She had no idea he came from the de Montforts, one of the oldest and most powerful families in England. He had mentioned his parents briefly and a few of his siblings in passing but he never brought up his past or anything about where he came from or what he did.

Amazingly enough, Elinor never asked. She was happy with what he shared with her. Content with an uncomplicated existence.

Other women in her position would have been after him without mercy to bare everything about himself. The Hal of old would have done exactly that, allowing them to wheedle information from him even as he charmed them through compliments and kisses. Instead, Elinor took him as he was, plain Hal, a man who had done his best to save her father—and failed. That was the only regret he had from the time he had known her, though new remorse would soon appear on the horizon. Hal dreaded his bones healing enough to allow him to continue his trek to Kinwick, for he would miss Elinor terribly.

He'd had no way to send word to Kinwick regarding his situation since he'd seen no other person during his stay. He should feel guilty keeping his whereabouts to himself but Hal took it in stride. He would return home when the time was right.

*Would Elinor be willing to go with him?*

The thought gave him pause. He doubted it. She seemed content in her work at Whitley and would become even busier once she began training the fledglings. As time passed, though, Hal had grown more than fond of her. With each new day, he longed for her. More than anything, he needed to taste her. Touch her. At night, he lay awake for hours, thinking of her only a few dozen feet away. So close—and yet an ocean apart. When he did finally sleep, dreams came of Elinor entwined in his arms. They seemed real, as if they were memories of a past life the two of them had shared and not some fantasy his imagination conjured up.

Elinor made him forget about everything he had ever known. Sir Hal de Montfort should be worried about his king, the man he had served and would have given his life for. More than likely, Richard now sat locked away in the Tower of London as the Lords Appellant ruled England in his stead. The knight Hal had been trained hard. Guarded his queen. Entertained her ladies. Avoided politics. All a life that seemed so foreign to him now, as if another person had lived it a long time ago.

He should want to go back to it. Find his way to London. Demand to be reinstated into the king's service. Fight with the king if the monarch still wanted to engage his oppressors. If Hal returned to court—and if Richard could once more reign as God intended him to do—Hal should be there by the monarch's side.

Even if that meant bringing Elinor with him.

Nay, that was the last thing he should do. Elinor would no more fit in at court than if he caged one of her falcons permanently. Living at the royal palace, she would die a slow death, being forced to live inside and put up with the nonsense of other women's petty gossip when all she longed to do was roam the woods freely with her birds. Besides, his feelings for her wouldn't be returned. Though he wanted nothing more than to explore her body with his tongue and hands every moment of the day, she had indicated no interest in him in that regard.

Elinor never spoke of her mother, who might not have lived long enough to tell her daughter of the ways between a man and a woman. She had no father. It seemed she had no friends either, other than Cleo and Horus. The possibility of her regarding him in a romantic light was not only unthinkable but far outside the realm of her experience.

Despite how much he enjoyed the company of women, Hal would never take advantage of a naive Elinor in any way. He would always obey his code of honor to respect women, Elinor above all others. She had a special way about her. He would not sully her. He would keep his thoughts—and his hands—to himself and enjoy what time he had left with her.

And be miserable the remainder of his days once he departed Whitley.

Cleo squawked and sat up. Hal stood and hobbled over to the mews, using the crutch Elinor had fashioned for him. The falcon glared at her eggs and then directly at him, sending a chill through him with her large, dark eyes.

"Am I to let you out?" he asked the bird, not knowing if the mother should be left with the emerging eyases. He remembered Elinor telling him if an egg cracked too early, how the parent would eat the young inside. He didn't want to be responsible for Cleo gobbling up her chicks. Elinor had eagerly looked forward to their births. He would not have her disappointed in any way.

Cleo's pointed stare prompted him to act. Hal swung open the door and the falcon flew from the mews. He thought to open the cage door next to the eggs. Sure enough, Cleo flew into it and settled in, her eyes focused on the two eggs. Hal shut the door and began to watch as the eyases struggled to come into the world.

Both chicks acted almost in tandem, poking at the cracks they had made in their eggshells. As pieces began to fall away, a head appeared. Then another. With quick, decisive moves, both chicks broke away from their bonds. The newly hatched eyases appeared to be wet and were covered with white down. Elinor had told him within three weeks, brown feathers would poke through this white fuzz and after another couple of weeks, the fuzz would be completely gone, replaced by brown feathers. That's when the tiny falcons would begin jumping about, testing their wings to get ready for flight.

He marveled at how tiny the two appeared, especially seeing Cleo so large in the cage next to them. Hal longed to open the door and scoop them into his palm but exercised control and left them alone. As small as the eyases were now, Elinor said in less than a week they would double in weight. By three weeks, thanks to the huge amounts of food they would consume, they would be ten times the size they were when they hatched.

As the two strutted around finding their way, Cleo ruffled her feathers. Elinor had said the mother would want to feed her young soon after their births. Hal supposed that the peregrine was eager to hunt. He opened the wire door and walked to the door of the cottage as the falcon studied him warily.

"Do you want to hunt?" he asked the bird as he opened the door and gestured the way he'd seen Elinor do.

Immediately, Cleo whizzed by him. Before he could shut the door to keep out the cold, Elinor appeared, wood for the fire gathered in her arms.

"They've been born?" she asked breathlessly, resting the logs on the floor.

"Aye. Both of them. Come and see."

Hal led her to the mews. Elinor took clean linen and rubbed it over each eyas, drying and fluffing them. She lifted first one and then the other from the cage briefly, turning them at various angles. A satisfied smile danced on her lips as she slipped the chick into the cage.

"Two females," she proclaimed, her smile wide.

Hal knew that females were preferred over males. They grew larger in size and proved to be fiercer hunters.

"What will you call them?" he asked.

"I've been giving it some thought." She studied each bird a moment. "The one on the left will be Bess. Her sister is Tris."

He nodded. "I like it. But will you know which is which if they move?" he teased since both tiny eyases looked identical to him.

Elinor grinned. "I am already like a mother to them. Of course, I will be able to tell them apart."

"When will we begin their training?"

"We?"

"Aye." He looked at her intently. "I know soon the braces stabilizing my leg can be removed. I have high hopes that the bone has mended properly. Even at that, I will need to take my time, building up my strength and letting the leg become accustomed to my weight again before I set out for home."

She nodded thoughtfully. "True. You will want to put your weight on it for small periods of time until it is strong enough for you to walk great distances."

"Till then, I would ask to continue to partake of your hospitality." He gave her his most charming smile, one that no woman at court had ever turned away from. "While I continue to heal, I would like to assist you in training the eyases. If that is acceptable to you."

"I wouldn't allow this with just anyone," she told him. "But in the weeks we have spent together, I have come to believe that you are a good man. You have proven interested in my raptors, well beyond polite conversation."

Elinor studied him a moment longer but Hal knew she had made up her mind.

"Because you will be here longer and since I could use an extra pair of hands, I would be happy to teach you what I know of falconry."

In another life, Hal would have bowed gracefully to her and swept up her hand, brushing his lips against her fingers in a sweet kiss. Instead, he tipped his head in brief acknowledgement.

"I am most grateful to you, Elinor. Working with the eyases will give me purpose and allow me to earn my keep for a while longer."

She moved to her gauntlet and slipped it upon her hand before retrieving a larger one. He realized this must have been the one Jasper wore and thought it must be hard for her to relinquish it.

Handing the gauntlet to him, she said, "This goes on your left hand since I have observed that you are right-handed."

As Hal placed the leather glove on, Elinor told him, "An ideal falconer rises early. He must have excellent hearing, keen eyesight, and possess an even temper. A loud voice is also needed to call out and gain your raptor's attention."

"I fit the description on all accounts. I am at your service, Elinor, a most willing pupil."

"Sit on the bench," she instructed. I will bring Tris to you."

Hal used his crutch to return to the bench and placed it beneath the table as Elinor thrust her hand into the cage and guided one of the eyases to the top of her gloved fist. She crossed the room and motioned for him to raise his hand.

"Form a fist. Keep your hand steady."

He did so and she transferred the eyas to him. Hal marveled at the tiny bird resting there and how it would grow rapidly into a magnificent falcon.

"The first stage in training requires the utmost patience and stamina. 'Tis called the manning period and is simply the time the eyas spends with you. Both Bess and Tris need to become accustomed to being around people. I will trade them off each day so they will have time with us both. They will merely sit on our fists."

"For how long?" Hal asked.

"Hours. That is where the patience and stamina come in. The chick will rest on your gauntlet, which you must always wear in order to protect your hand from its sharp talons. They are small now but they will grow longer and sharper as the days go by. Bess and Tris will need to become familiar with your voice, so not only will we speak to one another, but you will converse with the eyas you hold." She grinned. "I'll even teach you how to coo to them so that they will think you are smitten with them."

Something stirred within him. Hal would love for Elinor to remain close to him for hours upon a time. He would coo endearments into her ear, telling her all the ways he would touch her, watching her body tremble in anticipation. He fought to concentrate on her words, though. He had gained her trust enough to allow him access to her falcons. Disappointing her in any way would only put distance between them.

As he observed Tris sitting calmly on his fist, Elinor returned to the mews and allowed Bess to perch atop her gauntlet. Elinor then joined him on the bench, their thighs lightly touching, bringing a warmth to him that had nothing to do with the nearby fire.

"Starting when they are young is important. It helps them overcome their fear of us as we try to establish a close relationship with them. That is why we will always be the only ones who feed them."

"Not Cleo? Or Horus?" he asked in surprise. "I would think the parents would want to feed their young."

"They would love to claim that right, Cleo, in particular. But food is the bond between a falcon and falconer. Teaching her to accept food from you is why she will return each time."

"So from the beginning only we will feed the eyases."

"Aye. They will become use to us by sitting on our fists and as we feed morsels of food to them. They will come to trust us as we provide for them."

"We place the food in the palm of our other hand?" Hal asked.

Elinor nodded. "Once Bess and Tris can fly, we will whistle to signal them to fly to our fist for food. In fact, every time we feed them, we must whistle. It helps them recognize they are about to be fed. I suppose I should have asked if you can whistle, Hal."

"I can," he said and saw it brought visible relief to her. "Louder than my two brothers but not nearly as loud as my sister, Nan, can."

She grinned. "I already like this Nan."

"You two would definitely get along. I'm sure you would enjoy ganging up on me."

Hal thought of how Nan and Elinor both dressed alike, in tunics and pants because of the time they spent outdoors and the activities they engaged in, despite the fact that they were beautiful women. But it wasn't only their manner of dress that proved similar. Each possessed a sweet spirit about her that drew him in. Spoke to him.

Though he loved both Alys and Jessimond dearly, Hal always had a special bond with Nan.

"What else?" he asked. "As far as teaching them goes?"

"Eventually, we will train them with lures and to fly the quarry and return to our fist for a reward. The goal is for them to leave their prey untouched." A grim look crossed her face. "We will also hood them once they turn a week old."

"I saw you making something that resembled a hood a few nights ago."

"It's used to cover the eyas' eyes. We will even deprive them of food for a short time in order to make it easier to tame them. That is why I wait until they are a week old, so they have some strength. Deprive them of food when they are too young and you can lose the bird altogether."

"You looked upset when you mentioned hooding. Why?" he asked.

Elinor drew a deep breath and expelled it slowly. "When I came of age to help Jasper train the falcons," she continued, "he did not use a hood. He temporarily blinded them instead."

Hal glanced at the eyas resting on his fist. A queasy feeling overtook him. "How did Jasper accomplish that?"

She shuddered. "'Twas a common practice, he told me. Many falconers train their birds by using a needle and thread to seal their eyes. The end of the thread is brought to the top of the bird's head and tied there to allow the falconer to open and close the bird's eyes. Jasper said having this control made it easier to train an eyas."

"You didn't like that," he said flatly.

"Nay. I thought it cruel and unnecessary. I watched him to do and it sickened me."

"How old were you?" Hal asked quietly.

"Six."

It angered him that such a young girl would be subjected to something so vicious, especially by her father. Still, the harsh practice must have existed for hundreds of years. He knew the art of falconry had come from the Far East and been practiced there even longer than in Europe.

"I'm sorry." Hal wanted to take Elinor's hand but Bess rested in her fist and her other hand was too far away. Instead, he placed his hand on Elinor's leg and gave it a sympathetic squeeze. But the thought of her pale, tender flesh under the material reminded him that she only considered him as a friend, so he removed it quickly and looked back at Tris.

"I finally stood up to Jasper the next season when a new group of eggs hatched. Two females and a male. I demanded that he not blind the eyases that way. He agreed to allow me to train one eyas the way I wished to see if it could even be done."

"Let me guess—Jasper gave you custody of the male peregrine since the females were of more value."

Elinor nodded. "After both females were trained, the baron sold them. But Jasper allowed me to keep the male."

Hal took a guess. "Horus."

"Horus," she echoed. "Jasper later said he was the best trained tiercel—male peregrine—he'd ever seen." She shrugged. "After that, he let me have my way. We never blinded another eyas again."

Respect for Elinor flooded him. She would have been a girl of seven, standing up to her father, an expert falconer.

"It took courage to insist on using a different method than one that was tried and true. I admire that you stood strong regarding your convictions, Elinor, and that you had the falcons' best interests at heart."

She rewarded him with a tender smile. "You do understand, Hal." Her gaze held his for a long moment.

Hal leaned slightly toward her, drawn to her lips, wishing to give her an affectionate kiss. Not one of passion but one of approval for the brave young girl she had been.

And the woman she had become.

A squawk from outside the cottage caused him to pull away.

"'Tis Cleo," Elinor said. "She's returned with the first meal for her chicks."

She placed Bess back inside the mews and did the same with Tris.

"I need to slice up whatever Cleo has brought back into small bites. Then we will feed Bess and Tris their first meals. I'll be back soon," she promised.

Alone now, Hal closed his eyes and imagined the kiss that had almost occurred.

# CHAPTER 10

"It's time to remove the splints bound to your leg," Elinor told Hal. "I have counted the days since I straightened it. I believe enough time has passed. The bone should have knit together by now."

"I have looked forward to this day for weeks," he revealed. "I am not a man used to such inactivity."

Elinor knew that to be true before he ever admitted this to her. Though Hal had exercised enormous patience when holding the eyases upon his fist for hours at a time, a restless air blanketed him when she returned the growing falcons to their mews. His large frame and well-muscled body told of long hours of physical activity on his part. She had not asked him how he earned a living and he had not volunteered the information to her.

In fact, she knew very little of this man whom she'd spent so many hours with—and yet he had revealed much to her in small ways.

Hal loved to tell stories and could keep her spellbound for hours with tales from his vivid imagination. She knew he enjoyed hot weather over cold and eating meat more than bread. He valued honesty and hard work and thought little of liars and those who did not treat others fairly. He possessed a quick mind and a generous heart. And though he didn't speak often of his family, Elinor could tell they meant a great deal to him. She wondered how much longer he would stay with her before returning to them.

"Where would you have me?" he asked, interrupting her thoughts. "The pallet or the bench?"

"I think the bench. Not only will it keep your leg straight and steady as I remove the wood and jesses but it will be easier to help you to your feet to test the leg. I don't know if I could pull you to a standing position from the floor."

"The bench it is," he said agreeably. Hal hobbled over, using the crutch she'd made for him, and placed it on the floor underneath the table before lifting his leg and stretching it out in front of him.

Elinor dropped to her knees next to him. She worked at the knots in the leather ties that held the splints to his leg, becoming frustrated when none of them yielded. Pulling her blade from her boot, her fingers grasped his ankle and held it steady as she slipped the knife under the first jess and sawed through it. The tie broke and she placed it in the palm he held out. Elinor moved her hand up his leg and cut through the remaining jesses, Hal collecting each one and putting them on the table.

As she cut through the last leather tie, she reluctantly removed her hand. It had given her a thrill to touch his ankle. His calf. His knee. Her heart continued to pound fiercely even after she rose to her feet and returned her blade to its resting place. She forced her hand to stay by her side when all her fingers wanted to do was reach out to stroke his cheek. Elinor swallowed hard, doing her best to tamp down the butterflies that seemed to erupt inside her belly.

"Are you ready to stand?" she asked, pleased that her voice sounded both steady and neutral.

Hal looked up at her and smiled. Her heart raced madly at the sunshine in that smile. "I am. But I may require your assistance."

"I am here. I won't let you fall."

His brow wrinkled a moment. He gave her a quizzical look. Elinor wondered if she had said something wrong. Then he shrugged it off and swung his leg from the bench to the ground, still keeping it straight.

His eyes flicked to hers. "I think I'm afraid to bend it," he said softly. "I cannot remember the last time I felt fear. Mayhap . . . never."

The words tore at her heart. Hal was larger than life, a man who brimmed with confidence. More than likely, he'd been healthy his entire life and this was the first setback he'd ever suffered. Yet she remembered some of the small scars along his torso, her fingers tracing them as he slept, wondering where they had come from.

Elinor shook off that memory. She needed to reassure him.

"It will be difficult at first. It's been weeks since you have put any real weight on it. You must convince yourself that it won't hurt in the least. That when you stand, you will be as good as new—because you will be." Determination laced her words.

Hal laughed aloud. "If I think it, it will be true. If I say it aloud, it *must* be true. All right, Elinor, I will try it your way." He paused, tossing back his shoulders and sitting straight. "My leg has healed. 'Tis stronger than it was before. I will stand now and walk as if nothing ever happened to it."

His hands went to the bench. Swiftly, he slid both feet back toward him so that his knees were bent. Then he swiveled and set his feet on the ground. Using the strength in his arms, he pushed himself from the bench and took a wobbly step. He paused. Took in a breath and let it out slowly. Then he walked from where he stood to the mews and turned to face her.

Elinor saw sweat had broken out across his brow. "How does your leg feel?"

"Weak," he admitted, a sheepish look crossing his face. "I won't be winning a foot race anytime soon."

He moved back to the bench and eased himself down. "I'm not as feeble as an old man but my strength seems gone. At least no pain came when I thrust my full weight upon the leg."

She wanted to placate him. "You yourself told me that it would take time to gain your strength back. You have no reason to be disappointed."

"It makes me realize that I won't set out for home anytime soon." He looked intently at her. "Are you sure you do not mind if I remain with you for now?"

*Mind?* Elinor wished Hal would always stay with her. That they would train the raptors together. Eat their meals together. Talk about any and everything. Live together. Lie together.

*Love one another.*

Oh, she had definitely lost her mind to fantasize about such things. No, not her mind. She was still sane. What had been taken—not lost—was her heart. This handsome stranger with dark hair and blue eyes and a smile that caused her to bask in warmth had stolen it before she could even notice. Her heart was hers no longer. When Hal left Whitley, he would carry it with him.

And never know he possessed it.

Hurt poured through Elinor, traveling through every limb. A physical ache tore at her. She wanted this man. Now. Forever. She, who knew so little about the world or others, knew one thing rang true within her.

*She loved Hal.*

Loved him with every breath she took. She needed him. More than that, she wanted him—as a woman wanted a man. Though she had no mother, no other female, to explain these mysteries to her, Elinor instinctively knew. Her body knew. Her mind knew. Her heart. Her soul.

How would she ever be able to let him walk away?

Brushing aside the storm that raged inside her, Elinor mustered a smile. "You know that you may stay as long as you wish, Hal. You can walk some each day. In fact, you should do so several times a day. Increase the amount and length over the next few weeks until you are confident that you can journey home without any problems."

"Then I will start now. Would you like to take Bess and Tris outside? I know they have never been before but you did tell me they needed to be exposed to the elements. You called it the weathering yard. We could slip on our gauntlets and take them to the clearing for a few hours."

She determined to focus on the eyases once they got outside. Not Hal.

"'Tis a good idea," she agreed. "I might suggest that you take your crutch along. You can use it for a few days to steady yourself. I wouldn't want you to fall again and do further damage to your leg."

A look of horror crossed his face, as if the thought had never occurred to him. "You are right."

He bent and retrieved the crutch and then hoisted himself to his feet again. He went to the gauntlets and tossed hers to her. Elinor placed it on her hand as he did the same and joined him at the mews. She opened the door and thrust her fist inside. Tris hopped onto it willingly once Elinor whistled. Bess did the same with Hal once she received his signal. Both reached into the pouches they wore on their waists and rewarded the eyases with a bechin for having come willingly.

"Lead the way," Hal said, holding Bess in his left hand and the crutch in his right.

Elinor opened the door to the cottage and allowed him to leave first since both hands were occupied. Closing the door behind her, she drew a deep breath of the cold, crisp air into her lungs. Hal went and stood in the middle of the clearing, glancing about in every direction.

"You can sit here," she offered as she sat on one of the stumps left in the area for that purpose.

"Nay. I am enjoying standing on my own two feet. Don't worry. I won't overdo it. I promise to take frequent breaks. But it feels good being able to stand again and distribute my weight evenly."

Hal held his arm steady and smiled at the falcon perched upon his fist. "And how are you enjoying your first time outside, Sweet Bess? Exhilarating, isn't it?"

Elinor thought any time spent in Hal's company was invigorating.

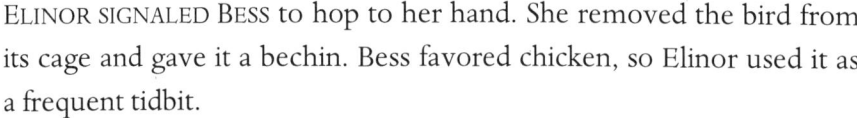

ELINOR SIGNALED BESS to hop to her hand. She removed the bird from its cage and gave it a bechin. Bess favored chicken, so Elinor used it as a frequent tidbit.

"Let's go, Tris," Hal commanded and whistled. The eyas responded quickly and received her reward. "I like that you've attached bells to their bewits," he said. "'Twill be easier to keep up with them as they start flying further distances."

They both slid a hood over their falcon's head and drew the braces until the hood tightened and closed. Then anklets were strapped around each bird's leg and jesses were attached. Jasper had sometimes called the anklets bracelets but that reminded Elinor too much of the silver bangles that had rested on her mother's thin arms. She preferred the term anklets so that no reminders of her former life invaded her work with the raptors.

Taking the falcons outside, they walked them to the block perch. Elinor loosened Bess' braces and then removed her hood. She held the falcon beside the perch and Bess hopped to it. Hal repeated the same actions with Tris and, soon, both young birds sat side by side.

"Are you pleased with their progress?" Hal asked as he began pacing in a circle around the clearing.

She noticed he no longer favored either leg as he walked. The crutch had long been discarded. In fact, Hal had spent many hours walking through the nearby woods, one of the raptors always riding on his fist. Both Bess and Tris had taken to him easily. If he chose to do so, Elinor thought Hal could become a falconer on his own. Knowing it was a skill few were trained in, it would allow him to work at any estate that kept raptors. She had not broached the subject with him, knowing it would require him to remain much longer at Whitley in order to glean all the knowledge she could pass along to him.

Selfishly, she thought it was a way to keep him with her. Elinor decided she wouldn't suggest it. But if he asked, she would be more than willing for Hal to continue living and working with her. If he chose to do so, that meant not only informing her cousin of a new falconer—but letting him know about Jasper's death. Guilt filled her and she realized whether Hal stayed or not, the time had come to inform the baron about Jasper.

Elinor told Hal, "I am happy with how quickly Bess and Tris are coming along. While all peregrines are highly trainable because of their strength and intelligence, these two are more versatile than any raptors I have worked with in the past. I believe they will be eager to hunt once they are shown how. Right now, they are learning to fly greater distances in order to return to our glove. I think it is time to start training them to the lure."

He smiled enthusiastically. "I've been looking forward to that. You said that they'll first eat off the lure?"

"Aye. They will need to recognize it as a food source, as much as they do our hands. We'll place the food face up on the lure so they can easily spot it in the beginning."

Hal grew thoughtful. "Will we still need to whistle?"

"Every time. They need to associate that signal and always link it to receiving food. If we whistle and they do not come, then we will put the lure away for a bit before trying again. A raptor should always wait on its falconer. We never wait on the bird for if we do, it will be training us."

He laughed. "It almost sounds like a way to raise a child."

"In a way, you are correct. They are new to the world so we must teach them about it. These two will catch on quickly. After a few days, I'm sure we will be able to start swinging the lure and have them fly to it in order to catch their food. That will be the next step. But we'll need to vary the pace of the swing. Sometimes, we'll need to let them catch it easily. Other times, we must give them more of a challenge. If not, they will bore quickly and lose interest."

"'Tis a lot to know," he pointed out. "It seems to come naturally to you."

"I have done this for many years, Hal. Ten and six. If you had been hard at work on something for that long, you also would be an expert at it."

They sat in silence for a long time. Elinor never felt awkward when they did so. Silence had always been a friend to her. She had spoken more to her raptors than Jasper over the years. Even as much as she enjoyed conversing with Hal, she appreciated the times they could sit together without words.

Finally, she said, "Before we begin teaching them with lures, I have something I must do."

"Can I help you?" he asked.

"I appreciate you wishing to lend me a hand but this is something I must do alone—take Jasper to the keep."

He nodded. "Though the wind still blows cold, winter is dying. That means a grave can be dug."

"Aye. It's time for Jasper to come to his final resting place."

Elinor had wrapped the falconer's body as tightly as possible in linen and two blankets. To keep any animals away, she had placed it in the wheelbarrow and draped another blanket over him, tucking it under the wheels of the cart. The cold had preserved him but with spring coming, he needed to be in the ground.

"Will you go to the keep to inform the baron of Jasper's death? I assume his soldiers can collect the body for the mass and burial."

"I plan to take Jasper to the castle. Today."

"Then I will come with you."

"Nay," she said forcefully. "They know nothing of you and I want to keep it that way. While you slept in those first days after your injury, two of the baron's soldiers came to the cottage. I was outside feeding the chickens when they appeared. They asked if I knew anything about the dead highwaymen a few miles away on the road that heads toward Long Bellbridge. I told them neither Jasper nor I had been to the village in over a week. That satisfied them and they moved on."

"Without asking for Jasper—or seeing me."

"Aye. Although I witnessed how the two robbers attacked you and Jasper, you did kill both of them, Hal. I did not want anything bad to happen to you."

"But 'twas in self-defense," he argued.

"Still, you are a stranger in these parts. They might have thought you were a part of this gang and, mayhap, you disagreed on how your ill-gotten spoils should be divided. I didn't want you blamed for anything. The highwaymen's death. Jasper's. Because of that, you must remain out of sight."

"Do you cut through the forest to reach the keep?" Hal asked.

Elinor nodded. "It is probably two miles through the woods before the castle comes into view, then another quarter hour to reach the keep itself."

His jaw set in determination. "I will accompany you and wheel the cart as far as the edge of the woods." His words left no room for argument.

"Then we should return Bess and Tris to the mews inside before we set out for Whitley."

They stood and whistled. Immediately, the growing raptors flew to their fists and were rewarded with a bechin.

"You are my good girl, Tris," Hal cooed to his bird. "I would smother you with soft strokes if Elinor would allow it."

She only wished he might speak to her in such a gentle, loving tone and shower her with affection.

"Despite our taming them, they are still creatures of the wild," she reminded him. "They don't tolerate being petted as a dog or cat might."

"I know. You have told me that they might take off one of my fingers if I tried to pet them in affection." Hal held his ungloved hand out before him. "I am quite partial to all five fingers on this hand. I promise I will keep them away from the falcons unless I'm giving a tidbit of food to them."

"Good."

They returned the birds to their cages inside the cottage and left to retrieve Jasper's body. Hal insisted on pushing the wheelbarrow for her as they made their way through the dense forest.

"I know this is hard for you, Elinor."

He didn't know how true that statement was. Jasper had meant everything to her.

"I will miss him dreadfully," she admitted. "When I came to him . . ." Her voice trailed off. She hadn't meant to reveal that.

"You came to him?" Hal asked, a frown creasing his brow as he stopped in his tracks. "Jasper wasn't your true father?"

Elinor danced upon the slippery slope between the truth and a lie.

"My mother died in childbirth. She had grown weaker over the years trying to produce a babe but I was the only one who had lived. When she passed away, Jasper offered to take me in."

She swallowed the bile that rose in her throat as she remembered her father's harsh words and angry tone as he banished her from his sight and the keep in front of everyone in the great hall. How Jasper had stood up and volunteered to bring her home when no other stepped forward to claim her.

"So that is why you refer to him as Jasper."

"Aye." She never would have called him father. That word only held scorn and hate for her. "Jasper had lost his own child and wife. The two of us formed a new family."

"I know on large estates that the falconer in residence trains one or more of his children to become the new falconer."

"That is how it usually works. I only hope the baron will allow me to remain in this position now that Jasper is gone. This baron is new to Whitley. He grew up somewhere else and only came to us near Christmas time when the old baron died. That baron had no son to inherit."

*Only a daughter who had ceased to exist for him years ago.*

They continued on. Elinor was grateful that Hal did not ask more about the estate or the baron, for she would not have been able to answer most of his questions. She knew next to nothing about life at Whitley, only the bits she'd gleaned from Jasper over the years and that wasn't much.

Finally, they reached the edge of the woods. Hal eased the wheelbarrow to the ground.

"I will wait for you here," he said. "For as long as it takes."

"You don't have to do that."

"I know. But I will be here, nevertheless."

Elinor took hold of the handles. "By the time I speak to the baron and let him know about Jasper, it may be too late to hold a mass today for Jasper's soul. If so, I will return to you and then come back to the chapel tomorrow."

"And if a mass is said and the burial does take place, stay for both. I will remain here out of sight and escort you back to the cottage once it is done."

"All right." A lump filled her throat. This man had only known her for a short while and yet showed her consideration and care far beyond what she deserved.

Elinor lifted the cart and wheeled it across the meadow, knowing Hal watched over her. She reached the road, which made for a smoother part of her journey, and finally came to the gates.

Calling up to the gatekeeper, she said, "I have Jasper the falconer. He has passed on. I must speak to the baron and the priest."

The gates swung open and Elinor went inside.

## CHAPTER II

ELINOR ROLLED THE wheelbarrow through the outer bailey, aware of the stares she received from those she passed. Still, she kept her head high and looked straight ahead. No one stopped or spoke to her. Coming to the inner bailey, she resolved to show no emotion when she met with her cousin. Nay, he was the Baron of Nelham. She must think of him that way. He was no longer family to her. She served him and Whitley by taming and training his falcons and readying them for the hunt.

The keep lay in front of her but Elinor rolled the cart to the right, toward the stone chapel. She halted in front of it, wondering if she should take Jasper inside or leave him next to the structure. Before she came to a decision, a priest appeared in the doorway, reed thin and with inquisitive brown eyes.

"What have we here?" he asked, his voice booming despite his thin frame.

"I remember you," she said, easing the cart to the ground. "You performed the funeral mass. For the baron." He looked to be a score and ten and had come to be the estate's priest after her banishment.

"I am Father Leo and I did say mass for our late baron. And you were the one who took the host from me."

Elinor started to defend herself and then saw his kind eyes were not judging her as others had that day.

"Aye," she said, defiance in her tone. "You offered and so I took it. Only after I did so, I realized I had made a mistake."

"To take Christ's body? Nay, that can never be a mistake. But in the future, you must allow me—or whatever priest is present—to place the host upon your tongue." He gave her a friendly smile. "Will you come again to mass, Lady Elinor? I hope so."

She froze, rooted to the spot. How long had it been since anyone had addressed her in such a manner? Panic swelled within her.

"I know who you are, my lady," he said gently. "I asked about you after you and the falconer came to mass that day." He shrugged. "I have always possessed a curious nature and asked countless questions, both as a boy and even now. About God. The world and everyone in it. And you. At first, no one would speak of you. Until Eunice came to me and shared your story."

Elinor dug her fingernails into her palms. "I knew Eunice. When I was a little girl."

"You mean when you were Lady Elinor and lived in the keep?" the priest prodded.

"Do not say that," she hissed. "Never call me that."

"But 'tis who you are," he pointed out calmly.

Sadness enveloped her for who she had once been and what had been lost to her. "Mayhap at one time. But no longer. My . . . the baron did not . . . he did not want me. So I left."

"I heard Jasper took you willingly." He looked down to the cart. "And now you have brought him to me, I see."

She nodded. "Aye. He had been ill for some time."

"I know. We spoke upon occasion though I have not seen him for some time. A persistent cough troubled him for months."

Elinor wanted to leave. This priest's prying made her uncomfortable. "I have brought him to you. You must say a mass for him. I need to tell the baron that Jasper is no longer with us."

"I will say mass for Jasper in the morning. Right now, you look as if you could use a bit of ale. You seem pale." The priest held out his hand. "Come inside the chapel. I have a room in the back. You can rest a few minutes and drink something before we go to Baron Nelham with this news."

"I have no need of rest. Nor do you need to accompany me," she said firmly. "I will tell the baron of Jasper's passing and then return tomorrow for the mass."

Father Leo bowed his head a moment. "As you wish, my lady."

Hearing those words, Elinor's heart began to pound. She latched on to his forearm. "Please. If you know what is good for you, you will never call me that again. I am plain Elinor."

He chuckled. "You aren't the least bit plain, Elinor, but I will respect your feelings."

"You must. The new baroness already does not like me. I want to remain at Whitley and continue training my raptors. If she heard you, she would take offense, Father."

A knowing look came into his eyes.

"I understand perfectly. Our new baroness is . . . opinionated. Very well. I will claim Jasper's body and bring it inside the chapel. I'll have a couple of men dig his grave. You may tell the baron on your own of Jasper's death." The priest paused. "But I think both the baron and baroness have done you a grave disservice, Elinor. You are a member of the Swan family. You should be treated as such."

Tears stung her eyes. "I have no family, Father. Only my falcons. I need no others."

Father Leo squeezed her shoulder and then gripped the handles of the cart. As he wheeled it away, he looked over his shoulder and said, "I will see you in the chapel tomorrow morning."

Elinor waited until he vanished inside and took a moment to collect herself. She willed her limbs to cease their trembling. She could not meet with the baron and appear weak in any way, especially if his wife made an appearance. After a few deep breaths, she had composed herself and returned in the direction of the keep. Mounting the steps to the top, she pushed everything from her mind.

Before she could knock on the large, oak door, it swung open. Eunice stood on the other side.

"Greetings," the old woman said. "I hear you have brought Jasper."

Though Elinor had only spoken to the priest since her arrival, she realized the castle's community was tightknit. The gossip must have started the instant she entered the gates with her wheelbarrow bearing Jasper's remains.

"Aye. I would like to speak to the baron."

"Follow me." Eunice turned and led her to the great hall.

As Elinor entered the room, it surprised her how large it was. The ceiling seemed to stretch to the heavens. The bulk of the room stood empty, with the trestle tables pushed against the wall. At the far end near the fire, she saw her cousin sitting, a dog at his feet. Giving a curt nod to Eunice, she traveled the length of the room, the sweet scent of the rushes wafting up from the floor. The dog rose, eying her warily. Elinor held out a hand and let him sniff it. Satisfied, he backed away and curled up again at his master's feet.

The baron frowned. "What are you doing here? You know the baroness does not want you inside the keep."

"I came to tell you that Jasper, your falconer, has passed on, my lord. I brought his body to the chapel and Father Leo has claimed possession of it. He said he will assign men to dig Jasper's grave. I wanted to tell you this in person."

The nobleman stood, his hands locked behind him, and began nervously pacing. He mumbled to himself, words Elinor could not catch. Worry shot through her but she kept silent.

Finally, he came to a halt in front of her. "Jasper was my only falconer?"

Elinor knew she needed to make a stand so she boldly said, "Nay. I am your other falconer."

"Only you are left?"

She nodded coolly.

"My steward tells me that you have never led any of the hunts. That you were kept from Uncle's sight."

"'Tis true that the baron did not wish to see me. Do not worry yourself about that, my lord," she said reassuringly. "Jasper raised me to be a falconer. I have trained raptors for ten and six years now and have two new eyases that I am working with. Both are intelligent females and are learning quickly. Though I have never led a hunt with others, have no doubt that I am most capable and trustworthy." She threw back her shoulders, her chin edging up a notch. "I will not disappoint you, my lord."

Anxiety flickered in his eyes. "I have no doubt you can do as you say but my wife might not be comfortable with you in this particular role."

Elinor stood her ground. Her future depended upon what this man would decide. She must convince him of her value.

"Then what would you have me do? Bring in another falconer to work with me? He could lead the hunts if you wish but even Jasper would tell you that my skills surpassed his as far as falconry was concerned."

Nigel ran a hand through his fair hair. "I don't know what to do," he said, his anguish obvious. "Let me think on it. We will speak again after Jasper's burial."

"As you wish, my lord." She lowered her eyes a moment and then turned, forcing herself to walk at an even pace and not flee the great hall as she wished.

She left the keep and the castle grounds, her pace brisk, and only slowed when she reached the meadow. It would all come down to Lady Rohesia. Elinor was certain the noblewoman would have the last word regarding Elinor's fate. She was powerless.

That frightened her more than Hal leaving for his home.

Approaching the woods, she scanned them without spotting him.

*He had deserted her.*

Though she didn't think she had been gone long, he hadn't waited as he promised he would. She had always looked at Hal as someone truthful. A man who, like a knight of the realm, would keep his word. Bitter disappointment filled her. It shouldn't bother her that he had returned to the cottage yet it did.

Elinor took a few steps into the forest.

"How did your talk with the baron go?"

She wheeled around, relief flooding her. Hal stood there, tall and incredibly handsome, concern written on his brow.

"I will tell you about it on the way home," she said stiffly, willing herself not to cry.

Wordlessly, he took her hand. Elinor drew strength and comfort from the gesture.

---

THE MASS RESEMBLED the previous one from when the baron had died. Elinor stood in the back, silently watching as Father Leo intoned the Latin words. When it came time to receive the host, she joined the long line that formed, relieved that she knew what to do this time. The priest placed the bread on her tongue. Elinor made the sign of the cross, imitating those who had gone before her. She almost burst into laughter as an audible sigh sounded across the chapel.

Father Leo gave the benediction. With the mass now concluded, the first to leave the chapel were Lord Nigel and Lady Rohesia. Elinor watched the couple until they grew closer and then deliberately dropped her eyes to the floor. She did not want to attract any undue attention and give the baroness an excuse to get rid of her.

Once the noble pair exited the chapel, others followed. Elinor stepped toward the door when someone tugged on her sleeve.

Turning, she saw a rotund man of two score next to her. He gave her a tentative smile.

"I am most sorry for your loss. Jasper was a good man."

Elinor nodded, uncertain how to reply.

Then others streamed forward, each offering her a few kind words and remarking on Jasper's good character. A glow warmed her, knowing how many people thought well of him.

She finally left the chapel and found Father Leo at her elbow.

"Thank you for coming, Elinor," the priest said. "I hope you see that Jasper was loved by many. He will be missed by all but most by you. May God's rich love bless you and keep you in this time of sorrow."

Once again, he placed a strong hand on her shoulder and squeezed it reassuringly.

"You are to go to the keep," he said, his voice low. "I will see to Jasper's burial. I hope for a pleasant outcome for you."

"Thank you."

Elinor walked slowly to the keep, dreading what the baron might say—or what words his wife might whisper in his ear to sway him. She climbed the steps and followed two women inside. Once again, she found Eunice waiting for her.

"I am to take you to the solar."

She followed the longtime servant upstairs. Memories flooded her as she passed the bedroom she had shared with her mother. Thoughts of peeking inside and seeing her mother shortly before her death caused a hitch in Elinor's breathing. She placed a hand over her pounding heart and told herself to remain calm.

They arrived at the solar and Eunice knocked at the door. A voice called out for them to enter. Eunice opened the door and motioned for Elinor to go inside. She stepped through the doorway.

Nothing about it looked familiar. If the furniture was the same, she didn't remember it. The solar had been her father's domain. She realized she might never have set foot in this place during her childhood.

The baron and baroness sat in chairs adjacent to the fireplace. The nobleman gestured for her to join them. No chair was near them, so Elinor understood that she was to stand throughout their meeting. She approached them and then locked her knees, hoping she wouldn't sway.

"I am sorry for your loss," Lord Nigel began, his knuckles white as he clutched the arms of his chair. "I know that it must be difficult—"

"Oh, get on with it," Lady Rohesia interrupted. When her husband fell silent, she glared up at Elinor, disdain written across her features.

"It simply won't do for you to be Whitley's only falconer," she began.

Elinor quelled the defiance rising within her. "If you feel the need to bring another falconer to the estate, I would be happy to work with him, my lady. Training raptors involves long hours and is a difficult task. I already work with a grown pair, Cleo and Horus. Cleo recently gave birth to two eyases."

"Male or female?" asked Lady Rohesia. "I hear females are more valuable."

"They are both females, my lady," Elinor agreed, keeping her voice pleasant. "Female peregrines grow to a much larger size and become fiercer hunters than males. Bess and Tris, the new eyases, already show great potential."

"How old are the first two?" Lady Rohesia demanded.

"Cleo is ten and three. Horus is ten and five."

"How much longer will they be able to birth new falcons?"

"A year or two. If that. As far as hunting goes, Horus has slowed down a bit but Cleo is still in fine shape and will happily lead hunters this upcoming season."

The noblewoman shook her head dismissively. "They are too old. My father's falcons didn't live as long. We would do well to sell them while we can and get a decent price then purchase a male to mate with the new, young females."

Elinor felt as if a heavy blow had landed to her gut. *Sell Cleo and Horus?*

"But they are as family to me, my lady. They could still be viable for more years to come," she pleaded. "At their age, they would never adapt to a new falconer after all their years with Jasper and me. Besides, the eyases need much more training before they can hunt, much less breed. It takes time and patience."

Lady Rohesia sniffed. "If we cannot get a fair price for the old birds, then I suppose we'll have to keep them. The king's laws are overly strict where falcons are concerned."

Elinor tamped down the anger surging through her. Just as a man could be legally blinded for poaching a falcon from the wild, she wished to poke out both of Lady Rohesia's eyes and throw them against the wall. She hated everything about this woman and her condescending manner.

"Still, I am not comfortable with you leading any hunts. 'Tis work for a man, not a woman," she mused. "In fact, I think we should only have a man as our falconer, my lord. Don't you agree?"

The noblewoman glanced casually at her husband before slyly meeting Elinor's eyes. "We will bring a new falconer to Whitley, one who has a son he can train to work with him. At that time, your services will no longer be required."

Elinor's anger dissolved in an instant as she felt deflated. Only now did she realize this had been the point of the conversation all along. That Lady Rohesia had previously determined to rid herself of Elinor once and for all and had steered the discussion to suit her purpose.

Still, she wouldn't give up without a fight.

"The raptors . . . they are mine. They are my family. I have trained them for years."

Lady Rohesia waved a hand about dismissively. "You yourself said these eyases are young. That will make it easier for someone else to step in since the birds are not yet so set in their ways." She looked pointedly at Elinor. "And remember that these raptors belong to the Baron of Whitley. *Not* you." Her victorious smile was the final blow.

Elinor reeled with this news. She had lost Jasper. She would soon lose Hal. And now this woman banished her from her beloved raptors.

Her head grew light. "Where I am to go?" she asked.

"The baron and I will decide your future. We will let you know once we have found a new falconer. In the meantime, carry on with your duties."

The noblewoman reached for a glass of wine and sipped it. Her husband sat mutely, staring into his own goblet.

Elinor began to rock and feared she might faint. Without a word, she fled the room.

# CHAPTER 12

ELINOR RUSHED DOWN the corridor, her hand pressed against her mouth to hold in the scream that threatened to erupt.

*She loathed that woman.*

The former baron had robbed her of her childhood and birthright but Lady Rohesia now stole Elinor's very family and livelihood away. How could she live without her raptors? Where would she go once the new falconer arrived?

She was utterly alone.

Elinor reached the top of the stairs. For a brief moment, she thought about flinging herself down them and ending her life. Lady Rohesia would not be able to ignore Elinor's broken body. But that would mean the noblewoman would be the winner in the game they played. Elinor refused to allow that to happen.

At the foot of the stairs, Eunice awaited her. Deep lines had been etched into the servant's face over the years. Elinor hurried down and joined the older woman.

"Did she rid herself of you?"

Elinor sighed. "Soon. She plans to bring in a new falconer. At that time, she will inform me what she and the baron have decided is to come of me."

Eunice spat on the ground. "She is a wicked one. And he is as weak as they come. She should have been the man and he the woman." Her face softened as she studied Elinor. "No one at Whitley likes what's been done to you, my lady. No one. But not a one of us has ever been in a position to stand up for you. For what is right."

Tears welled in Elinor's eyes. "Thank you for telling me that."

Eunice gave her a swift hug and stepped away. "You look so much like your mother." She choked and turned away—but not before Elinor saw the guilt in her eyes.

Elinor walked back to the cottage, deliberately keeping her mind a blank. Thinking about her circumstances wouldn't change anything. She had no control over her situation. Neither did the baron, it seemed. His wife ruled Whitley with an iron fist.

*Unless Elinor left on her own.*

She wasn't a serf tied to the land. Despite being exiled by her father, the fact remained that Elinor Swan was a member of the nobility. They couldn't hold her here as if she were some low-born soul.

And that gave her a sliver of hope.

She continued across Whitley lands, through the meadow and into the forest. Spending as much time as she could with her raptors would be her chief concern, especially since she had no idea how long she would be allowed around them. Then there was Hal. Her feelings had grown for him as rapidly as the eyases had developed. Soon, he would be gone, as well. She must cherish each day in his company before he departed and returned to his former life.

Arriving at the clearing, she paused when she spied Hal sitting on a stump, Tris perched on his gloved fist. Bess stood on the block perch alongside Cleo and Horus. The falcons preened their feathers as Hal conversed with Tris, his back to Elinor.

"You are my best girl, Tris. You are beautiful and smart and eager to please me." He looked up. "And you are also my sweet one, Bess. I have come to admire you both. I will miss you once I leave Whitley but I must return to my family. I have been away far too long and know they are worried about me."

Hal stood and encouraged Tris to hop onto the block perch. She joined her sister and began grooming her feathers with her bill as the others did. Hal stripped off his gauntlet and rested it on the stoop.

Elinor's heart rent in grief and despair, knowing she was about to lose him and how eager he sounded about leaving. Yet, as a mother bird knew when the time had come to push her babes from the nest, she must do the same with Hal and free him to return to his people. He had stayed with her far too long out of some sense of obligation for her helping him recover from his injuries. She needed to insist that he leave because she wouldn't be able to bear it if he had to witness her cast out from Whitley. Knowing Hal, he would feel a responsibility for her and offer to take her with him. Elinor couldn't allow that to happen. He had a life of his own, away from her.

With determination, Elinor stepped into the clearing, ready to insist that he leave in the morning. It wouldn't be easy to see him depart but the longer he stayed, the more it would hurt her to see him go. Better now in order to give her time to deal with that heartbreak before she faced being turned away from Whitley and her raptors.

Hal must have sensed her presence. He swung around and as he caught sight of her, he broke out into the most brilliant smile.

Elinor promptly burst into tears.

He closed the distance between them in seconds, encircling her in his arms, drawing her to his chest. Her fingers clutched his soft tunic as she buried her face in it and wept a river of tears. Elinor cried for the mother she barely remembered and the life she'd been forced to give up because of her father's selfish whim. Tears fell for the hole in her heart with Jasper dead and buried. Her body shook as she sobbed in misery because her time with her beloved raptors soon would come to an end. Everything she had known was being wrenched from her. She stood alone against the world and didn't know if she even wanted to continue living in it.

The longer she cried, the more Hal stroked her back with firm but gentle hands, murmuring comforting words that she didn't bother to listen to. Immense warmth radiated from him, bringing her a sense of solace. His hand touched her head, wrapping around it, his thumb moving back and forth, soothing her scalp.

Though everything was wrong in her life, his embrace eased her suffering—and felt so right. She gazed up at him with watery eyes only to find his a brilliant blue and stormy. They scared her, depths to them she'd never seen. Hal had been so quiet in the beginning. Through time together, he had opened up to her, but this was a new side to him that she'd never witnessed before.

It frightened her. It thrilled her.

She knew when he came to a decision—and knew what that decision was even as he lowered his mouth to hers. Softly, he brushed his lips against hers. The tingling she'd experienced when she'd touched him began in full force. His lips grew more insistent. The tingling spread through her limbs.

Elinor needed him. She'd never needed anyone or hadn't thought she did. Until this man. Sudden desire for things she didn't understand burned within her. Her hands slipped up his rock-hard chest to his neck. Her fingers danced along it and pushed up into his hair.

A deep groan rumbled within him. Hal clutched her as his tongue gained entrance into her mouth. It possessed her, dominating her, causing her bones to melt. Elinor clung to Hal as if a tempest swirled about them and they would only survive it if they held on to one another. He was her anchor amidst this storm. She determined never to let go.

His hands roamed down her back and cupped her buttocks. She felt something stiff pressing against her belly, something between them, and realized his manhood hardened.

*He wanted her.*

Exhilaration filled her. He *wanted* her. No one other than Jasper had laid claim to her and even then, Jasper had left her on her own much of the time. But Hal desired her as a woman. He didn't know she was an outcast from the nobility. He only knew her as a falconer. He wanted Elinor for her true self.

The kiss deepened as he kneaded her buttocks with strong fingers. Elinor returned his kiss with everything she had, wanting to remember the taste of him in the years to come.

He began to pull away but she was having none of that. Her fingers tightened in his thick hair, forcing his lips back to hers. Elinor kissed him as he had kissed her, with a longing and passion that rocked her to her core.

Hal tried to break the kiss again but Elinor refused to cooperate. Her hands locked behind his neck and she hoisted her legs up, wrapping them about his waist. A deep growl came from him. His lips traveled down her throat, nipping her with little love bites that sent a frisson of pleasure through her. He began walking as she tossed her head back, giving him better access to her neck. They crashed against something and Elinor held on securely. She heard a noise and felt warmth before a door slammed. Opening her eyes, she saw they were now inside the cottage.

Hal spun around and pushed her against the door, her legs still locked around him. His teeth now teased her earlobe, causing a pounding to begin where her legs joined. No, it had drummed since their mouths met, picking up the pace until it throbbed enough to gain her attention.

It told her that she needed him to touch her there. To do something to quell the restless feeling that rippled through her. Her nipples ached as they pressed against his chest. They, too, begged for his attention. Elinor released her legs and slowly lowered them to the ground.

"Touch me," she said, her voice quivering.

Hal's tongue, which swirled about her ear, stopped. He raised his head, a question forming on his lips.

"No questions," she ordered. "No words."

"But—"

She silenced him, pressing two fingers against his beautiful mouth.

"I don't know what I need but *you* know what to do to satisfy me. Do it. Now."

"Elinor," he murmured against her fingers.

"Hush," she told him.

He captured her hand in his and pulled it from his mouth, kissing the tips of her fingers tenderly. Her breasts swelled against him, the nipples aching.

"Do it," she urged again and saw desire spark in his eyes. When he still hesitated, she said, "I have always loved my birds more than people, for they have never let me down. But they cannot fill this emptiness inside me.

"Only you can."

He swept her off her feet and crossed to her pallet, placing her gently atop it. Elinor trembled with need as he stripped her tunic from her and tossed it aside. Hal lowered her to the straw and then yanked his own tunic away, exposing his splendidly muscled chest, a dark matting of hair on it. She itched to touch it. To touch him. Folding his tunic, he lifted her head and placed the garment under it.

His mouth hovered over hers a moment, his warm breath mingling with hers. Then he kissed her softly and continued to trail kisses down her throat and to the top curve of her breast. His tongue traced the curve from the top and rounded to the side before dragging across her nipple. He licked and nipped at it as he kneaded her other breast with his hand.

The thumping in her nether region pulsed violently as his lips and tongue and teeth continued to tease her. Elinor's head began to whip from side to side. Hal's hands rose, his fingers pushing into her hair to still her as he sucked at first one breast and then the other. She thought she might go mad from the wild pleasure.

Then he abandoned both breasts and trailed his tongue down her body. It began shaking uncontrollably. Hal loosened her belt and pulled her pants over her hips and slowly down her legs until they reached her feet. She wriggled as he removed her boots, her blade spilling out, and then he eased the pants over her feet.

Elinor lay bare before him and shivered, not from the cold but at the admiring gaze in his eyes as they traveled up her body. His hand lightly stroked her thighs.

"So soft," he whispered. "So silky."

His fingers traveled to her inner thigh, brushing it softly. Her core now pounded fiercely, calling out for his attention.

He gave it to her.

A finger slipped inside her. Elinor gasped. Hal's eyes held hers as his finger explored her with delicious slowness. Another joined the first, stroking her. Her hips rose and fell as she clenched around his fingers.

"That's it," he murmured. "Oh, you are so tight. So lovely."

Hal continued to watch her. Elinor felt her face flush as her entire body heated at his touch. His fingers petted her languidly until she wanted to scream then he began pushing them in and out, picking up the pace as he stroked her.

Elinor's breath caught. The tingling now brought her to a precipice. She danced at its edge, ready to dive headfirst, knowing something wonderful was about to happen.

"Let go, sweetheart," Hal encouraged as his thumb rubbed against a nub, circling it, teasing it, as his fingers continued to move inside her.

Then Elinor was falling, hard, fast, dizzy from the burst of intense pleasure that radiated through her.

"That's right. Go with it," he said as she bucked and twisted and gasped. The pleasure went on and on until she shouted in utter joy.

And all the while, Hal watched her, a satisfied smile playing on his sensual lips.

The waves of pleasure began to ebb and finally petered out. Elinor felt more spent than ever before. She could not have lifted even her smallest finger.

Hal lay down beside her, drawing a blanket over them. Elinor turned and snuggled against his bare chest, her cheek next to his beating heart.

"Sleep, sweetheart."

And she did.

## CHAPTER 13

HAL LISTENED TO Elinor's soft breaths as she slept. He glanced down at her, toying with a lock of her deep brown hair. Though they were close in age, in sleep the years fell away from her. She appeared so very young.

And vulnerable.

That was why he hadn't coupled with her. He'd wanted to bury himself inside her—more than any woman he'd ever known—but it wouldn't have been right. Elinor's life was here at Whitley, while his was . . . where?

He didn't fit in anywhere.

His gut told him the king hadn't been successful against the Lords Appellant. Hal had witnessed the armies that de Vere and Molineux raised crumble in front of him. Richard had depended upon those two men and the soldiers they led to join him in battle against the noblemen who usurped his power. Without receiving those reinforcements and facing the seasoned forces of the five Lords Appellant, the king didn't stand a chance. At best, he had been taken into custody and languished in the Tower while the quintet tried to rule England. At worst, Richard had lost his head.

If so, that would plunge England into civil war. Hal knew none of the Lords Appellant wanted that, which was why he hoped the young king was in custody. Only two things would save Richard—reaching his majority in the next year or his uncle, the Duke of Lancaster, giving up trying to win the crown in Castile and returning to England to support his nephew.

If Richard's powerful uncle did not return, Hal supposed once the Lords Appellant relinquished power next year and handed it back to the rightful monarch, he could rejoin the king's royal guard. But the thought left him despondent. Both his brothers had been members of Richard's elite protectors and found reasons to leave—and women to love.

As Hal had.

He would freely admit it to himself. He loved Elinor, a mysterious woman with no known last name. No family. No friends—except for her wild raptors. The woman who had nursed him back to health. But his love didn't boil down to gratitude. He knew better than that. His parents had always told their children they would know when they found their soul mate.

Elinor was his.

She had taken a broken man, physically and emotionally, and her healing hands and kind heart had brought him back to himself. The true Hal from long ago, not the arrogant knight at court who flirted outrageously and only thought about training and battle. He had been stripped of everything dear to him—his position at court, his honor as a knight, his social circle. As Elinor helped rebuild him without even knowing she did, Hal realized how shallow his life and thoughts had been before now. That what mattered most was love and family.

He was fortunate to have a large, affectionate family who supported him no matter what he did or where he went. Hal knew they would support his pursuit of Elinor, though she was so different from the rest of the mates three of his siblings had chosen. Ancel's wife, Margery, was the daughter of an earl. Alys had married Kit, who'd become the rightful Baron of Brentley. Even Edward's wife, Rosalyne, who grew up in humble circumstances as the niece of an artist, was, in reality, the daughter of Lawrence Bowyar, Baron of Shallowheart.

Yet, he couldn't help but think that every de Montfort would welcome Elinor with open arms. Hal's parents believed in love. Geoffrey and Merryn de Montfort had wanted love matches for their children and so none of them had been betrothed to another while still in their cradle. They would understand his feelings for Elinor.

Even when Hal barely understood them himself.

Physically, he was attracted to Elinor, for what man wouldn't be? The dimple alone in her left cheek that appeared when she smiled was enough to bring him to his knees. He could lose himself in her warm, brown eyes and dark waves of hair for hours. He'd just spent time caressing the beautiful curves on her slender frame, finally touching with hands and mouth what he'd dreamed about night after night.

Yet her inner beauty outshone her looks. It was a mixture of many things that he'd admired about her. Her patience could outlast Job's, thanks to her work training falcons over the years. He adored her intelligence and practical nature. Elinor was not a woman who made time for those who proved idle or flirtatious. Obviously, she'd had a hard life, losing her parents when she was so young and being taken in by Jasper. Nothing had been given to her and she was the kind of woman who wouldn't have accepted it if it had been offered to her. Elinor was generous and giving, especially to a stranger. She had the strength of character to rescue him and nurse him and then teach him to train raptors. He believed, though she seemed to be a woman with a simple life, that she had more depth than most anyone of his acquaintance.

Hal thought she had a great capacity for love. If the fierceness and devotion with which she guarded and trained her falcons was any indication, it would be tenfold with a husband and children.

He wanted to be that husband. He wanted to plant his seed in her belly and watch it grow. He wanted to father a dozen children with her, hoping each would get her fine looks and sweet spirit, be they sons or daughters.

Still, she had shown no romantic interest in him. Until today.

Guilt rushed through him as he thought he might have taken advantage of her emotional state. She had returned from Jasper's funeral mass and must have been feeling terribly alone by the time she reached the cottage she had shared with the falconer and their raptors. Hal hoped he hadn't forced himself on her. Then he remembered the heat of desire flaming in her eyes. Begging—no, ordering—him to fill the emptiness within her. Almost against his will, he did what he had longed to do for weeks.

Hal had stopped short of taking her virginity. For all the confidence she displayed in her work, Elinor seemed naïve about what occurred between a man and a woman. She had caught on quickly and returned his kisses with passion and enthusiasm but he forced himself to draw a line and not breech her maidenhead. The possibility of creating a child always existed when a man coupled with a woman. He wanted that choice to be hers. He could not make it for her.

Would she be able to give up her life at Whitley and come with him to Kinwick?

Hal's heart told him that's where his future would unfold. He decided to return home to speak with his parents about his plans and then return for Elinor. The time apart would allow her to know if she had true feelings for him, ones that might grow, hopefully, into love. He wouldn't try to talk her into leaving Whitley once he returned. It wasn't up to him to convince her. She must come willingly because it was what she wanted. That *he* was what she needed to exist.

Because of that, he would make no declarations of love to her before he left. They would part as friends. Hal only hoped that his absence would create a void in her heart and allow her to realize they were meant to be together, now and always.

He rose from the pallet and placed the blanket snugly around her then slipped his gypon back on. He would spend what remained of the afternoon training Bess and Tris and then head for Kinwick in the morning.

ELINOR AWOKE, STRETCHING her legs and pointing her toes. A deep contentment filled her. She also felt more rested than she had in months. Her eyes slowly opened and scanned the small cottage. Hal wasn't present. The fire needed to be built up. Mayhap he had gone for more wood.

As she pushed her arm from under the blanket warming her, she realized it was bare. *She* was bare. Then delicious thoughts of Hal's hands caressing her naked body caused her to heat. They had been gentle and thorough. Elinor licked her lips and still tasted him. A sigh of satisfaction escaped as her hand searched for her clothes. She found her tunic and sat up, pulling it over her head and smoothing it down.

But the rough wool only made her aware of her breasts and how sensitive her nipples now were since Hal had lavished attention on them. She dragged her pants to the blanket and kicked it aside. Drawing the material up her legs only made her relive his hands skimming her thighs. She brought her pants up to her waist and collapsed again, recollecting everything that had passed between them.

Hal cared for her. Mayhap, he even loved her. A smile tugged at the corners of her mouth. Oh, she had pushed aside these very thoughts to a far corner of her mind, locking them away, refusing to let them out.

Now she could.

After what had passed between them, Elinor knew she must tell him that the baroness wanted her gone from Whitley lands. She hoped that the strong feelings he'd displayed for her would encourage him to invite her to accompany him when he returned to his home. It must lie somewhere south of Whitley since that was the direction he journeyed when the highwaymen attacked. If what she believed of the baroness was true, a new falconer would arrive soon. After a few days working with him and making sure her raptors were in good hands, Elinor would be free to leave—with Hal.

Surely, he *must* want her to go with him. What they had done together seemed only the start of what could come. His actions had sated her but she thought she could have done something in return to help him feel the same soaring passion. She'd always been a quick learner. Just look at how fast she'd understood what kissing was all about. Who would have thought kissing involved more than pressing lips together? But it did and Elinor knew Hal could initiate her into all of the ways of love play between a man and a woman.

Tamping down the giddiness that threatened to erupt in bubbling laughter, she sat up and located her boots. As she slid the first one onto her foot, the cottage door opened.

Hal entered and nodded pleasantly at her. "Good morning, Elinor."

His words startled her. "Morning? I slept until the next day?" Her stomach gurgled noisily in response, letting her know it had been a long time since she'd eaten.

He tended to the fire, adding another log as she pulled on her other boot. "Aye. Your body needed the sleep. Putting Jasper to rest yesterday was trying for you, both physically and emotionally." He indicated the table. "I have set out food to break our fast."

She joined him at the table, where bread and ale awaited.

"I trained with Bess and Tris all yesterday while you were gone to the castle and then after you slept."

Elinor tried not to let hurt feelings arise. Hal had not once mentioned what occurred between them. In fact, he looked at her today as he had every other day.

*Had she dreamed of his kiss?*

Nay, she couldn't have. Even in her wildest imaginings, she would not have known to think of such things. Her body today was sensitive in places she had ignored in the past. Hal had awakened some sleeping giant within her and it longed for his touch. That alone told her that she couldn't have imagined yesterday's events.

So why did he ignore speaking of it?

Unless he regarded their intimacies as a mistake. Or mayhap, she had not pleased him. In her inexperience, she had not made him feel as he had her. Should she say something? Elinor didn't think she could stand his rejection.

"I am concerned about Horus, though," Hal continued, chewing his bread thoughtfully. "He's seemed out of sorts for a few days. He did not come home last night and he isn't outside on the perch this morning. I freed Cleo from the mews so that she might search for him."

She chewed on her bottom lip. "I have also been worried about Horus," she confided, pushing aside the wild thoughts bouncing inside her. "He hasn't preened or roused as he should for a few days and his appetite has been lacking."

"You have said he is ten and five. Is that old for a peregrine?"

Elinor nodded, a lump forming in her throat. "'Tis near the age that raptors . . . cease." She dropped her head, not wanting to face the possibility of Horus dying.

He frowned. "I am sorry to hear that. I was hoping to see him before I left this morning."

Her head shot up. "You . . . are leaving? Now?" Her stomach churned uneasily. She blinked her eyes several times, fighting to keep the tears at bay.

"Aye. Dawn occurred as you awoke. 'Twill give me an early start on the road if I leave now." He turned his cup up and drained the last of its contents. "I fear I have overstayed my welcome. My leg is as strong as ever, thanks to your healing hands. You also forced me to take my time and not rush things once the splints came off."

Hal pushed the cup aside and leaned his arms on the table. "I have no more excuses left. I have built up my strength so that I may make my way home. On top of that, I have learned a small fraction of what it takes to work with raptors." He gave her a warm smile. "And I have made a friend in you."

"A friend," she echoed dully, mustering a weak smile. She looked across the table at him and saw everything she wanted. Everything she needed. He was handsome and kind and intelligent.

And he only thought of her as a friend.

The kisses they had shared would not be mentioned. She refused to be the one to bring them up. Elinor resolved to remain strong in the next few moments. Hal mustn't suspect how she truly felt about him.

He rose. "Come outside with me as I say goodbye to the falcons." He took both their gauntlets and headed out the door.

She followed him with a heavy heart, forcing herself to put one foot in front of the other. Obviously, he did not feel about her as she did him. The last thing she wanted to do was send him off with guilt hanging over him for not returning her sentiments. They *were* friends. Over their weeks together, they had built a friendship to be treasured, even though they would never meet one another again. Elinor would see her companion off in good spirits. He deserved that much from her.

Placing a smile on her face, she joined him. Both slipped on their gauntlets and removed Bess and Tris from their mews. Hal held each bird for a few moments, telling them both goodbye as he returned them to their cages. Cleo swooped from the sky and landed on the perch and he bid her farewell, too.

Hal pulled off his gauntlet and handed it to her. "Thank you for everything you taught me in my time here, Elinor. I enjoyed every moment working with your raptors. Though I am sorry about the circumstances that led me here, I appreciate you taking me in and befriending me."

"I have enjoyed coming to know you, Hal," she said brightly, consciously keeping a smile on her lips. "Your stories have kept me amused for many hours. I, too, am grateful for your friendship." She paused. "I hope one day that we can renew our acquaintance."

"I'd like that. Very much," he said, his gaze meeting and holding hers.

For a moment, Elinor thought he might kiss her. Then the unreadable look on his face vanished and he smiled broadly.

"Then I am off." He gave her a courtly bow, triggering a memory of how she and her mother had been greeted by knights in the great hall so many years ago. "Till we meet again."

Hal strode from the clearing without a backward glance. Elinor waited until he was out of sight and gave in to the feeling to follow him. She knew these woods better than anyone on Whitley lands and silently tracked him at a distance, not ready to let him go.

Finally, he reached the road and she lost sight of him. By the time she came to the edge of the woods, he was a good ways down the path. Elinor clung to a tree, watching until he became only a speck and then disappeared from view. She collapsed to her knees, a mournful wail piercing the surrounding quiet. Heaving sobs erupted as her fingers dug into the earth.

He was gone. Hal was gone. For good. She would never see him again, despite their final words to one another. He marched jauntily off to his old life, one that held no place for her.

Elinor dragged herself to her feet. She wouldn't think about him. She couldn't. Not with everything she faced in her immediate future. She returned to the clearing and stopped in her tracks.

"Horus!" she cried.

She rushed to the tiercel, who lay on the ground only a few feet from his mews. Cleo stood next to him, keening softly as she nudged him with her beak. Not taking time to place her gauntlet on, Elinor sat and placed Horus in her lap. She gently stroked the peregrine as the life ebbed away from him. The faint heartbeat beneath her fingers eventually ceased as his eyes closed a final time.

Cleo hopped into her lap and lay her head next to her mate as Elinor cried for the loss of Horus.

And Hal.

## CHAPTER 14

Elinor held a lethargic Cleo in her lap. For two days and nights, the peregrine had mourned her life mate. The raptor did not preen and refused to eat or drink. Elinor feared Cleo would soon follow Horus into death. She didn't know how much her heart could take. She'd only left the falcon to feed Bess and Tris, neglecting to eat much herself. Because of that, her head pounded fiercely while her stomach churned noisily.

A rap at the door startled her. No guests ever came to the cottage. Elinor sat silently, not bothering to acknowledge the visitor's presence.

"Elinor!" a muffled voice called from outside. "'Tis Father Leo. Open up." More knocking ensued.

She did not respond. Hopefully, he would go away. Then she noticed that she had not bolted the door when she'd come in from feeding Bess and Tris. Would the meddlesome priest try to enter without permission?

He did.

"Elinor?" he called out as he came through the door. He squinted and caught sight of her. "Oh." He closed the door behind him and crossed to her, a grave look on his face. "Is your bird ill?"

"She is," Elinor said dully. She had no wish to carry on a conversation with anyone, much less a priest. Her anger at God had built slowly over the past few days. If Father Leo did not watch himself, he would take the brunt of it.

The priest sat on the floor beside her. "I have brought Gerald with me. He is the new falconer from the far north who arrived yesterday.

Lady Rohesia would like you to work with him today and tomorrow and then report to her at the keep on Gerald's progress with the falcons."

His words confirmed her suspicion that the noblewoman had already sent for a falconer and had merely planted the idea of bringing in a new one with her husband since it would have been impossible for this Gerald to arrive so quickly from so great a distance. Anger now boiled inside her at Lady Rohesia's deception.

"I will do my duty," she ground out. "See if this man is capable of working with my raptors."

Father Leo looked to Cleo. "Will she live?"

"I doubt it," Elinor said harshly, regretting her tone as Cleo shuddered.

"Life and death are all a part of God's plan, Elinor," the priest said placidly, as if he remarked upon the recent weather.

Rage poured through her at his thoughtless words.

"What else is a part of your God's plan?" she demanded in a low tone so as not to upset Cleo any more than she already had. "He must be an angry God, for He has shown me no mercy."

"Our Lord Jesus Christ is full of mercy," Father Leo countered.

Tears of fury spilled down her cheeks as she asked, "Then where was He when a young, motherless child was turned out of her home? Why did He allow that to happen to me? My mother died. *Died!* And yet my father, who never once referred to me by name since I was an insignificant girl, offered me no comfort. Instead, he ejected me from the keep and said I was never to return. I was placed in the hands of a man I had never met and taken from everyone and everything I had ever known."

She wiped the tears from her cheeks, embarrassed that they showed weakness. "And now what has happened to me? After years of serving Whitley, raising and training its raptors, I have lost everything. Jasper. Hal. Horus." She glanced down at her lap and softened her tone. "And now my precious Cleo." Swallowing, she added, "Soon, I will lose this home for when I speak to Lady Rohesia, she will send me far away. I already know this."

Elinor glared up at the priest. "So where is the mercy in all of this, Father? I am a penniless noblewoman who never learned how to act as one of my class should. I dress and live as a male peasant. I have no coin and will soon be an outcast. What kind of God would do that? What did I ever do to injure Him so that He would punish me?"

Before she received an answer, a knock sounded. The priest rose and ushered in a man who looked achingly like Jasper. He had the same lean frame and was close to Jasper's height. His eyes were kind and his face weathered by years spent in the sun.

He smiled at her. "Greetings, Elinor. I am Gerald and I must compliment you on what you have done with the young raptors. I've only spent a few minutes with them but I can already see how well you have trained them. They are most intelligent and eager. I look forward to working with them."

Then he frowned as he looked at her lap and came to her. Kneeling, he pulled off his gauntlet and set it aside. He studied Cleo, deep sorrow reflected in his compassionate eyes.

"How old is she?" he asked gently.

"Ten and three," Elinor told him.

"Her feathers are dull. Her appetite?"

"She has none." Elinor paused. "Cleo just lost Horus, her life mate. She had spent every day she lived in his company."

Gerald reached out and stroked Cleo's head. "Ah, the poor thing. She's grieving. Horus was her soul mate. She won't want to go on without him." He looked to the priest. "Falcons mate for life," he explained. "Cleo will mourn Horus' loss until she wastes away. I have seen it happen before."

Elinor's eyes welled with tears. She, too, grieved. Not only for Jasper and Horus but for Hal's absence from her life. She still hadn't gotten used to him being gone and expected him to walk through the cottage door at any moment.

She watched Gerald gently pet Cleo, a falcon he'd never seen, and saw his anguish at the raptor's impending death. Despite wanting to hate everything about this new falconer who would replace her, she realized he would take excellent care of Bess and Tris. Knowing her girls would be in good hands gave her some solace.

"I will leave you together to care for this bird," Father Leo said. "Elinor, you know when to come to the castle." He bowed his head and left the cottage.

Elinor lost track of how long they sat with Cleo. Gerald attempted no conversation, which she appreciated. He merely comforted the raptor as she did.

Cleo shivered and made a soft mewling sound. She opened her eyes and glanced up at Elinor.

"I love you, my sweet Cleo," she managed to say, her voice breaking. "You have been like a child to me. I will always remember our time together." Elinor dipped her head and brushed her lips on the falcon's crown. "Go. Be with Horus. Give him my love."

The bird expelled a last breath and grew still. She swept her hand along Cleo's coat one last time. Gerald helped her to her feet and Elinor wrapped her favorite falcon in clean linen.

"Have you already buried Horus?" he asked, his eyes bright with unshed tears.

"Nay. When Cleo and I found him, her distress caused me to spend every waking moment by her side. I placed Horus in the mews." She indicated the small cages inside the cottage, where Cleo's mate also lay wrapped in linen. "I wanted them to be close together."

"We can place them next to one another. I'll dig them a grave they can share. Show me where you want them laid to rest," he said gruffly, mopping his eyes with his sleeve.

Elinor led Gerald outside, knowing exactly where her raptors should be buried.

"Here. At the foot of this oak," she told him. "Since they will lie next to the clearing, they can be here in spirit as Bess and Tris complete their training and mature over the years."

"So that's who these two beauties are." Gerald looked at the young females sitting in their mews, each watching with interest what the humans did.

"Bess is on the left. Tris is slightly smaller than her sister."

"Have they worked with the lure yet?" he asked.

"Aye. They've even begun stooping to it," she said with pride.

Gerald nodded in approval. "Good. Then find me a shovel and let us bury their lovely parents. I hope after that you'll be up to showing me all they can do."

"I will," Elinor promised, pushing aside her grief.

HAL'S FEET HAD grown weary as he walked the last few days but his leg had held up well. In the next quarter hour, he would reach Sandbourne, home of his cousin, Elysande, and her husband. Michael Devereux had served as one of Geoffrey de Montfort's knights when Hal had begun to walk, and the family loved telling stories of how Hal would call Michael's name over and over, chasing the knight about and being chased in return. He could still remember Michael bringing him up into the saddle to ride with him.

Michael left Kinwick when he became the Earl of Sandbourne and had married Elysande soon after. No one in England knew more about horses than Elysande did. Since by horse it only took a full day and until noon of the next to arrive at Kinwick, Hal hoped his cousin would loan him one of her beloved horses so he could shave off time from his long journey.

Besides a horse, he needed new clothing and a shave and probably a day's rest before he set out again. He looked forward to seeing Elysande and Michael and hoped also to visit with their son, David. They had been close growing up and David had been knighted several months ago when he'd turned one and twenty. Hal had not been able to get away from court because of the charged political atmosphere and regretted not attending David's Oath of Knighthood Ceremony. David now resided permanently at Sandbourne, preparing for the day he would take his father's place as its earl. David's sister had married the previous year and his younger brother, Tucker, served as a squire to Geoffrey de Montfort's cousin, Raynor Le Roux.

Coming around a bend in the road, he spotted Sandbourne perched on a hill. Hal picked up his pace, eager to arrive. As he made his way toward the castle, he wished Elinor could be here with him. She would have gotten along well with the Devereux family and he would have given anything to have introduced them to the woman he loved. He could hear David teasing him about having fallen in love. Michael, too, would laugh that Hal loved a woman crazy for falcons just as he loved a woman who was mad for horses. Hal vowed that once he returned and claimed Elinor as his own, they would marry in front of as much family as could attend. Those who couldn't make it to Kinwick for the nuptial mass would be in store for a visit, for he wished Elinor to meet everyone he loved. His family would become hers.

And they would make a family of their own.

Arriving at the gates of Sandbourne, he greeted the gatekeeper by name and gained quick admittance. He decided to head straight to the training yard, hoping to see Michael and David in action. Though he'd enjoyed his time working with Elinor's raptors, Hal longed to swing a sword or mace once again.

As he drew near, it startled him to recognize his sister passing near his right. What would Jessimond be doing at Sandbourne?

"Hal?" He heard astonishment in her voice before she broke out in a smile and came running toward him. "Hal!" she cried with enthusiasm.

She flew at him, her arms and legs wrapping tightly about him. He laughed as he twirled them in circles.

"What are you doing here?" she demanded as she released him and stepped away, her hands going to her waist.

Hal grinned. "I was about to ask you the same thing. You're growing up, Jess. You look quite pretty."

Jessimond would be two and twelve sometime in June and she had blossomed since he'd last been home. He could see more than traces of the woman she would become, a true beauty. Her wavy, thick hair shone like spun gold in the sunlight and her unusual violet eyes darkened in color at his compliment. She blushed a pretty pink, twisting her hands in front of her.

"Don't be embarrassed," he chided her. "Simply say *thank you* when a man flatters you. But watch for those who flatter you overmuch," he warned, as a good brother should.

"Thank you," she said sweetly, batting her lashes coyly at him.

"Enough of that." He drew her into another hug and then released her. "I'll ask again—why are you at Sandbourne?"

"We came so Nan can work with Michael's archers. Mother and Father are here, as well. They will be so excited to see you." Jessimond frowned. "They have been worried about you, Hal. We all have. No word has come for ever so long."

He threw an arm about her. "I know, Jess. But I am here now, in the flesh, and eager to see them."

"I was going to fetch Mother and Elysande from the stables to the training yard. Nan has set up a contest between various soldiers. Michael and Father wanted them to come watch."

"Let's retrieve them," Hal suggested.

Jessimond chattered happily as they walked to the stables. Being with her reminded him how much he had missed home. They entered the stables and he put a finger to his lips. She stopped talking as they wound their way down the stalls in search of Elysande and his mother.

They turned a corner and Hal stopped in his tracks. Elysande's beauty had only grown and matured over the years. She had to be a couple of years older than two score but she still was a lovely woman.

But Merryn de Montfort's beauty stunned him.

His mother would turn two score and ten this year and yet she radiated eternal youth. Hal had often laughed when his father referred to his mother as a goddess but Hal also knew how fierce his father's love was for his wife. Pride at being this woman's offspring rippled through him.

Sensing their presence, Merryn turned. Though a few laugh lines had appeared around her eyes, the rest of her face remained smooth.

Her eyes lit up as she caught sight of him.

"Hal!"

He hurried to embrace her, holding her a long moment as he drank in her familiar scent and felt the comfort of a mother's arms. Finally, he drew away.

"You could stand a bath. And a change of clothes," she admonished, though he saw the teasing light in her eyes. "And sending a missive our way every now and then would be something for you to consider in the future. Or else you might have to be summoned home to attend my funeral mass because I will have dropped dead from worry."

He kissed her hands. "I agree, Mother. To everything you say. I'm sorry that I wasn't in a position to send word to you and Father. I was indisposed for several weeks with a broken leg."

Her eyes flew to his legs. "You are all right?" Her hands clutched his arms as she scanned his face.

"I am quite well now. I have much to tell you and Father, though." He glanced to his left. "Greetings, Cousin Elysande. I did not mean to ignore you." He stepped over and gave her a kiss.

"I am happy to see you alive and well, Hal. Michael will be delighted to find you at Sandbourne. David, too. We should go find them and celebrate your return to our fold."

"Nan has an archery contest about to begin," piped up Jessimond. "She wanted you all to come and watch."

Merryn put an arm around her daughter and took Hal's hand. "The contest can wait. I want to spend time with my son."

"I will return to the keep and have food and drink sent to the solar so that we may enjoy a long visit," Elysande said. "Bring Geoffrey and Michael back with you. Nan and David, too."

Hal escorted his mother and sister to the training yard. When they grew near, he spotted his father and Michael standing on a platform observing the action. Geoffrey de Montfort glanced in his direction and beamed. He jumped down and strode toward them.

Hal broke away and met his father. They shook hands then

hugged. Michael arrived and slapped Hal on the back, grinning broadly. Hal heard Nan cry out his name as she ran across the training yard, casting her bow aside. She clung tightly to him.

"Oh, where have you been?" she agonized. "We thought the worst, Hal." Her eyes brimmed with unshed tears. "I couldn't have lived without you."

He whispered reassurances to her, feeling guilty for what he had put his family through.

Suddenly, Michael shouted across the training yard to the soldiers standing, watching the reunion. "The archery contest is canceled. You men can continue your training in other ways."

Hal protested. "Nay, Michael. Nan has been preparing these men for it. I wouldn't want her to be disappointed."

Nan snorted. "It can wait, Hal. I would have beaten every one of them anyway. This way, they can have another day of practice and think that they might have a chance against me." She grinned, full of confidence and mischief.

He might not be at Kinwick yet, but where family could be found, there was home.

# CHAPTER 15

THEIR GROUP LEFT the training yard, David falling into step behind them after greeting Hal. They made their way across the bailey toward the keep. Jessimond held his hand while Nan took the other.

"So Jess told me you've been training Michael's knights."

"'Tis the same as I've done at Kinwick," Nan said. "Only it took a few days to win over the Sandbourne soldiers. They did not trust a woman with a bow in her hands, much less one who could best them."

He laughed. Nan's skills had far surpassed what he had taught her many years ago. "You could probably teach even the Cheshire bowmen in the king's royal guard a thing or two," Hal replied. "And they are known to be the best in the kingdom."

Her brows knit together. "Things are nasty at court," she confided.

"How? I know nothing of it."

"Father knows more than I do. He has received several missives. I heard him telling Michael. Ask him."

Elysande greeted them once they arrived at the solar. Hal's mouth watered at the feast spread out on the table. He smelled rabbit stew that had been simmered in garlic and pepper and spiced eels and couldn't wait to sink his teeth into the soft manchet, which he hadn't eaten since last summer before he left court for the Midlands. It made the simple fare he'd partaken of with Elinor seem meager. It had been, he now realized. She lived a life on the edge of poverty. If not for Cleo and Horus providing meat on a regular basis, she might actually have starved. It angered him that the nobleman who held the estate treated her so poorly. If the baron did that to a treasured falconer, how must others at Whitley suffer? Hal determined to rescue Elinor from the place as soon as he could—and that meant sharing with those he loved what he planned to do.

"Have a seat, everyone," Elysande told her guests. "I had the kitchen bring up platters of cold meat, fruit, and cheeses and several hot dishes." She winked at Jessimond. "A few sweetmeats, too."

Michael brushed a kiss upon his wife's cheek. "I'll pour the wine."

All present begin to fill their trenchers with food as cups of wine were passed around. Hal savored his first taste of wine in months, allowing it to roll along his tongue. Not since before he'd marched from London with the king had he drunk wine. Then he allowed himself to enjoy eating a few minutes before he opened up the conversation.

Looking to his father, he said, "I'm sure you have wondered where I was for several months now. Especially since you've already received news from court about the Lords Appellant revoking the king's power. We marched from London so quickly, I didn't have time to send word to you where I might be."

Geoffrey sipped his wine thoughtfully before speaking. "We did hear of Richard's attempts to make peace with the French so that he could focus his full strength against the armies of the Lords Appellant. After they defeated the king, the five lords convened Parliament so that they could expose his attempts to reconcile with France. As of now, Parliament has reacted swiftly. Most all of the king's advisers have been convicted of treason. A few have been forced into exile but many have—or will—be executed. Robert Tresilian, the chief justice, was one of the first to lose his life."

Bitterness rose in Hal. He'd liked Tresilian a great deal. The judge had a keen mind and had been loyal to a fault when it came to supporting Richard. What country did they live in where a man who supported his king lost his head?

His mother's hand covered his. "We feared you might be one of those punished, Hal, especially when we heard nothing from you."

Though she appeared calm, he knew how much she had been affected by his absence.

"Where is the king now?" he asked, almost afraid to hear their response.

"Locked away in the Tower," Michael informed him. "Supposedly, he's being looked after by a few of his guardsmen. That was our hope—that you were one of them and simply couldn't get word out to us."

"Let me tell you where I've been since autumn," Hal said.

He related to them how he'd accompanied Richard to the Midlands and how the king had wished to assemble an army there to fight the Lords Appellant.

"The king sent me on a mission. He said he trusted de Montforts and mentioned how well Ancel and Edward had served him during their time in the royal guard, as well as Father's service to the Crown."

"Where did you go?" David asked.

"I met up with de Vere and Molineux, who were in the West Country. Both had orders to gather as many men as they could and rendezvous with the king." He paused. "We never made it to Richard's side, though."

Hal told them about how untrained—and unwilling—many of the men were that had been gathered to fight for the king. How the two leaders deserted the assembled mass near Radcot Bridge to save their own hides.

"I've never witnessed such cowardice. With no way to cross Radcot Bridge or any of the other bridges, thanks to the Earl of Derby's troops dismantling or physically blocking the way, the so-called volunteers chose not to fight. Derby commanded them to lay down their arms and return to their homes. They did as he ordered so fast, my head spun."

"Leaving only you standing there, I take it?" Geoffrey asked, his eyes narrowed in anger.

"Aye, Father. In front of all of his troops, Derby had me strip off my armor and demanded my sword and remaining weapons. He refused to let me return to the king's side. Instead, he told me I was no longer a member of the royal guard. He even kept my horse." Hal slammed his hand down on the table. "And I did as he asked, without protest. Oh, Derby's a decent sort. He could have run his sword through me. Made an example of me in front of all of his men. As I began walking home to Kinwick, I almost wished he had."

He paused. "I felt not only stripped of what physically made me a knight but it's as if I left my honor on the battlefield that day. I admit that shame ran deep through me."

His father shook his head. "Nay, Son. Your honor is intact. You took your oath and will always be a knight. You know I never wanted you to belong to the king's royal guard because of the direction of where Richard took the court. I'm sorry your service to him had to end this way but you are forever a knight. You have more integrity and loyalty than any man who serves at court, be he a knight or councilor." Geoffrey squeezed Hal's shoulder. "I am proud of you. Always."

"Thank you, Father." Hal had worried that his actions might have cost him his father's respect. Hearing it hadn't brought him some comfort.

"But the events at Radcot Bridge happened before Christmas, Hal," Nan interjected. "Why are you only now coming home to us? Even without a horse, I could have walked home blindfolded and been at Kinwick long before now." She paused, a smile playing about her lips. "I know what kept you. A woman. With you, 'tis always a woman."

"How about a broken leg, dear sister?" Hal countered. "Might that have kept me from walking since I was without a horse and only possessed a few coins to my name?"

Nan gasped. "Oh, Hal, I beg your pardon. What happened?"

"While I journeyed toward home, I came across two highwaymen. They attacked a man."

"And you're a knight, so you had to stop and help," Jessimond added.

Geoffrey ruffled his youngest daughter's hair. "'Tis so, sweetheart. A knight must always come to the aid of those in need." He looked to Hal. "Continue."

"Suffice it to say by the end of the encounter, both highwaymen lay dead. Unfortunately, so did the traveler I tried to help. In the mayhem, I was injured. A stab wound to the torso and my lower leg broken."

"Did you crawl to help?" Jessimond asked, her eyes wide and round.

"The daughter of the traveler who was killed—his name was Jasper—came to my aid. She used a wheelbarrow to transport me to their cottage, where she was able to splint the leg and cleanse and cauterize the gash."

Nan snorted. "I knew a woman had to be involved. And I'm sure she was beautiful."

"More beautiful than any woman I'd seen at court," Hal retorted playfully, though only he knew that he was not teasing.

A knock sounded and a servant entered. "Pardon the interruption, my lord, my lady, but the men in the training yard are clamoring for Lady Nan. They are demanding more instruction before tomorrow's contest. And they've asked Lady Jessimond to come help judge."

Nan rose and crooked her finger for Jessimond to join her. "Come on, Jess. We already know the rest of this tale. The beautiful women nursed our dear Hal back to health before tenderly kissing him and sending him on his way. End of story."

She came and stood behind Hal and wrapped her arms around his neck. Kissing him on the cheek, she said, "Despite my teasing, I am happy my favorite brother is home."

Hal patted her hand. "Just don't tell Ancel or Edward that."

Nan shrugged. "They already know. And I love them both dearly, but you are the one who spent the most time with me. Without you, I would never have gained such skill with my bow and arrow." She kissed the top of his head.

Both his sisters left the solar. Hal emptied his cup and Michael poured him more wine.

"What else, Hal?" prompted Merryn. "I know there's more to your story."

"Both injuries kept me in bed with a fever for some days. The bones in my leg mended properly. Once the splints had been removed, Elinor, Jasper's daughter, kept me on a strict leash. When I wanted to walk, she only allowed baby steps. And when I wished to run, I had to be satisfied with walking. She insisted that I take it slowly in order to heal properly before I set out again on the long journey home. I must admit that she was right."

"And?" His mother's eyes wore a knowing look.

"How do you do it, Mother? Can none of your children ever keep a secret from you?"

Merryn gave him a triumphant smile. "I gave birth to you, all except Jessimond, and I have mothered her since she was but a few days old. Tell us more. About Elinor."

"Elinor is a falconer," Hal began.

"Oh, Nan shouldn't have left," Elysande said. "This is an interesting twist to the tale."

"Her adopted father, Jasper, was a falconer. He taught her everything about raptors that he knew over many years. While I was there, the female peregrine, Cleo, gave birth to two eyases. Elinor named them Bess and Tris."

Hal ran a finger along the rim of his pewter cup. "I helped in the early training of these eyases. Wore a gauntlet and had a falcon perched on my hand for much of my time there. As I began to walk finally, I helped in training them to leave my hand and return for bechin—a food reward. The two were beginning to learn about the lure just before I left. Not only did working with raptors help pass the time but I found I had an affinity for it.

"And for Elinor," he finished.

"Do you love this falconer?" his father asked.

"I do. You and Mother were right. I wasn't looking to fall in love. Elinor wasn't someone I would have ever met at court. It took being shamed and stripped of all I knew before I fell into her path. But once I met her?" he asked. "I fell. Hard."

Hal glanced at the two loving couples at the table, shining examples of what it meant to love another and how to build a life together. "I haven't declared for her yet. She has no idea that I am of the nobility and a knight of the realm. I wanted to speak to my family first before I asked her to be my wife."

His mother placed her hand on his forearm and squeezed. "It was thoughtful of you to do so, my boy, but you didn't need our permission. If you love Elinor, then that is all we need to know."

Though Hal believed he would have his parents' support, nonetheless, her words warmed him. "Oh, Mother, she is everything I could have dreamed of in a woman. She is beautiful, both inside and out. Wells of patience lie within her. She has a keen intelligence and a pure heart."

"Then what are you waiting for? Go fetch her now," Merryn told him.

Another knock sounded and the same servant entered. "Beg pardon, my lord, for interrupting again. A missive has arrived from Kinwick for Lord Geoffrey and Lady Merryn."

Geoffrey accepted the parchment and broke the seal as the servant exited. He pushed aside his trencher and smoothed the scroll on the table. His eyes scanned the page and a smile appeared on his face.

"It seems that Benedict has passed away in his sleep. Edward and Rosalyne are the new Baron and Baroness of Shallowheart. They ask that we come home immediately to see them off since they are needed at once."

Hal looked at his mother. "Then I will come home first and bid Edward and his family goodbye before I bring Elinor to Kinwick. And if Edward and Rosalyne cannot break away for our wedding, then Elinor and I will go to visit them once we are man and wife."

# CHAPTER 16

TIME WITH GERALD passed quickly. Elinor's respect for the falconer grew as she watched how well he handled Bess and Tris. Not only was he skilled but he had a gentle demeanor and patient nature. Both falcons took to him quickly. She could leave Whitley knowing her raptors were in capable, kind hands. Gerald had convinced her of his worth from the moment he had shown respect and a tender heart as Cleo went to join Horus. He was a born falconer.

She joined him at the table, where he had set out the last of the bread and ale. How many mornings had she broken her fast seated here? Hundreds? Thousands?

And this time, most likely, would be the last.

Gerald tore a piece from the crust he held and washed it down with the ale. "Are you ready for us to work with the lures again?"

"Nay. Only you will be training the raptors today. I am to report to Whitley this morning to meet with the baroness."

Elinor saw an odd look on his face and rushed to reassure him. "You'll be fine, Gerald. I trust you with Bess and Tris. You have proven your worth as a falconer a dozen times these past few days." She paused, unsure if she should speak about the future and then decided that it would be best if she addressed it.

"You must know you were brought here to be Whitley's falconer. I will soon be gone."

He flushed a dark red. Elinor knew he must feel guilty and didn't want him to blame himself for circumstances beyond his control.

"The situation wasn't explained to me properly, Elinor," he said, his frustration obvious. "I was told Whitley's falconer had died."

"Aye, Jasper—my father—recently passed."

"But you're a falconer in your own right, Elinor. I would be privileged to work alongside you."

She gave him a sad smile. "We both know Lady Rohesia wouldn't allow that." Then she decided to probe him. "Did you know her before she came here?"

He nodded grimly. "I worked for her cousin. Knew her from the time she was a girl since she visited each summer. When her offer came, I truly wanted it. To work with falcons on my own and to escape the frigid winters in the north? I couldn't get here fast enough."

Gerald shifted uncomfortable in his seat. "I hate that I'm taking your place, Elinor."

She chuckled. "I don't think Lady Rohesia and I can exist on the same estate. 'Tis better that I go."

"You will find new raptors to work with," he promised. "I have never seen another with your talent."

Elinor finished the last of her ale and rose. They washed their mugs and set them aside. She couldn't put off her conversation with the baroness any longer.

"I will see you later, Gerald. Continue to work on swinging the lures. Have the girls go out a farther distance from what we practiced yesterday."

She took her time, drawing out the walk in the familiar woods. If she had the chance to demonstrate her skills, she would easily be hired as a falconer. What worried her was not receiving the opportunity simply because she was a woman. Mayhap she could start as an assistant to a falconer, as she had with Jasper. The thought gave her some hope for her future.

Elinor arrived at the meadow. It was greening up with spring in the air. Flowers had started to bloom. She saw masses of fresh, delicate daffodils and cowslip and tossed aside the urge to pass them by. Picking a blossom, she held it under her nose and inhaled deeply. Spring had always been her favorite time of year. Everything came to life after the cold of winter. Any eyases born weeks before showed tremendous progress in their training during that season.

The road to the castle lay ahead. Elinor reached it and made her way along the path, seeing serfs in the fields sowing. A few gave her a tentative wave and she returned their greeting, wondering if everyone knew Lady Rohesia was sending Elinor away. It wouldn't have surprised her if the noblewoman had stood in the great hall and declared with glee that Whitley would soon be rid of Elinor Swan once and for all.

She strolled through the open gates, still in no hurry to reach her appointment with the baroness. Both the outer and inner bailey buzzed with activity. The blacksmith hammered away, while she saw the carpenter sawing through wood. Both men concentrated so that they did not even see her pass by.

Finally, Elinor arrived at the keep and started up the steps. She halted when she heard her name called. Looking over her shoulder, she saw Father Leo hurrying toward her. She sensed the blush tinging her cheeks, reflecting her embarrassment over her recent outburst to the man of God. Elinor might not believe in a merciful God but she should have respected that Father Leo did.

He gave her a broad smile. "Elinor, how are you? I have been thinking of you."

"I am well, Father."

A shadow crossed his face. "And your falcon that was so ill?"

"Gone," she said softly. "But she is with her mate."

The priest touched her elbow. "I know that must have been difficult for you. How is Gerald working out? Have your young falcons taken to him?"

"Gerald is a good man, Father, and he will train them well. The baron will be pleased."

Father Leo's eyes darkened in anger. "I've learned that our new baron is your cousin and knew you when you were children." He frowned. "I cannot understand why he would treat his own flesh and blood this way."

"Why not? He is only holding to the example set by my father. One baron removed me from the keep. Today, another baron will banish me permanently from Whitley."

He drew in a quick breath. "Nay. The baron is not even at Whitley now. He is away on business. You will be safe for now."

Elinor gave him a pointed look. "I think we both know who runs this estate, Father, and it is not the coward who is absent today. Nay, I am to report to the real power at Whitley and tell her how Gerald fares with the raptors. Once I have confirmed that he is a worthy successor to Jasper, the baroness will see me gone. For good."

"Then I will tell her 'tis a sin," the priest boldly proclaimed. "She cannot wrong her husband's kin without suffering the Almighty's wrath."

She gripped his forearm tightly. "You will do nothing of the sort, Father. Anyone who is not the baroness is in a precarious position. She would make your life miserable." Elinor released her hold on him. "Besides, I will be happy to shake the dust of Whitley from my feet and leave this place. I have known no kindness here. I plan to make a new life far away."

Elinor only hoped he believed her words. She had spoken with conviction.

*When nothing but doubt and despair plagued her.*

He took a long time until he spoke, assessing her words. "If you truly feel that way, then may our Lord Jesus Christ bless you and keep you always, my child." He made the Sign of the Cross on her forehead and embraced her.

Her throat grew thick with unshed tears. After all this time, it took a man of God to show her an inkling of kindness. "If you will excuse me, Father. I must see Lady Rohesia now."

"Go with God, my lady," he said softly.

Steeling herself, she climbed the stairs to meet her destiny. With each step, Elinor resolved to show no emotion—no matter what the baroness said to her. Emotion portrayed weakness. She would not let the baroness see any sign of that in her.

Entering the keep, Elinor went directly to the staircase that would take her to the second floor and the solar. She ignored the fluttering in her stomach as she passed her former bedchamber. What she would give to lie on that soft mattress again, curled next to the warmth of her mother. To go back to a time before her mother lost so many babes. To when she spent time with her only child.

Going back was never an option. Life had taught her that cruel lesson. Elinor continued until she reached the solar. Taking a deep breath and exhaling, she knocked firmly on the oak door.

"Come!" a voice called.

Elinor pushed open the door and saw Lady Rohesia standing on a small stool in the middle of the room. She wore a cotehardie of rich gold, embroidered with tiny sprigs of green. Eunice knelt beside the stool, pinning up the hem.

The noblewoman's eyes swept up and down Elinor judgmentally. Then she clapped her hands twice.

"Eunice. Stop. You can finish later. I have business to conduct."

"Very well, Baroness. Shall I help you from this?"

"Nay. I won't be long. 'Tis simpler to leave it on. Come back in a quarter hour to complete the hem."

"I can stay if you wish, my lady."

The noblewoman's eyes narrowed. "What I have to say to this woman will not be a matter of gossip to be spread. Is that clear?"

The old woman winced at the harsh words. "Aye, my lady."

"And I will expect my garment to be completely hemmed by tomorrow morning. No excuses."

Eunice rose shakily and faced Elinor. As she walked away, Elinor saw defeat in the servant's eyes. Her blood boiled at the baroness' cruelty to the old woman. Elinor warned herself to rein in her emotions as she heard the door shut.

"Come closer."

Lady Rohesia remained standing on the stool. Elinor thought it comical that the woman wanted to physically lord over her. She crossed the room and stopped before the stool and the person perched atop it. Elinor stifled a smile, thinking Lady Rohesia was like a peregrine sitting on its perch.

With a disdainful look, the noblewoman said, "I'm ridding myself of you."

Knowing she had nothing to lose, Elinor boldly replied, "Do you have the power to do so, my lady? Shouldn't it be your husband, the Baron of Nelham, who makes such an important decision? After all, I am blood kin to him. You are only related by marriage."

She watched shock and then outrage ripple over the baroness' face and knew no one ever spoke with such impertinence to the noblewoman.

"You think Nigel is responsible for any significant decision?" A cruel smile played along her lips. "My husband is merely clay that I form into whatever shape I deem necessary." A low, throaty chuckle sounded in the room. "I questioned my father when he betrothed me to such a weak, simple man. I told him I refused to marry sweet, unassuming Nigel Swan. I wanted to wed a strong man, one like my father and brother. One who was hard. Forceful. Persistent. I needed a husband who could make certain I would want for nothing."

Lady Rohesia paused. "Father beat me senseless. Locked me in my bedchamber for three days without food or water. When he finally opened the door, I listened. And understood."

She licked her lips. "My father deliberately bound me to a man who was soft. One I could control. Sometimes, I handle Nigel with soft words and softer caresses to see my wishes fulfilled. Other times, I manipulate him without him even being aware of it." Lady Rohesia looked down triumphantly at Elinor. "*I* am the one who wields power over Whitley. Its people and fortunes. I've endured being wed to a weak, despicable man for years. I loathe my husband's touch. I despise how kind and generous he is. I had to wait far too long to become the Baroness of Nelham. Now that I am? I will not have anyone question my authority—especially you.

"You will be sent to the property of one of my distant cousins. He lives near the Scottish border." The baroness' nose crinkled she studied

Elinor. "Of course, I cannot think to send you . . . this way. You will need a bath. And a cotehardie to wear. I have an old one that will suit you well enough."

"Why?" Elinor asked.

"Why?" The baroness echoed, looking puzzled. "Because you are unacceptable as you now are. I will not be embarrassed by the likes of you, even with lowly relatives I despise." Lady Rohesia paused. "In truth, I've realized you remind Nigel of another time, one before me. I can't have that. You're a threat to me and everything I want. So, I will clean you up and send you far away. My husband need never think of you again."

The noblewoman lifted her skirts and stepped down from her stool. "Take off that disgusting tunic and those filthy pants."

Elinor held her hands out, palms up. "*This* is who I am, my lady. I was forced from the nobility years ago by *my* father, the former baron. This is how I dress. This is how I look. I refuse to change my clothing and hide who I've become. Not for you. Not for anyone."

When the noblewoman's mouth gaped open at this open rebellion, Elinor drove a stake into her heart. "You might have changed everything for me, Baroness. You could have allowed my cousin—your husband—to welcome me back into the fold of my family. It was within your power to restore me to my rightful place as the daughter of a baron and once again be recognized as a Swan. Instead, you deliberately choose to act uncharitably toward me. You refuse to acknowledge me by name. You prefer to cast me out by sending me to the far north, knowing what you do is wrong."

Lady Rohesia glared daggers at her. "You must have been an awful child—a monster—for your father to remove you from the keep. I would never expose my precious children to someone such as you. We are all better off without you."

"Nay," she denied. "I was a good child, quiet and dutiful. 'Twas my father who was the cruel one, a man with no love in his heart for me or my mother. He ignored me because I was a girl. Females meant nothing to him. My hope had been that when Whitley became Nigel's property and he held the title, my cousin would treat me with respect and restore me to my birthright."

Elinor took a step closer. "I believe Nigel would have done that very thing—except for your meddling." She stared with determination into her enemy's eyes. "I don't wish to go to this distant cousin of yours whom I have never met. I refuse to live in the north. I would rather find my way as a falconer. I plan to start my life over, far from the Baroness of Nelham and her wicked ways."

Without waiting for a dismissal, Elinor whipped around and headed for the door.

"You can't do this!" Rohesia shouted at her.

She ignored the angry noblewoman and opened the door.

"You must obey me!"

Elinor moved into the corridor and strode down it.

"Stop! I say—"

A loud thud sounded. Elinor glanced over her shoulder and saw Rohesia had followed her, tripping over the unhemmed gown. She lay on the stone floor, pushing herself to her feet, a dazed look on her face. Whether it was from her fall or the fact that Elinor had chosen to ignore Rohesia's commands, Elinor didn't care. She kept walking. The angry baroness hurried after her, threatening her now with vile language.

As Elinor reached the staircase, she turned in defiance.

"Can't you understand? You are no one to me. I will go if it pleases me. Not you. I alone determine my fate."

The noblewoman had bunched up the cotehardie in her hands and trotted down the hallway.

As she hurried along, she cried, "My husband is your legal guardian. He is the head of the Swan family. He will force you to obey him. To obey *me*."

"I am of age. A score and two. You wanted your hands washed of me? So be it. You will never see me again. Of that, you can be sure." Elinor flew down the stairs, rage bubbling inside her, as Rohesia continued to yell at her.

"You are betraying your family," the noblewoman accused, the whine in her voice revealing her desperation.

At the foot of the stairs, Elinor stopped and glared up. "I have no family."

Rohesia huffed and quickly turned away but her feet must have tangled in the material of the hem which had come undone. Her arms waved violently as she tried to catch her balance but she had nothing to grab on to for support. She tumbled down the stairs in a blur, landing at Elinor's feet.

And lay there silent. Unmoving.

Elinor bent to feel the pulse in her neck and changed her mind, withdrawing her hand. Rohesia Swan's neck had twisted, making her head sit at an odd angle. Lifeless eyes stared up at the ceiling. Elinor had no need to check. Lady Rohesia was dead.

*And she would be blamed.*

Elinor looked around wildly. No one was in sight. Panic poured through her. She had to get out. Escape. Now, while she had a chance. Before they took her away and hanged her for murder. With no witnesses, they would say Elinor pushed the noblewoman to her death. Nigel, Gerald, and probably others knew that Rohesia planned to send Elinor away. It would be the perfect motive.

"I will not suffer the blame," she whispered.

Instead, she ran to the door and hurried outside. Scrambling down the steps, she decided to leave through the sally port instead of the front gate. She kept close to the structure of the keep and finally rounded the back of it. Elinor made her way to the western side of the inner bailey and continued through the outer bailey until she found the little used doorway. It took her a few shoves before the door gave way and she scurried through it, closing it carefully.

She must leave Whitley immediately. Her only regret was that she hadn't told Bess and Tris goodbye when she left them earlier. But the first place they would look for her would be at the cottage. Returning to it would be impossible.

Elinor ran as fast as she could, circling the meadow and crashing through the woods until she reached the road to Long Bellbridge. The road Jasper had died on.

The road that had brought Hal to her.

Pushing aside all thoughts, she kept to the edge of the road. She had no idea what lay beyond the village, for she had never gone past it.

She had wanted to leave Whitley. Now she did so, forever, without looking back.

# CHAPTER 17

Hal's eyes eagerly surveyed the road before them. Soon, they would spy Kinwick Castle perched high upon a hill. It had been far too long since he'd visited home. Simply breathing the surrounding country air made him realize how different life would be for him now. Away from London. Away from his duties at court in the royal guard.

But with Elinor by his side.

At least he hoped she would agree to come live here with him. Wed him. Bear his children. He'd never experienced rejection by any woman. His life had been a charmed one. Yet, Hal realized that a life without Elinor in it would be no life at all. She had to want him as he wanted her. Oh, she had cleverly hidden her interest in him but the intimacies they had shared—the sounds she had made—the tenderness he'd felt for her as he touched her silken skin—let him know she needed him as much as he needed her.

And if she didn't love him? He could only pray that love would come. That she would give it a chance to blossom between them. It meant he must convince Elinor to abandon everything about the life she knew at Whitley and come on a lifetime of adventure.

With him.

Kinwick came into sight. Hal spurred his horse on, one that Michael and Elysande had insisted he take as a gift since Derby had kept his steed that day at Radcot Bridge. Elinor would also need a horse of her own. He doubted she'd ever ridden before and he couldn't wait to teach her to do so. With her affinity for birds, he knew she'd take to riding with ease and have all the horses in the stables eating from her palm, much as Elysande did with hers at Sandbourne.

The gates swung open as he charged down the road. Hal glanced over his shoulder when he heard thundering hooves approach and saw Nan turned the last portion of their ride into a race. He adored this sister of his, with her competitive nature and giving heart. The man who captured it would have a treasure beyond measure.

Together, they passed through the Kinwick gates at the same time, both laughing as the wind tore through their hair. Hal pulled on the reins, slowing his horse to a trot. Nan did the same as they headed toward the keep.

"Will you go back to Sandbourne?" he asked.

"In a few weeks. I want to see Edward off and give the Sandbourne men time to practice." She grinned. "And time to miss me. Only then will I return and see if they've taken my lessons to heart."

They entered the inner bailey and he spied Edward and Rosalyne waiting for them at the bottom of the stairs that led to the keep. He would recognize Edward's muscular frame anywhere. His hair, which normally seemed dark brown, picked up Merryn's chestnut highlights whenever Edward stood in the shining sun. How he would miss this brother of his. Hal had always led, while Edward blindly followed him. Close in age, they had spent their childhoods together, then years of fostering with Lord Hardwin and Lady Johamma, and they'd finally joined the king's guard together after Edward was knighted on the battlefield for bravery.

His younger brother had changed in recent years, though, all because of the irresistible beauty standing next to him. Edward's arm wrapped protectively around Rosalyne's shoulder. Her dark blond hair gleamed in the sunlight. Even after birthing a son then a daughter in the past two years, she still remained slender.

Hal halted his horse and sprang from it. Edward met him and wrapped him in a bear hug, pounding him on the back.

Pulling away, Edward smiled. "I had no idea we'd be treated to a visit from you. Mother and Father have been sick with worry, Hal."

"I know." He turned and embraced Rosalyne, drawing in a deep breath before he pulled away. "You still smell of paints," he teased. "And I love that about you."

Hal had met Rosalyne when she came to London from Canterbury to paint the portraits of the king and queen. If Edward had not staked his claim and declared his love for the artist, Hal might have done so himself, for Rosalyne was not only a beautiful woman but one with depth and talent and kindness. Looking at the two of them, he saw how well they fit together.

Besides, he'd found love of his own and couldn't wait to share the news with them.

"I am delighted to be welcomed by the new Baron and Baroness of Shallowheart," Hal told them. "No one deserves a title and estates more than the two of you."

By now, Nan had approached and greeted the couple warmly.

Rosalyne said, "Though we are sad to hear Uncle Benedict passed, Edward and I are excited to begin this new part of our lives. With the children so young, Shallowheart will be the home they always remember. They will have the childhood there that I never did."

Hal recalled how Rosalyne lost her parents as a babe and Benedict's wife had refused to allow Rosalyne to be raised at Shallowheart. Instead, she'd gone to live with her mother's brother, Templeton Parry, who gained recognition as an artist in Canterbury. While not raised in poverty, her life had none of the luxuries she should have had access to if she'd grown up at Shallowheart. Now, she had the love of her husband and would return to bring up her children at the place of her birth. The title and lands would remain in the family, passing from Edward to his oldest son.

"When do you leave Kinwick?" he asked.

"Tomorrow," his brother told him. "There is much to tell you between now and then."

The rest of their riding party arrived. Geoffrey, Merryn, and Jessimond dismounted as stable hands took charge of their horses. Greetings were exchanged and then the entire group headed up to the solar. Fruit and cheese awaited them, with Tilda fussing over everyone as they gathered around the large table. Hal kissed the longtime servant's cheek and she swatted at him as if he were still two years of age. He remembered Tilda having to chase after him many times when he was young and perpetually in motion.

Edward spoke of the missive they'd received a week ago, informing him and Rosalyne of Benedict's death.

"He went peacefully in his sleep. The steward who wrote to us said Benedict had spent the morning hunting and the afternoon reading. He ate a light dinner and retired then never awoke."

"Uncle enjoyed life at court until the king was removed from power," Rosalyne told Hal. "But I am glad he spent his last days at Shallowheart. He had a true love for the place."

"I used to see Benedict in the palace every now and then. He was always friendly and had a kind word for me. Many courtiers will miss his presence," Hal said.

Rosalyne looked to her mother-in-law. "Merryn, I have a favor to ask of you since we are speaking about Shallowheart."

She smiled warmly. "You know I will do whatever I can for you, Rosalyne. You are as a daughter to me and have already given me two precious grandchildren."

"Would you come to Shallowheart with us for a few weeks?" pleaded Rosalyne. "You make running a castle seem effortless. I know I have learned much from you in the two years I've lived at Kinwick but I fear there will be so much to do once we arrive, especially since Uncle Benedict never remarried. Shallowheart has been without a baroness for many years. I don't want to make any mistakes."

Merryn shook her head. "I must refuse this favor, Rosalyne. Hear me out. First, you have already learned everything I could teach you about managing a great castle and need to have confidence in yourself. Second, the people of Shallowheart must look to you as their lady from the very start. Not me. You. We can talk over some of the things you should do upon your arrival but you are the one who needs to put her mark on the place.

"Find out who is to be trusted and can help you oversee the keep.

Then check continually at different times in various areas so that the servants know your eyes are everywhere and see all. Set high expectations and they will live up to them." Merryn smiled. "Once you have established yourself as a strong but fair baroness, you will still have plenty of time for your painting. Only then will Geoffrey and I come for a visit."

Rosalyne took in the words, nodding in agreement. "I understand, Merryn. 'Tis wise advice you give me. But that reminds me, I finished my latest portrait. Transporting it to Shallowheart half-done would have been too much trouble, so I worked quickly in order to complete it before we left. I hope you don't mind that I sent word to the Le Rouxs for them to come for it. I neglected to tell you that they should be here soon."

It pleased Hal to know Raynor and Beatrice would arrive today. Raynor had made a wooden sword for each de Montfort child through the years. The tradition had started when he did so for Ancel and Alys demanded she also should receive one in order to learn swordplay. Raynor had reluctantly given in to Alys' demand but found her to be a willing student who worked hard and took his lessons to heart. Since the twins had received swords, all de Montforts, be they male or female, had been awarded a wooden sword crafted by Raynor for their sixth birthday.

The door swung open and Raynor and Beatrice entered. A joyous reunion took place among those gathered. Hal grinned down at Beatrice before embracing her. As a boy, he'd been taken by the petite beauty who could outsing any songbird in the land.

"I still remember how you would come and sing us to sleep when you visited Kinwick or we came to Ashcroft. It was as if an angel had come down from heaven and lulled us to sleep. I fancied myself half in love with you," Hal confessed.

Beatrice laughed merrily. "And I wanted little terrors exactly like you. Fortunately, Cecily was our first and a perfect babe. But her two brothers? I fear their Cousin Hal had a bit of influence on their wild behavior."

"A toast!" Geoffrey called out. "For the return of our beloved son and the visit of my closest friend and kin, along with his beautiful wife."

Raised goblets clanked together. Happiness permeated the room. Hal could only hope the same scene would be repeated in the near future, with Elinor by his side, as their upcoming wedding would be acknowledged.

"Enough of this. Hal must tell Beatrice and me where he has been," Raynor said. "We've been anxious since you went missing when the king rose up to fight but we're delighted to see you back at Kinwick."

Hal explained what he'd shared with the others about the trials Richard had undergone as he went up against the Lords Appellant and how unsuccessful uniting an army had proven to be. Then he related the story about the injuries he'd suffered, which kept him from returning to Kinwick sooner.

He took a long swallow of wine, his mouth parched after speaking for so long.

"The rest, Hal," his mother urged.

Before he spoke, his eyes met Beatrice's. He saw that she knew.

"You've found love," she said softly, her eyes misting.

"Aye," he confirmed. "How could I not with so many shining examples around me?"

Jessimond giggled while Nan's jaw dropped. Hal realized they'd both been in the training yard and didn't know anything about his feelings for Elinor.

Raynor clasped his shoulder. "Tell us of her."

Hal did, describing everything he could remember about Elinor, from the way she looked to how she'd nursed him back to health to her vast knowledge regarding raptors.

"Elinor even allowed me to help her train the two newborns, Bess and Tris. They're called eyases. Those weeks working with the young raptors while I healed passed quickly."

"It sounds so romantic," Rosalyne said. "And to think she loves you for yourself, with no idea you are a member of the nobility."

"Speaking of love," Edward prompted, his fingers entwining with his wife's as he looked at Raynor and Beatrice, "you must see your portrait. Rosalyne did something unusual."

Beatrice's eyes sparkled. "What? Oh, I cannot wait to see them. I've loved the ones you have already done of the family."

"Actually, there's only one," Rosalyne said. "I have always painted couples separately but, this time, I decided to put the two of you together."

"Once you see it, you'll wonder why Rosalyne has never done this before," Edward added.

Merryn said, "I'm already jealous and have yet to view it." She looked at her daughter-in-law. "Promise me, Rosalyne, you will do the same for Geoffrey and me once you've settled in at Shallowheart. Between birthing Edward's babes, of course."

Everyone laughed and rose to follow Rosalyne to the chamber she had taken over as her studio. Entering, all conversation ceased as the group studied the portrait of the pair in front of them.

Beatrice walked toward the canvas and gazed upon it reverently. "We are so lifelike." A smile danced upon her lips. "And 'tis obvious that we are very much in love. Even after all these years." She gave her husband an adoring glance.

Raynor joined his wife and wrapped his arms around her, pulling her to him possessively. "You've always had my respect, Rosalyne, when I've seen your art. But this? You have more than earned your commission. I can tell that Beatrice will want all of our children painted now."

"I promise I will paint every Le Roux," said Rosalyne, "as soon as I become familiar and comfortable with my duties at Shallowheart." She glanced at Merryn, whose eyebrow was raised. "That is, after I do one of Geoffrey and Merryn together."

Tilda appeared in the doorway. "The evening meal is ready, my lady."

"Thank you, Tilda." Merryn looked around. "I hope everyone is hungry."

As they filed from the room to join with the workers at Kinwick, Hal found himself near the end of the line, with only Edward and Rosalyne behind him. Happiness radiated from the couple as they engaged in a long, heated kiss. Hal turned away and followed the others, giving them privacy. He was eager to share this special bond with Elinor. He'd already gone too long without tasting her. Touching her. He decided when Edward left with his family in the morning, he would do the same and head toward Whitley to claim the woman who'd stolen his heart.

Edward and Rosalyne caught up to him as he entered the great hall.

Rosalyne slipped her hand through the crook of his arm. "Once I meet your Elinor and get to know her as my new sister, I look forward to painting her portrait. And yours, too. I haven't yet done so and now I know why. You are a wonderful man, Hal de Montfort. A good son. Brother. Friend. A dedicated, skilled knight.

"But love adds a dimension to your life and your appearance changes because of it." She squeezed his arm. "I cannot wait to capture you and Elinor."

"Together," Hal insisted. "As you did Raynor and Beatrice."

Hal swore to himself that once he found Elinor, he never would be parted from her again—not even on canvas.

# CHAPTER 18

Hal waved a final farewell as the escort party left the inner bailey. Edward returned his salute, his smile one Hal wouldn't forget. For a family's youngest son to receive his own land and titles was a remarkable accomplishment. Hal couldn't be prouder of Edward and was eager to see what his little brother would do at Shallowheart in the coming years as he built a legacy for his growing family.

He watched his mother brush away a tear as his father's arm went about her shoulder in comfort.

"Are you sad to see them go?" Hal asked.

"Nay. Can't you tell these are tears of happiness?" Another cascaded down Merryn's cheek. "Well, mayhap one or two possess a little selfishness. I have enjoyed having Edward and Rosalyne at Kinwick these past two years. Rosalyne fit into our family as if she'd been born one of us. And her birthing two little ones only made their time here all the sweeter."

"But they are off to start a new life," Geoffrey said. "The time together without us hovering about them will be good for them as a couple. They will learn to depend upon each other." He brushed a kiss against his wife's hair. "Besides, it gives us an excuse to visit them. I know you'll like that, my love."

"You're right," Merryn admitted. She looked to Hal. "And I suppose you're off, as well. At least you plan to bring Elinor home to us." She brightened. "I will have a new daughter added to my family. Hopefully, more grandchildren, too."

"Aye," Hal agreed, ready to fill Elinor's belly with his seed and know the joys of sharing a child between them.

"Let me consult with Gilbert," his father said. "You'll need to take some men north with you. Gilbert can also see that you are fitted with new armor for the trip."

"That's not a good idea," Hal said. "Elinor has no idea that I am a knight of the realm. It would probably frighten her to find armed knights riding into her clearing." He paused. "Remember, Father, I go to win Elinor's hand and her heart. I don't need a dozen armored men surrounding me while I try to do so."

Geoffrey frowned. "I won't let you go alone as you did when you left the Midlands. Looked what happened to you, Hal. I refuse to allow my son to suffer or be set upon by brigands on the road."

"I think this calls for a compromise," Merryn said smoothly.

Hal bit back a smile. His mother had run Kinwick alone during the long years his father was locked away. She had the head—and heart—of ten men and had often led individuals that clashed toward peace.

"What would you suggest?" he asked.

She mulled it over. "You should allow Gilbert to see that you have weapons and armor for the ride there. Being part of an armed escort party, you will reach Whitley quickly and safely. Once you near the estate, have the men camp nearby. Discard your armor and convince Elinor of your love and invite her to return with you to Kinwick. After you are successful, you can rendezvous with our soldiers and proceed to Whitley's castle."

"Why?"

"You'll need to discuss with the baron about Elinor leaving. Who knows what type of arrangement they have? He may wish her to stay on until he can find a worthy falconer to replace her."

Hal didn't know the particulars. Jasper had been the baron's falconer, not Elinor. When she'd returned from burying her adopted father, she hadn't mentioned if things had changed or if the baron had agreed that she should remain to tend and train his raptors. Hal had left an important part left unsaid because he'd been too interested in comforting her—and pleasuring her.

"'Tis a sound plan," Geoffrey said. He flicked his wrist and a servant came running. "Tell our captain of the guard to come to the great hall at once."

Geoffrey led them back inside as they waited for Gilbert. He mentioned that Joseph, Kinwick's falconer, was getting up in years and that Elinor would be welcomed to work with their raptors if she wished. Once Gilbert arrived, Geoffrey explained how he wished ten men to accompany Hal to Whitley and stressed that Hal was to be armed to the hilt. Hal accompanied the knight to the armory first, noticing that Gilbert moved more slowly than he did before. He wondered how long the man would be allowed to remain in his position as Kinwick's captain. Hal couldn't remember a time when another man served in that capacity.

By the time Gilbert helped Hal into new armor, his horse and ten men awaited him outside the keep. He kissed his mother's cheek and offered his father a hand.

"Be safe," Geoffrey said. "And don't come home until Elinor is with you. Do whatever it takes to win her heart, Hal. If you love her, she will be life itself to you. And every day with Elinor will be one rich in happiness."

"Thank you," Hal said. He knew the separation his parents withstood years ago had been difficult but the strong love they possessed for one another had seen them through that dark time. The years that followed had been ones blessed because each day had been wrapped in love. For each other. For their children. For Kinwick and its people.

Hal mounted his horse, ready to ride to Elinor's side. His mother blew him a kiss as their group started out. All he could hear were thundering hooves as they rode through the gates of Kinwick and north on the road to Whitley.

He tamed his impatience, wishing they could ride straight through the day and night. Instead, they stopped and camped twice overnight and then rose early the following day to complete their journey. By mid-morning, they'd reached Long Bellbridge. Hal had them ride through the village and stop on its outskirts near where he'd first seen

Jasper.

"Wait here," he instructed. "I hope to be back in several hours if all goes as planned. If not, we'll make camp here and then leave sometime tomorrow."

Ronald, the squire who'd accompanied them, helped Hal from his armor. He left all weapons behind save for a baselard tucked inside his boot. As he wove his way through the thick woods, his heartbeat picked up. Excitement rippled through him. All he could think about was wrapping Elinor in his arms and kissing her senseless.

Reaching the clearing, he saw a man standing next to the empty broad perch. His right hand was raised, shadowing his eyes as he searched the skies. His left hand wore a gauntlet.

Had the baron already added a new falconer?

Hal strode into the clearing, taming the anger and uncertainty that raced through him.

"Greetings," he called. "I seek Elinor."

The man dropped his hand and faced him. "Elinor is no longer at Whitley," he said, his words tinged with sorrow.

"Not here?" Hal stood a moment, dumbfounded. "Where is she?"

"Gone."

His heart pounded fiercely in his chest. "Gone where?" he ground out.

The man shrugged. "No one knows. I am Gerald. I was hired by the baroness to be Whitley's falconer. Elinor helped me get to know Bess and Tris as she evaluated my skills. She went to the keep to let the baroness know I would be a suitable replacement. Then . . ." His voice trailed off as his feet shuffled in the dirt. "There was . . . trouble. She's gone. Never came back to tell the two raptors farewell."

This sounded nothing like the Elinor he knew, a woman both responsible and caring. She never would have left her falcons without saying goodbye to them.

"Wait," he said, puzzling over the man's words. "You said two raptors. There are four. Did she take Horus and Cleo with her?"

"Nay." Gerald shook his head. "Horus took ill. He died only days before I arrived. And poor Cleo?" The man's lips trembled. "She grieved herself to death. Elinor took their deaths hard."

Hal's head spun. Elinor had lost Jasper and then the very raptors she'd spent most of her life with. He'd also deserted her by heading back to Kinwick. Why hadn't he told her who he was before he left? Declared his feelings for her? Or better yet, taken her with him? His foolishness had only left her with heartache.

And he had no idea where she was. She could be anywhere. Anywhere.

A calling startled him from his thoughts. Hal looked overhead and saw Tris sailing through the air toward him.

He called out, "Toss me your gauntlet!"

Gerald responded quickly. Hal barely had time to slip on the glove before Tris landed upon his fist. He sighed in relief, knowing the raptor's sharp talons would have sliced his hand to pieces.

"How's my pretty girl?" he crooned as he held out his free hand to Gerald.

The falconer understood and placed a bechin in his palm. Hal brought it to Tris and the falcon gobbled it down.

"You're such a good, good girl," he told her. "I've missed you and Bess."

Gerald stepped closer. "So you know the pair?"

"Aye. I saw these eyases born. Worked with Elinor for a couple of months with them."

Hal heard Bess overhead and prompted Tris to take her place on the perch. Bess swooped down and greeted him. She even pecked him on his cheek. Gerald whistled low.

"I've never seen a falcon do that," he said in wonder.

Hal rubbed the pad of his thumb on Bess' forehead and placed her on the perch before he gave Tris a fond stroke in the same spot. He removed the gauntlet and handed it back to Gerald.

"I am going to see the baron. He might know where Elinor went. Thank you for letting me see my girls."

Gerald looked as if he wanted to say more but shook his head. His eyes fell to the ground.

Though Hal had gone most of the way to the castle with Elinor and could have walked to it from her former cottage, he decided a show of strength would be important in dealing with the Baron of Nelham. He returned to his men and told them where they would ride next. Replacing his armor with Ronald's help, he led the guard of ten to the castle. They easily gained entrance. The gatekeeper had fought in France years before and had met Geoffrey de Montfort at Poitiers.

"Your father was one of the bravest men I ever met," the man said in awe. "England is better off with soldiers like him fighting for our country."

Hal brought his group to a halt near the keep. A balding servant hurried down the steps and asked him his business.

"I am Sir Hal de Montfort. I need to see the baron at once. And the baroness," he added since Gerald had mentioned the woman hired him. Something seemed odd about their conversation. The falconer had mentioned trouble but did not elaborate. If this trouble involved Elinor, Hal wanted to know so he could remedy the situation.

"Have your men take their mounts to the stables," the servant said. "They can water their horses while you speak with Lord Nigel."

Hal handed his reins to Ronald and followed the servant into the keep.

"Wait here, my lord."

The servant scurried up a flight of steep stone steps and disappeared. Hal turned slowly in a circle, taking in everything around him. At one point, an older woman with graying hair passed by him, a curious look on her face as she openly studied him before exiting through the front door. He wondered who she might be.

The servant returned. "Come with me, my lord."

He led Hal upstairs to the keep's solar, where a nobleman he estimated to be close to a score and ten sat in a chair near a blazing fire. A heavy air of sadness enveloped him.

"Sir Hal de Montfort?"

"I am he."

"Please, have a seat." The baron indicated a chair across from him. "I am curious as to your business with me since we have never met. I am Lord Nigel Swan, Baron of Nelham."

"I came to find out what happened to Elinor. Where she is now."

The nobleman sputtered. "Elinor? You know Elinor? How? She has lived in the forest for almost a score with the falconer who took her in after . . ." He abruptly stopped.

"After?" Hal prompted, his voice low and menacing.

"After . . ." The baron pushed his sleeve against his forehead, wiping away a trickle of sweat that had begun to roll down it. "You said you knew Elinor. Then you must know about . . . it."

"Enlighten me. About *it*."

Hal's gut told him something was terribly wrong here. The baron's hands shook. His eyes kept darting about, looking for an answer that did not appear.

"I had nothing to do with it," Lord Nigel began. "I was merely a cousin to Elinor. I didn't live at Whitley then."

*This nobleman was Elinor's cousin?*

Masking his surprise, Hal merely nodded.

"If my uncle did not have a son, then I was to inherit. My aunt produced Elinor less than a year after her marriage but Elinor was the only babe to survive. Several times, she lost the babe a few months after conceiving. Twice, she had stillborns. Each time she failed to produce an heir, my uncle grew more angry."

Understanding began to dawn within Hal.

"We came for a visit, my father and I, the year I became a squire. We came each year so that he could visit his brother. That is when we learned that Uncle had exiled Elinor. He had no need for a female child. My aunt and the final babe, a boy, died during childbirth. Uncle told us he chose not to be reminded of all the failures and demanded Elinor be removed from his castle. He never wanted to see her again. The estate's falconer spoke up and said he would take her in."

Anger sizzled through Hal. "You are telling me that Elinor's father *gave away* his only child?"

Nigel Swan nodded. "We were never to mention her again. In all the years I came to visit Whitley, I never saw Elinor until after my uncle died. I came to Whitley as its new baron a few months ago."

"A few months ago," Hal echoed, menace dripping in his tone.

The baron licked his lips nervously. "Aye. I saw Elinor when she came to the funeral mass for her father. Apparently, she had not set foot inside the castle walls since she was a small child."

Hal leaned forward. "I'm sure you wished to right the wrong your uncle had done all those years ago. Surely, you invited Elinor to return to her home in order to be restored to her rightful position."

Lord Nigel stood and began pacing. "Frankly, she was like a wild thing. Dressed as a young boy. No manners to speak of whatsoever. My wife and I were appalled. I asked Elinor about her life. She claimed to be happy as a falconer. My wife . . . that is, we thought it best to allow Elinor to remain where she was. Rohesia—my wife—believed Elinor would be an unsuitable influence on our children if she lived with us in the keep."

Hal saw everything clearly now. How Elinor had been rejected by a savage parent and sent to live with a man she didn't know. How she'd gone from a privileged life in the castle to a life of little means. And probably her hopes had risen when she learned of her father's death because her cousin, whom she would have known as a young girl, would assume the title. Then Elinor had met with rejection again because the man in front of him had allowed his wife to dictate to him.

"She said . . . she said she liked birds better than people. Who was I to take that away from her and force her to return to—"

"Who were you?" roared Hal. "You were the man with the power to change her life for the better. She's had nothing for years, not her name or position or a family's love. No material wealth. No attention. Elinor is a woman who has her pride and little else. When your wife made it clear that Elinor would not be welcomed again as a true family member at Whitley, of course she would have claimed to be happy with her life as it was. Her fate lay in your hands, Lord Nigel, and you dashed all her hopes. You are a coward, man. A sniveling bastard. I hope you rot in Hell for the wrongs you have done to her."

Red mottled the nobleman's face. "You dare come in here, a total stranger, and make such accusations? I am a man in mourning. My beloved Rohesia died while I was away on business. For that, I will never forgive myself. I now have two motherless children to raise."

Hal shot to his feet and narrowed his eyes. "Then I hope you show them more love and care than your cousin ever received. As for me, I intend to find Elinor and make her my bride. I'll see that she never sets foot on Whitley lands again."

He stormed from the room before he pummeled Nigel Swan to a bloody pulp. Hal knew if he didn't leave now, he would kill the idiot.

As he hurried down the corridor and stairs, emotions swirled inside him. Rage and shock at how Elinor had been treated for most of her life dominated them. He pushed those aside and concentrated on the good.

He loved Lady Elinor Swan. He intended to make her his wife and never let any of her hideous Swan relatives near her again. Hal and all the de Montforts would wrap Elinor in love and never let her go. She might have suffered rejection and isolation for years but he would make it up to her every day for the rest of their lives together—even beyond the grave.

Throwing back the front door to the keep, he stepped into the spring day and its sunshine. His mission now would be to find Elinor.

*But where would she have gone?*

She had no other relatives to turn to. The baroness had brought in a new falconer, so Elinor no longer had a purpose at Whitley or a place to live.

He looked about in frustration, unsure where to begin his search.

"My lord?"

Hal turned and saw a priest making his way toward him. He smiled. Experience had taught him that priests heard and observed things that others didn't. If anyone might be able to help him, it would be this man of God.

"Greetings. I am Sir Hal de Montfort from Kinwick," he said, using his most charming smile.

"I am Father Leo. 'Tis not often we get such important visitors at Whitley. I hear a guard of ten accompanied you and are at our stables now. Are you friends with the baron?" the priest asked nonchalantly.

Hal stifled his smile, knowing the priest wanted information. "Nay. I only met the man today and cannot abide the fool."

Father Leo's eyes widened. "So you say." He studied Hal. "Wait. You said your name was Sir Hal?"

"Aye."

"Then you know Lady Elinor."

Hal's senses went on full alert, hearing her called lady. "I do," he said cautiously. "You know Elinor?"

The priest nodded. "All of Whitley knows of Lady Elinor and the wrongs done to her. By this baron and the previous one, her own father. I did not know she was Lady Elinor Swan and a daughter of the house until recently. I only came to Whitley a few years ago and had never caught sight of her until her father's funeral mass. After Lord Nigel arrived, I found out from Eunice what had occurred years ago."

"Who is this Eunice?" Hal demanded.

"I am Eunice, my lord," a voice behind him said.

Turning, Hal saw it was the gray-haired servant who had looked at him with interest inside the keep.

"You seek Lady Elinor?" she asked hopefully, her eyes bright with unshed tears.

"I do. I love her. I plan to wed her," he declared.

"Thank the Living Christ," she murmured. "That child has suffered so much."

"Do either of you know where she has gone?"

Both Eunice and Father Leo's mouths set. They shook their heads.

"What are you not telling me?" he asked.

Eunice spoke first. "The baroness summoned Lady Elinor. Lady Rohesia had sent for a falconer from her home in the north. Lady Elinor was to see if Gerald was suited to the task and report to Lady Rohesia about his skill with the birds."

"Did she?" prodded Hal.

"She came to the keep and met with the baroness. I overheard some of their conversation. Gerald was to be the new falconer, while Lady Elinor would be sent to live near the Scottish border with Lady Rohesia's cousin."

New waves of anger poured through Hal. "Banishing her from the castle wasn't enough? Lady Rohesia wanted her exiled to the far north?"

"Aye," Eunice confirmed. Then a tiny smile tugged at the corners of her mouth. "But Lady Elinor was having none of that, my lord. She told off the baroness but good, though the baroness continued to demand blind obedience from her. The baroness chased after Lady Elinor. In her fury, Lady Rohesia was careless and tripped. She fell down the stairs," Eunice said, not a hint of compassion on her face. The servant shrugged. "No more baroness."

"Unfortunately, no Lady Elinor, either," Father Leo added. "She vanished soon after. No one saw her leave the castle grounds. I went to the cottage but she never returned there. She still hasn't."

"You are saying Elinor is the last person to have seen Lady Rohesia before her accident? Before she died?" Hal asked, trying to understand everything that had unfolded.

"Aye," Eunice said. "I was upstairs, waiting to continue hemming the baroness' hem. She had just put on a new cotehardie when Lady Elinor arrived. 'Twas the extra material dragging the ground that Lady Rohesia tripped on when she chased Lady Elinor, screaming at her to submit to her authority."

"So Elinor witnessed the baroness fall?" Hal asked.

"She must have," said Eunice.

"And she disappeared right after that?" He expelled a long breath. "Elinor ran—because she thought she would be blamed for the noblewoman's death."

It made perfect sense now that he had all the pieces of the story. Why she hadn't returned to the cottage to bid her raptors farewell. Why no one had seen her once she'd entered the keep. Elinor fled because she thought no one would have believed that the baroness' death had been an accident.

"Did the baron accuse Elinor of causing Lady Rohesia's death?" he demanded.

"Nay," Eunice said quickly. "I made sure that no one mentioned to him Lady Elinor was at the keep when the accident happened. Gerald had already taken her place. The baron only needed to know that he had a new falconer and that the old one was gone." Eunice set her mouth in a firm line.

"So no one knows which way she might have gone?"

"Nay, my lord," Father Leo said. He told Hal how long Elinor had been missing.

Hal cursed under his breath.

It would take a small miracle to find the woman he loved—but he would search to the ends of the earth to reunite with her.

## CHAPTER 19

ELINOR COLLAPSED A few feet from the road. She leaned against a thick oak for support. Hunger gnawed at her belly. She couldn't remember the last time she'd eaten, other than picking a few unripe berries in the woods. Though she'd never had an overabundance of food, the raptors had always provided enough game for her and Jasper throughout the year.

But she had no raptors. No home. No coin. Only the clothes on her back, and they were wearing thin, the same as the soles on her boots. She resorted to stealing food a few times but felt guilty that she'd taken it from the mouths of others and had stopped doing so. When tempted to try it again as hunger pangs caused her belly to spasm, she feared being caught. She already was wanted for murder. If someone caught her stealing and handed her over to the authorities, she would certainly swing from a gibbet.

She'd lost count of the number of estates she'd stopped at as she'd pushed south. Trying to gain a place as a falconer—or even an assistant to one—without a gauntlet or lure to her name had proved impossible. If only one person would have given her a chance to show what she could do. Instead, she'd been met with everything from laughter to derision.

Putting falconry aside might be the only way to survive. Though her skills lay with training raptors, Elinor knew she was capable of other tasks. If she could find work, she could put aside money to purchase a new gauntlet or even buy the leather and create the glove herself. Her decision made, she pushed herself to her feet and continued trudging down the road. Her steps grew slow due to how weak she was. Eating soon had to be her priority. Starving to death couldn't be an option.

Not when in the back of her mind she looked for Hal.

That was why she had set out heading south. Because south was the direction he had taken when he left Whitley. Part of her knew it to be impossible. He only thought friendship lay between them. He had a life and family. She did not even know his last name, though he'd once mentioned having two brothers. She also recalled he had a sister named Nan because she could whistle louder than any of the three boys. It wasn't much to go on. But something drove her to continue on, hoping to catch a glimpse of him. Find someone who knew him.

So far, no one did. Elinor had only spoken to a handful of others when she'd stopped at various places, trying to find work. She did more listening than talking. Hal's name never came up. The few times she mentioned or described him, no recognition appeared on the faces of those she conversed with. It was as if Hal had vanished into thin air.

If by some slim chance of fate she found him, how would he react? What if he'd left a sweetheart behind and had reunited with her? Or mayhap, after he'd spent a short time with his family, wanderlust caused him to set off again?

Elinor couldn't think those things. Finding Hal was the only thing that kept her going. She pushed all thoughts from her mind and trudged on mindlessly, ignoring the loud grumblings that caused her belly to cramp painfully.

Rounding a bend in the road, she spied another castle in the distance. Despite her recent experience of repeated failure, a glimmer of hope sprang within her. This might be the place that needed her. The lord of this estate might be the one to believe that she was a falconer without dismissing her or laughing in her face. Elinor fell to her knees in the middle of the road.

And prayed in desperation.

"I am sorry that I said you were not a merciful God," she apologized. "You have punished me enough for my foolish words, Heavenly

Father."

The image of the Virgin Mary came to her, one she'd seen as a statue in the chapel at Whitley. "Mary, Mother of God, help me. Oh, I pray for you to help me. I ask your Holy Son to help me." Tears flowed freely down her cheeks, falling into the dust. "I am not a bad person. I did not mean for Lady Rohesia to fall, much less die. Please, God Almighty, forgive me of my sins. Help me to make it up to you. I beg you—give me another chance. If I cannot find Hal, please let this estate make a place for me. I promise I will go to mass every day. I will learn to be obedient. I will make something good of my life.

"Please." Elinor's voice cracked with the emotional plea. "Please."

Slowly, she dragged herself to her feet, resolve filling her. She didn't know if God had bothered to listen to her. She was only one person. No one important. But she would be the best person she could be if only He gave her the chance. Wiping the tears from her face, she set out again.

It took an hour to reach the castle she'd seen. On the road leading to it, serfs weeded the fields. A few of them looked at her in curiosity. Elinor ignored their stares and focused on reaching the gates. They were open. People came and went through them. She fell into a group bringing in some sheep. No one questioned her as she peeled away from them and headed toward the noise she heard. Clanging swords meant the training yard. She hoped to find the nobleman who owned this estate there.

Elinor followed her ears and the sound of steel striking steel grew louder. She came around the stables and saw a large group of soldiers, probably three score or more, fighting one another. As she approached the yard, she located a well-dressed man standing on a platform. He spoke with a soldier. Both nodded their heads. The soldier leaped from the platform and went to a pair and halted them. While he instructed the two fighters, she made her way to the lone man who looked to be two score or so.

"Are you the nobleman who holds these lands?" Elinor called out.

He glanced down at her. "I am Lord Hardwin. And who might

you be?"

When she left Whitley, knowing they would search for her, Elinor had decided not to use her true name. But in this man's searing blue eyes, she could not lie anymore.

"I am Elinor." She stood straight and with more confidence said, "Elinor Swan. I am a falconer in search of a place who needs my services. Or any other work," she added.

"Hmm." The nobleman came down from where he stood.

She had to crane her neck to look him in the face, much as she'd done with Hal because of his great height.

"Winterbourne has no need of a new falconer, Elinor Swan, but my neighbor an hour's ride to the south might. His man has been at Kinwick for many years. If you have any talent, you might serve as Joseph's assistant and then one day take over. That is, if you have the skills necessary. Falconry requires patience."

"Aye, my lord, you are right. I have worked with raptors since I was six years of age. I have the necessary skills and experience. If you will share the name of Kinwick's lord, I would be most grateful and will set out for this place now."

Lord Hardwin studied her with kind eyes. "It is close to our evening meal, Elinor. Why don't you dine with us and stay the night? You can travel to Kinwick in the morning on a full belly and a good night's rest."

Elinor thought it over quickly. He'd said it was an hour's ride, which meant much longer walking the road. She'd barely made it to Winterbourne. If she didn't eat soon, she wouldn't be able to walk at all. As it was, she grew dizzier by the moment and her vision had started to blur.

"I thank you, my lord. 'Tis gracious of you to ask me to stay. I accept your kind offer."

"Let me give my captain of the guard a few instructions and then I will escort you to the keep. My wife, Johamma, would enjoy visiting with you."

Lord Hardwin strode off and spoke to the man who'd stood next to him on the platform. He soon rejoined her.

"Come, Elinor. Accompany me to the keep. You can tell me more about how you came to work with falcons." He gave her a smile, something so rare that she couldn't remember the last time she'd received one. "I have never met a woman falconer before. I'm sure your story is a fascinating one."

She tried to match his long strides and found herself practically running to keep up with him. Suddenly, her belly cramped as if a knife sliced through it and she cried out.

"Elinor?" Lord Hardwin marched back toward her. "Elinor?"

She heard him say her name a few times but a loud roaring sounded in her head, blocking out his next words. She tried to straighten but her belly knotted in agony, forcing her to her knees. Darkness obscured her vision. Elinor fell to the ground.

---

MERRYN DE MONTFORT left morning mass with her husband by her side. Their fingers entwined as they left the chapel. She looked up at the profile of her husband, still so handsome after all the years they had known one another. To her, Geoffrey was the man who still made her heart flutter when he entered a room. After decades together, her body craved his caress. She counted her blessings each day and chief among them all was that she had the love of this good man.

"You seem quiet this morning," he remarked as they walked back toward the keep. "What are thinking about?" His fingers squeezed hers gently in encouragement.

"I was thinking how fortunate I am to be wed to you. To be your partner in everything that we share."

He brought their joined hands to his lips and pressed a fervent kiss against her knuckles. "We are lucky, Merryn, for we are a love match. I hope we will have many more years together."

"I am also grateful that three of our children have found love," she added. "I see how Alys, Ancel, and Edward look at their spouses and rejoice that they know great love."

Geoffrey smiled. "The fact that they've all given us grandchildren is simply a gift—to us and to them."

They began ascending the steps leading to the keep.

"I am worried about Hal, though. He has been on my mind since he left a month ago."

Merryn had assumed their middle son would return with a smile on his face and the woman he would wed on his arm but Hal had sent word that Elinor was no longer at Whitley as its falconer and he needed to find her. After that, nothing.

"Hal will find Elinor," Geoffrey assured her. "His search will prove fruitful. The fact that Hal has fallen in love surprised me. I feared it would be many years before he settled down. Elinor must be quite a special woman to have tamed his wild ways."

They entered the great hall and made their way to the dais.

"What if he cannot find her?" Merryn asked. "His missive was brief. I can't help but wonder why she left Whitley, much less why no one would know where she went. How is Hal to find her, not having any idea where to search?"

Geoffrey seated her and took his place beside her. "For Hal to love a woman enough to wed her, he will move heaven and earth to find her. Quit worrying about him, sweetheart."

"Is that an order?" Merryn's lashes fluttered at him.

He placed a hand on her thigh. Warmth filled her. "Look at me like that again and we will skip breaking our fast."

She gave him a lazy smile. "And what might we do instead, my lord?" she asked coyly.

His fingers traveled up her leg, causing her pulse to quicken as his gaze held hers.

"My lady?"

Reluctantly, Merryn tore her eyes from her husband's. "What is it, Tilda?" Her heart continued beating rapidly as Geoffrey's hand tightened on her thigh, his thumb making small circles.

"A messenger just arrived from Winterbourne and wishes to speak with you."

Merryn glanced to the door and saw a soldier waiting. She motioned him to come.

"Thank you, Tilda." As the servant turned away, Merryn said under her breath, "As much as I enjoy where your fingers are, Husband, kindly remove them so I may give this messenger my full attention."

"As you wish, Wife." Geoffrey leaned in and gave her a soft kiss below her ear, sending a shiver down her spine. His hand went back to his lap.

"Good day, Lady Merryn, Lord Geoffrey," the messenger greeted them.

"Is anything wrong with Lady Johamma or Lord Hardwin?" she asked.

"Nay, they are both in excellent health but one of their guests has fallen ill. Lady Johamma cannot break the fever and asked if you would come to assist her."

Merryn rose. "I will leave at once."

Geoffrey also stood. "Let me accompany you, my love. 'Tis been a few weeks since I have seen Hardie. The men who escort us can spar with the Winterbourne soldiers while your healing hands help their visitor."

She looked at the messenger. "I must collect my satchel and Lord Geoffrey will gather a few men. Meet us at the stables."

They galloped through the gates of Winterbourne a little over an hour later and handed their horses to waiting stable hands. Geoffrey led her and the Kinwick men to the inner bailey, where Hardie welcomed them.

"Good day to you, Merryn." The earl kissed her cheek. "And I was hoping you would come, too, Geoffrey." The men clasped hands.

Merryn thought how Hardie's courage long ago had not only kept her husband alive but allowed Geoffrey to come back to her. She would be forever in his debt. Geoffrey and Hardie had become as close as brothers, and all three de Montfort sons had fostered at Winterbourne. Hardie had treated the boys as he would his own, helping them to grow into fine men that she was so proud of.

"A few soldiers came with us. I thought we might enjoy watching them in the training yard while Merryn tends to your guest."

"An excellent idea," Hardie proclaimed as he turned to her. "Johamma is inside. You'll find her in the blue chamber."

"I'll go to her now. Behave yourself," she told her husband. "No fighting. You need only observe."

Geoffrey pulled her close for a quick kiss. "As you wish, my love."

The two men headed toward the training yard while Merryn entered the keep. She and Geoffrey had stayed in the blue chamber several times over the years so she knew exactly where to go. She nodded as she passed a servant and then slipped into the chamber without knocking, not wishing to disturb whoever this ill visitor might be.

Johamma stood over the bed, running a damp cloth over the face of someone. Her friend turned when she heard Merryn's footsteps. A smile crossed her tired face and she came to greet her. Merryn embraced her and looked to the bed in curiosity. A feverish woman lay there but despite the flush, her great beauty shone.

"Thank you for coming," Johamma said. "I was up all night trying to break her fever. When it lingered today, I felt I must send for you."

She wondered who the young woman was but knew that could wait. "Let me examine her."

Merryn went to the bed and looked over her latest patient. "Tell me what you have done for her."

Johamma recounted everything she'd tried. Merryn instructed her to send for boiled water, which arrived as Merryn spoke the words.

"I anticipated whatever remedy you used would most likely include boiled water," Johamma said.

Merryn mixed in heather from her satchel with the hot water and dipped a clean cloth in so she could bathe the young woman's forehead. That would help if the woman had a headache and would also soothe her fever.

"You have the healing touch," Johamma complimented her.

"So who is your visitor?"

Before Johamma could reply, the woman began murmuring. Merryn leaned close and brushed the dark brown waves away from her face.

"Hal . . . Hal . . ."

Merryn's hand stilled. Her eyes met Johamma's.

"That is another reason why I summoned you," the countess said. "She arrived yesterday and collapsed. I think the poor thing hasn't eaten in some time and she was feverish to the touch. She's called out the name Hal several times and even mentioned Nan twice, so I thought somehow she had to know them."

Merryn stilled. "Do you know this woman's name?" she asked, her heart pounding.

"Hardie told me her name is Elinor. Elinor Swan. She came and inquired about a position as a falconer. He told her we were not in need of one but that his neighbor might be. Hardie said Kinwick's falconer was close to retiring and he suggested she try there after staying with us the night. But she fainted dead away. Hardie brought her inside and I have tried to nurse her ever since."

Merryn told Johamma, "Hal intends to wed Elinor Swan." She caressed the cheek of the woman who'd won her son's heart. "Now we need to find him and bring him home."

# CHAPTER 20

ELINOR FOUGHT TO open her eyes. The lids felt heavy as she forced them to remain open. She glanced around the room, unsure of her surroundings.

What was the last thing she remembered?

*Soothing hands . . . and a low, melodious voice . . .*

Who had those belonged to?

She pushed herself to a sitting position and found she was in a bed. A luxurious one, with smooth covers and soft pillows behind her. The curtains had been drawn away, allowing her to see the chamber more clearly. When was the last time she had slept in a bed? It had to have been before she came to Jasper's. For years, she had fallen asleep on a pallet of straw on the floor with a rough blanket covering her when the weather turned cold.

Vaguely, an impression came to her of a woman with fiery hair who'd always seemed to be by her side. Elinor remembered waking several times. The woman spoke to her in soft tones. Fed her soup. Wiped her brow with a cool cloth. Then Elinor had drifted back into a heavy slumber.

The estate. The kind nobleman. Memories at the edge came rushing back. He'd offered her a place to stay for the night. She'd been so hungry. So tired. And she now knew, very ill. Her limbs seemed weighted down, as if she couldn't lift them of her own accord.

"You're awake."

The chestnut-haired woman glided into the room. Though she was much older than Elinor, an incandescent beauty glowed about her. She must have been stunning in her youth, for she was still remarkable now.

She came and set a tray on the floor before drawing a chair next to the bed.

"Let me help you get more comfortable."

Fluffing the pillows, she helped Elinor lean against them and drew the soft linen sheets up again, smoothing them before she placed the tray in Elinor's lap.

"I'm Merryn," she revealed. "And I'm sure you have a great many questions for me. Do you know where you are?"

Elinor nodded. "I do not know the name of the estate but I remember stopping here. The nobleman who owns it spoke with me. He invited me to stay overnight before I journeyed to his neighbor." She frowned. "I think he called it Kinwood."

"Kinwick," Merryn prompted. "And 'tis Lord Hardwin's estate where you are. Winterbourne."

"How long have I been here?"

"This is the third day I have nursed you. You arrived the afternoon before that, so you have been here four days."

"Thank you for tending to me."

"You needed food and rest above all. You did have a fever but it soon left you. You probably still feel somewhat weak from it, though."

"I'm so tired, 'tis hard to even smile," she admitted.

Merryn laughed. "Go ahead and eat first. We can talk in a few minutes. Every bite you take will help you to grow stronger."

She did as Merryn asked. Though she hadn't realized it when she awoke, she was ravenous. She ate the bread and broth on the tray and drank the wine. She couldn't remember ever having had wine and it felt rich and thick on her tongue.

Merryn removed the tray once she'd finished eating. "That's good for now, Elinor. In a few hours, I will bring you broth with meat in it. More bread and cheese, as well. And the wine will also help build your strength."

Elinor leaned back into the pillows. "You know my name."

"Aye. You spoke it to Lord Hardwin before you fainted. He said you were Elinor Swan. Is that true?"

Fear clutched her heart. Did this woman want to know because she knew what Elinor had done? What she'd run away from?

Merryn took her hand. Her warm touch brought comfort.

"I ask because you have called out my son's name when you were restless. My daughter's, too."

Elinor licked her lips. "Hal? You are Hal's mother?" She tried to see Hal in this woman but no trace of him was reflected in her face.

Merryn nodded. "Aye. And Nan is my daughter. I suppose Hal spoke of her to you while his bones and side healed. I must thank you for taking such excellent care of him."

Her heart began pounding fiercely. "So Hal . . . reached home? Oh, he told me you were a healer. Does he live here, at Winterbourne? Are you Lord Hardwin's healer? May I see Hal?"

Merryn squeezed her hand. "I am a healer but not at Winterbourne. I am Lord Hardwin's neighbor and reside at Kinwick. In fact, I am the Countess of Kinwick."

Elinor frowned. Surely, she had heard wrong. Hal's mother was . . . a countess? How was this possible? That made Hal the son of an earl. She absently rubbed her temple with her free hand as shock poured through her.

"I know you must be confused, Elinor." Merryn patted her hand. "You have nothing to worry about. Hal may be a knight of the realm and not someone of your world but he loves you. Very, very much. You were all he could speak of once he reached home."

"Hal . . . *loves* me?" Elinor whispered.

Uncertainty filled her. She was wary of what this woman had just revealed. Could she actually believe that Hal loved her—a man who could claim an earl as his father? One so far removed from her way of life. Tears filled her eyes and spilled down her cheeks. Then great, heaving sobs began. Merryn climbed onto the bed and held her close, stroking her back and murmuring soothing words. Her actions made Elinor cry all the more.

"But . . . Hal is of the nobility. I am a lowly falconer. And not even that. The baroness replaced me. I . . . I . . ." Elinor's throat thickened. No more words came out. A man she thought she had known well wasn't anything she had thought him to be. Despite being born into the nobility herself, Elinor felt unworthy of Hal—and somehow betrayed by him at the same time.

Merryn gripped her shoulders. "Look at me," she commanded, her voice quiet but full of authority.

Elinor did so, afraid not to obey this woman.

"You have nothing to fear, Elinor. Hal loves you. He loves *you*. He told us over and over during his brief stay at home. That's enough for us. My husband, Geoffrey, and I are a love match. It is what we've wanted for all of our children. For them to find that one person who is their soul mate. To wed and love this person every day for as long as they live.

"You and Hal are two halves who will make a most perfect whole. You will be as Geoffrey and I. As Hal's siblings are. Alys and Kit. Ancel and Margery. Edward and Rosalyne. You will come to know each other better than any two people in the world. You will rejoice together in good times and cling to one another in bad. You will make love with a fierceness that frightens you and then so tenderly you fear you might shatter in two. But never be afraid, Elinor. Hal loves you and because of that, all the de Montforts will, too."

Elinor sucked in a long breath and slowly expelled it. She tried to understand everything Merryn de Montfort had said. That Hal loved her. That his parents and family approved of the match. It didn't matter that she was a falconer. Hal loved her.

*He loved her.*

Elinor had never known love from another. She hadn't really believed in its existence, though her heart told her she loved Hal. And now to hear that her love was returned?

Merryn released her shoulders and cupped her face. "Hal went to Whitley to claim you. He sent word to us that you'd left there. He's been searching for you ever since."

Guilt washed through her. If Hal had gone to Whitley, then he would know of her role in killing Rohesia Swan. How could she tell Merryn that her son didn't hunt for her because he loved her—but because he wanted to see justice meted out. As a knight, his code of honor would demand it.

Fresh tears sprang to her eyes. Elinor rolled away from Merryn and buried herself in the covers.

Merryn stroked her hair tenderly for a few minutes and then said, "It is a lot to take in. You need to rest. I will be back in a few hours with something for you to eat."

The noblewoman left the room. The door softly shut.

Elinor threw back the linen sheets. She couldn't face Hal, now that he'd been told that she was a murderess. She needed to escape Winterbourne and go as far away as possible so that he would never find her. Glancing down, she saw she wore something soft and feminine, something so unfamiliar that it tore her heart asunder. Once she had possessed fine clothes such as this. Once she had been a member of the nobility.

That part of her life was over. She could never go back. Elinor ran a hand along the fabric, knowing she couldn't keep it. She eased from the bed, gripping the post to steady herself. Her faded clothes lay folded in a chair. She stripped off the chemise—that's what it was called—and folded it neatly, leaving it on the bed. Dressing in her tunic and pants, she felt less vulnerable.

She must escape this castle without being seen. Elinor opened the door and crept down the hall.

*Don't think of Hal*, she told herself. *Find a way out.*

Scotland. That's where she'd go. She would travel as far north as she could and leave England behind. Leave Hal behind.

Leave her broken heart.

DESPONDENCY FILLED HAL as they rode the last league to Kinwick. He and the band of soldiers had searched for weeks now, to no avail. They were no closer today to finding Elinor than they had been when he'd first discovered her missing from the cottage in the clearing.

His men had proven supportive of the quest but he could see now how weary they were. His plan was to take them home to get a hot meal in their bellies and return to their duties at Kinwick. He would ask his father for new soldiers—even more than before—and fan out again in different directions. A part of him agonized that the time and manpower would be wasted. That the new search for Elinor would again be fruitless. She had disappeared.

If she had, he didn't know if he could go on.

The castle appeared in the distance and Hal picked up the pace, allowing his horse to gallop freely. He sensed the anticipation building in the soldiers behind him, knowing they were happy to return home. They passed workers in the fields who waved a welcome to them, ready to see their friends and loved ones return home, and various soldiers returned the greetings.

Only he was miserable as they approached the castle walls.

Hal guided his horse to the side, allowing the ten men to ride past him as he slowed to a trot while the others picked up speed. He dreaded having to tell his parents he hadn't succeeded in locating Elinor. The gates opened and the Kinwick men rode through them. He followed reluctantly.

When he arrived at the gates, though, the gatekeeper signaled him to halt.

"You're to wait for Lord Geoffrey, Sir Hal," the man informed him. "Those are his instructions. Hold fast."

Hal wondered why his father would want him to linger at the gates instead of heading to the stables to water and feed his horse. Moments later, he heard the sound of hoof beats and spied his father riding toward him from the outer bailey.

Pulling up alongside Hal, he said, "Elinor has been found."

"What?" Disbelief took hold of him. He'd traveled far and wide without discovering a clue to her whereabouts.

"She arrived at Winterbourne a few days ago," Geoffrey explained, "looking for work as a falconer. She took ill and collapsed so Johamma sent for Merryn. But Elinor is alive, Hal. She's waiting for you there."

Hal whipped his horse around and raced like the wind down the road, kicking up the dust. He couldn't reach Winterbourne fast enough. He wondered if it could really be true that Elinor had found her way to him. Part of him refused to allow his hopes to be raised, only to be dashed. He'd lived with too much disappointment the past month. Yet he knew his father wouldn't have told him of her presence unless he was certain. Glancing over his shoulder, he saw his father gaining on him. Geoffrey de Montfort gave him an encouraging nod.

Faith. He must have faith. That Elinor was truly at Winterbourne. That whatever illness which had possessed her had been vanquished by his mother's healing touch. Hal uttered a prayer under his breath, over and over.

*Let it be her, Dear Lord. Let her be fine.*

They reached Winterbourne and the gates opened since they were expected. Hal and Geoffrey flew through them side by side, arriving at the keep minutes later. He leaped from his horse as a stable hand took the reins.

"He's been ridden hard and needs special care," Hal warned.

"Aye, my lord."

The two men hurried inside the keep. As his eyes adjusted to the dim light inside, Hal spotted his mother coming from the great hall, a tray in her hands.

"Hal!" she called, her brilliant smile warming his insides. No one had a smile like Merryn de Montfort. She'd given it to him when he'd first walked. When Raynor had put Hal's first sword in his hands. She'd beamed at him on the day he took his oath to become a knight. And now she smiled upon him, knowing he would soon be reunited with the women he loved.

He rushed to embrace her, tray and all. "She's here?" he asked eagerly, his heart beating rapidly.

"She is. Oh, she is so lovely, Hal."

"But is she well?" he demanded. "Father said she'd been ill."

"She has passed through the worst of it. I fear she hadn't eaten much in a long time. She needed food and rest."

Something flickered in her eyes. "What's wrong? What aren't you telling me?"

Merryn sighed. "I fear I have done something foolish. I hope you won't be angry with me."

"Mother, you've nursed Elinor back to health. I could never be angry with you." He paused. "Tell me."

She handed the tray to her husband and took Hal's hands. "When Elinor came to her senses, she was unsure of her surroundings and somewhat frightened. I called her by name and told her that she'd called your name over and over. When I explained that you were my son, it made her so happy to know you'd reached home safely. But when she found out you were the son of an earl, all the color drained from her. I did my best to reassure her that she had nothing to fear. That you loved her. That we would love her because you did."

Hal knew why she was upset. "And you realized I had not told her of my feelings."

She nodded unhappily. "You should have been the one to tell her that, Hal. I stole that moment from you. It should have been a private time of joy between you. I am so sorry."

He hugged her tightly, brushing his lips against her hair. "You have no need to worry, Mother. I will tell Elinor again and again how much I love her for the rest of our lives. So many times a day that she will grow weary of hearing it. She will see me coming and run the other way," he teased.

Hal released her. "Where is she? I cannot wait any longer. I have to see her."

"Come with me." She motioned for Geoffrey to follow them with the tray. "She's in the blue room."

The time for waiting had ended. Hal ran up the stairs to the second floor. He'd fostered for years at Winterbourne and was familiar with every inch of the estate. Knowing exactly where the blue room lay, he arrived at the chamber's door long before his parents did. Without bothering to knock, he flung the door open and stepped inside, ready to kiss Elinor until she fainted from all the attention he lavished upon her.

Elinor was nowhere to be found.

He rushed about the room, turning in circles. Mayhap she had gone to the garderobe and would return at any moment. He saw a chemise lying on the bed and picked it up. Bringing it to his nose, he inhaled deeply.

The cloth smelled of her. Hal clutched it to him.

His parents entered and paused. His mother's puzzled look alarmed him as she glanced around.

Without her speaking, Hal knew the truth.

*Elinor was gone. Again.*

# CHAPTER 21

ELINOR STRUGGLED TO stay on her feet. Her stomach gurgled noisily as she fought her drooping eyelids. Each step became more of a struggle as she made her way through the thick woods. Stopping by a large tree trunk, she leaned against it and closed her eyes a moment.

Leaving Winterbourne had been easier than she'd expected. She'd spied a cart carrying a bed of straw and waited for the driver to pass her. Expending every bit of energy she possessed, she'd hurried toward it and thrust herself into the back of the wagon, falling into the sweet smelling hay. Elinor lay still a moment before pulling some of the straw over her to disguise she was in the bed. She could see above her and watched the clouds passing by in the sky. When they approached the wall, she covered her face with hay, hoping no guard on the wall walk would notice her, especially since their job was to keep threats outside the castle's walls. They passed through the gates without being stopped.

After lying there a bit longer, she pushed the hay aside and sat up. The driver looked straight ahead, whistling a tune to himself. Elinor scooted to the end of the cart and hopped down, quickly diving into the woods before anyone might spot her. She decided to keep to them instead of the road for now but weariness began to overcome her. Forcing herself to push away from the tree trunk, she continued through the dense forest with no end in mind.

She hadn't a clue how long she'd walked when she reached a small structure. Elinor came into a clearing and saw what she gathered was a hunting lodge by its size and shape. The baron had one at Whitley. Though she'd never been inside it, she had passed it many a time when she lived with Jasper. It wasn't hunting season now though it would be soon. Elinor decided to take a chance and go inside. It was starting to grow dark and she had no desire to spend the night in the cold, black woods.

Finding the door unlocked, she pushed it open and entered. Looking about, she saw it had a couple of rooms to either side of the door and a staircase leading to a higher floor. She wandered about and found a barrel with some apples in it. Greedily, she ate one and then gobbled down another two before her stomach started aching. Deciding to explore upstairs, she found a bed. Her hands stroked the soft linen sheets, which were as fine as the ones she had awakened upon at Winterbourne.

Might this be the Earl of Winterbourne's hunting lodge? Elinor had lost track of direction and the distance she'd traveled and this bed looked inviting. Despite knowing she should move on, her body rebelled, especially now with her belly full. She doubted the owner would be using his hunting lodge tonight. She would sleep here and continue in the morning.

Elinor pulled back the sheets and climbed into bed. At least her clothes had been washed and mended while she'd been ill so she wouldn't dirty the sheets. She pulled them up to her chin and then curled on her side as her head sank into a feathered pillow. Fighting to stay awake a moment to enjoy the utter bliss of being in a cozy bed, Elinor lost the battle and fell into a deep sleep.

---

"WHY WOULD SHE leave?" Hal asked, his heart wrenching.

"I cannot say," his mother replied. "She did cry a great deal. I thought she shed tears of relief once she knew she was in a safe place and that you would soon return to her." Her mouth turned down. "I'm not so sure now."

He couldn't imagine why she'd vanished. Elinor had been told he was coming home to her. That he loved her.

*Is that why she fled—because she discovered that he loved her?*

Impossible. They were meant to be together.

"Do you think 'tis because she's a commoner?" Geoffrey mused. "Mayhap, she was intimidated when she learned of your background, Hal," he suggested.

Hal raked his hands through his hair in exasperation. "That wouldn't be an obstacle," he shared. "Elinor Swan is the daughter of a baron."

"What?" his parents cried in unison, surprise on their faces.

"I thought her of lowly birth. The adopted daughter of Jasper, the falconer, until my recent trip to Whitley," Hal said.

Quickly, he explained what he'd learned from Father Leo and Eunice, the longtime Whitley servant.

"So instead of mourning the wife who died in childbirth and comforting his frightened daughter, this baron *exiled* Elinor merely because she wasn't a son?" Anger and disgust filled his father's features.

Merryn placed a hand on her husband's arm. "Geoffrey, not all men are loving fathers such as you. Many noblemen care little for female children."

Sorrow crossed Geoffrey's face. "My heart goes out to this future daughter of ours. Elinor *will* be loved. By her husband. His siblings. The two of us. I cannot imagine how she felt growing up in total rejection. Knowing who she'd once been and losing all she'd ever known."

"It gives me even greater respect for her," Merryn proclaimed. "To have remained strong and believed in herself. To have become a falconer, which takes years of hard work and dedication. Elinor is as accomplished as any noblewoman I've known. Even more so."

Hal adored how his parents already championed Elinor. Their steadfast belief in him and Elinor together would see him through now.

"When was the last time you saw her, Mother?"

"About two hours ago."

"She can't have gotten far. Not in her weakened condition."

Geoffrey spoke up. "I'll have Hardie send men in all four directions. They can ride two leagues out and then slowly work their way back toward Winterbourne. Surely, they'll come across her. I'll see to it now."

After he left, his mother said, "I know better than to ask you to wait here for Elinor's return." She kissed his cheek. "Go, my son. Find your one true love and return her safely."

Hal left the keep and went for his horse. Mounting it, he rode to the gates. The gatekeeper saw all who passed. He might have a clue where Hal could start to look.

"Who has left the castle grounds in the past few hours and not returned?" he asked the man.

The gatekeeper scratched his chin, his eyes scrunching up in thought. "John, who oversees the workers in the fields. Our blacksmith. He went to the village but he should be back soon. No one else, my lord." He paused. "Oh, wait. A cart full of hay bound for—"

"Thank you," Hal interrupted.

He had his answer.

Elinor was clever enough to have disguised herself using the hay to remain hidden in order to make her escape. He kept his horse at a trot, heading through Winterbourne's gates. She wouldn't have stayed long in the vehicle, not knowing its destination yet she wouldn't have left its cover too soon.

Glancing about, he spoke aloud. "She would have taken to the woods."

He slowed the horse to a walk, his eyes sweeping the ground, damp from last night's rain. There had to be a sign of her progress. And then he found it—a bent branch.

He steered the horse toward it and saw footprints. They led him to a tree near the road before they continued into the woods.

Hope flickered within him as he began his search. Methodically, Hal tracked Elinor to a place familiar to him—the de Montfort hunting lodge. It lay at the most northern part of their estate, closer to

Winterbourne than Kinwick.

His gut told him Elinor sheltered inside.

Riding into the clearing, he saw no sign of her outside. Hal dismounted and secured the reins of his horse. Slowly, he walked toward the door, anticipation building inside him. He recalled how his parents came to the lodge every year for a few days, always in August. They went alone and never failed to return looking more deeply in love than when they'd left. Hal had asked Alys once about these annual visits. His sister had given him a mysterious smile and merely said the place held special meaning to them. They went every year to rediscover and repledge their love to one another.

Mayhap, this safe haven for them would also prove to be his and Elinor's place of salvation.

Hal entered and softly closed the door behind him, not wanting to startle her. He searched the bottom floor and decided she had to be upstairs. He moved up the steps, not wanting to face what would happen if he didn't find her there.

His breath caught in his throat.

*She was here.*

Silently, he closed the chamber door and went to stand beside the bed where she slept. Raw emotion overcame him, causing him to shake as if he'd come down with a fever. He blinked back tears while he stared at the angelic beauty curled upon her side. Hal knelt next to her, assuring himself she was flesh and blood and not some figment of his imagination as he watched her breathe in and out.

Elinor's face was thinner than when he'd last seen her but she was as he remembered. He stroked her hair softly, not wanting to awaken her but unable to keep from touching her. She murmured something and he bent close, his ear near her lips.

"Hal."

'Twas all she said but it moved him to his very core. Her soft, warm breath tickled his ear. Hal lifted his head and stared at the face that he'd searched for. The one he wanted to see every day of his life and never be parted from again. His palm nestled against her cheek.

Elinor sighed. The corners of her mouth turned up slightly, causing that sweet dimple to appear.

And then she opened her eyes.

ELINOR AWOKE, BURROWING toward the warmth near her face. Her eyelids fluttered open and she tried to understand the dream. It made her think she was awake because the warm hand resting against her cheek belonged to Hal. She saw him drink her in, deep longing in his eyes.

*Wait. This was no dream.*

Elinor sat up with a start and edged away from the knight, her back pressing into the wall behind her as her heart pounded loudly, the blood roaring in her ears. He had come for her. She would be dragged back to Whitley to atone for her role in Lady Rohesia's death, all at the hands of the man she had fallen in love with. The fact that he knew her to be a murderess was hard enough to deal with but to find he would be the one responsible for bringing her to justice was more than she could bear.

Panicked, Elinor threw back the covers and leaped from the bed. She had to escape. Now.

She reached the door and before she could open it, Hal's strong arms encircled her waist and above her breasts. He yanked her to him. She strained against the rock-hard chest, her hands beating against his thighs in a futile effort to find release. But he was having none of that. His grip tightened around her.

Elinor gave up. It was over. She couldn't break free nor could she outrun him. Like an animal who had stepped into a snare, she had been captured for good—and would now lose her life for a single mistake.

Hot tears spilled down her cheeks as she went limp. Callused fingers tenderly wiped the tears from her face. Hal's lips hovered near her ear, causing a tingle to ripple through her.

"Elinor. Talk to me. What is wrong? Why do continue to flee from me?"

She heard the hurt in his voice, hurt she had put there. Her head fell back against his chest. His hand dropped to her throat and stroked it, his thumb moving up and down. Despite her misgivings about his presence, something stirred inside her. The pull came from her womanly parts and started to pulse with need. Her body remembered his touch and cried out for it.

Hal turned her in his arms. Elinor couldn't back away with the door nudging her from behind. He caged her between it and his body, his palms flat against the wood.

"Does my love so repulse you that you must run from me?"

Confusion roiled through her. Merryn had told Elinor that Hal loved her but that had been before he sought her out at Whitley. Surely, he now knew her grievous actions had caused Rohesia Swan's death. He couldn't possibly love her.

*Could he?*

He lowered his forehead until it rested against hers. She inhaled the familiar scent and longed to taste him. They stood together this way for some minutes until Elinor thought he was trying to lull her into a false sense of confidence. Why was he toying with her, as a cat did a mouse, pretending to feel some great affection for her?

Then his arms fell away. His hands found hers and he threaded their fingers together.

Hal lifted his head and met her gaze. "Hear me out, Elinor. Please."

His voice cracked on the last word. A flood of tenderness swept through her. She nodded mutely.

"You not only healed me physically but emotionally. I was broken and did not even know it. You gave me a gift—the gift of rediscovering myself. With you, I learned to be the man I once was. And the one I want to remain."

His fingers tightened around hers. "I left so many things unsaid before we parted but I feared I had taken advantage of you when you returned from Jasper's burial. I longed to tell you how much I care for you. Desire you. Need you. How much I always want you by my side."

Hal gave her a crooked grin. "I love you, Elinor. I believe we are soul mates. I want to see your face next to mine when I awaken each day after having spent the night holding you in my arms."

His words left her with unanswered questions. "Then . . . then . . . why did you leave me? Why did you not say what was in your heart?"

"Because I'd never told a woman that I loved her. I didn't know how."

Elinor drew in a sharp breath.

"Though we'd spent hours talking, I had never told you who I truly am—a knight of the realm. One who served King Richard at his court and had flirted with hundreds of women who meant nothing to me. I was afraid you would think a match between us impossible." His eyes fell. "I am ashamed to tell you that I was afraid you would choose your falcons over me."

She found it hard to take in everything he said.

Hal continued. "I stupidly thought if I declared my love for you, you would turn away. I hoped my absence from Whitley would help you realize that we were meant to be together. And I did want my family to know I was unharmed. England is in turmoil, Elinor. I know you haven't heard what is happening in our kingdom since you've lived in isolation for so long, but battles have been waged as to who should hold the power to rule. I owed it to my loved ones to let them know I was alive.

"And that I'd found the woman who would become my wife. If she would have me."

Elinor trembled at those words. "But surely you could have found another at court? Someone to love—"

"The royal court is the last place to find love, sweetheart. 'Tis full of conniving schemers who speak falsely." His determined gaze warmed her blood. "God sent me to you, my love. He gave us time alone to be who we truly are, with no other trappings."

Hal's eyes heated with desire. Elinor's bones began to melt.

"Tell me you feel the same about me as I do you," he said, his voice rough. "Tell me your heart has told you that we should be together forever."

"Aye."

# CHAPTER 22

HER WHISPERED WORD was all he needed.

Hal's mouth crashed down on hers. His body pressed Elinor against the door.

But she tensed under his fingers and he realized how overwhelmed she must be. His kiss should not only convey his desire for her but should also let her know how much he cherished her. He forced his own body to relax from the weeks of tension coiled inside and brushed his lips softly against hers, over and over. He released her fingers and brought his hands to rest against her waist.

Slowly, he ran his tongue along the seam of her lips, teasing her mouth open. She responded and gave him entrance into heaven.

*Holy Christ . . .*

Hal had forgotten how sweet this woman tasted. He took his time, gently exploring her mouth with his tongue and smiled when hers began to mate with his. Soon, Elinor was an active participant in their kiss and he let her take the lead. Her hands crept up his chest and came to rest along his shoulders. She kneaded him as a kitten might, bringing a swell of deep emotion within him.

His palms glided up her ribcage, his thumbs slowly weaving back and forth under the curve of her breasts. She murmured into his mouth and though he didn't know what she said, it encouraged him. He cupped each breast and kneaded them as she had done with him. Her fingers tightened on his shoulders as he dragged each thumb across her nipples. They puckered in need. Elinor sighed, causing his manhood to rise to attention, brushing against her belly.

He leaned into her now, the door supporting her, as he broke the kiss and allowed his tongue to run down her pale throat and back up. He brought it to her ear and outlined it before gently sinking his teeth into her earlobe. Her gasp of surprise—and satisfaction—swept through him as his heart slammed against his ribs.

Reluctantly, Hal released her earlobe and lowered his hands, encircling her waist again. Elinor pressed her heated body against his, the back of her fingers stroking his neck before she tugged his head back to her.

"Wait," he told her, his hands capturing her wrists. "I want to give all of myself to you, my love, and I want all of you in return. Do you wish for us to be together in the way a man loves a woman? If you'd rather wait until we're wed, I will understand." He kissed her swiftly. "But we will need to stop soon if you do."

Any lingering doubts melted from her eyes and Hal only saw trust within them. This bond of trust would be the foundation for everything they built together for their rest of their lives.

"I'm not certain of everything that is to come between us," Elinor began, "but I only know how my body craves your touch. I want everything from you. Everything you can give me. Love me, Hal. I am yours. Now and forevermore."

Barely had the words left her mouth when he swept her into his arms. Hal took Elinor to the bed and placed her on it. He lifted the hem of her man's tunic and pulled it over her head. Her arms went straight up to allow him to remove it. Another, lighter one lay underneath it and he pulled it away, too. Perfect, creamy globes greeted him. Hal stared in awe. Elinor lowered her arms and her gaze fell as a blush crossed her cheeks.

He lifted her chin with two fingers until their eyes met. "You have no reason to be self-conscious, sweetheart. You are beautiful."

"Really?" she asked, wonder in her voice.

He realized she had never been told so before. "Aye. Everything about you is beautiful. Your rich, brown hair. Those warm, brown eyes. The dimple that creases your cheek when you smile at me."

She smiled and he tenderly kissed the dimple.

"And your body, love." He brought his fingers to her breasts and began to rub them. A small moan escaped from her. Holding her gaze, he said, "I look forward to exploring every inch of you."

Her eyes widened before a teasing smile crossed her lips. "And will I be able to do the same with you?" she boldly asked.

Heat sizzled through him. "If you wish."

Elinor cocked her head to the side as if she considered it a moment. "I think I would like that. Very much."

Hal couldn't help but laugh and she joined in with him. He eased her back onto the bed, his lips finding her throat again before trailing down the valley between her breasts. He lavished attention on one, nipping and licking until she writhed under him before turning to enjoy the other one. As he sucked on one and Elinor's fingers pushed into his hair, he heard satisfaction in the small sounds she made.

Gradually, his lips made their way down the tender, white flesh of her belly. Her fingers continued raking through his hair, making his scalp tingle and sending a delicious ripple from his head down his spine. He had hit more clothing, though, and raised his mouth from her. He worked her pants down her legs and removed her boots before he discarded both. Leisurely, he worked his way back up, his fingers brushing against the sweet curve of her calves and gliding along the silken skin of her inner thighs.

When his mouth reached her apex, Elinor suddenly pushed him away.

"Nay," she said firmly. "You have seen me bare. I want to see you the same way. Now."

A wide grin spread across his face. "At your service, my lady," he said smoothly.

Hal climbed off the bed and took his time in removing his clothes and boots. He wanted Elinor to see what she had committed herself to and give her time to change her mind if she so desired. He enjoyed watching her face as he tossed aside each bit of clothing he wore. Finally, he stood before her, naked.

"Are you pleased with what you see?" he asked, hoping she was.

"Not yet," she said saucily. "I want to touch you." She swallowed. "I need to touch you."

He lay on the bed next to her, his back against the mattress. "Explore as you wish."

And she did.

Hal soon craved those slender fingers, which left nothing undisturbed. She stroked his arms, grasping his forearms and biceps. Her fingers danced along his chest, toying with the hairs there, smoothing and teasing them. Elinor's lips kissed his and trailed downward, eventually reaching his nipples, where her tongue playfully glided around and across them.

By this time, his manhood had grown so hard, he ached for release. Her hand came lower and encircled his shaft. Hal sucked in a quick breath. She began running her fingers along it.

"The head is like fine silk but the rest is so hard," she marveled. She pressed a kiss upon it. When her tongue lightly flicked against it, Hal grabbed her and roughly brought her against his chest.

"Did I do something wrong?" she asked, her voice small.

"Nay." He gave her a long, lingering kiss. "'Twas very right," he assured her. "But I want you so badly that if you continued to do that, I might explode."

Her hands cupped his cheeks. "Then what should I do?"

He rolled her to her back and rose over her, his large body covering hers. "I would like us to join together. Only if you truly wish it."

Elinor's eyes shone with trust—and love. "I do. More than anything."

His fingers found and parted her fold. She was definitely ready for him. Hal slid a finger inside her and she gasped and tightened around it.

"Your body remembers me," he told her. "Let me give you pleasure and then you can return the favor."

He brought her to the edge of climax twice and pulled back each time, her breath growing quick and short and her face flushed.

Knowing he had teased her long enough, he found her nub and rubbed it with his thumb, pressing just hard enough to hear the hitch in her breath. Her hips began to rise and buck against him.

"That's it, sweetheart. Come for me," he encouraged softly.

His fingers continued to work as her climax hit. Elinor's nails dug into his back as her small moans became much louder and longer. Hal let her ride the wave of pleasure and as it began to subside, he quickly slipped his shaft into her with a single thrust.

"Oh!" she cried out, startled.

He remained motionless, allowing her body to get use to him. "'Tis the only time it will hurt. I had to break through your maidenhead," he explained as he covered her face in soft kisses.

"It did hurt. But it doesn't now."

"Good."

Hal began rocking slowly with her, withdrawing and plunging into her tight sweetness again and again. Elinor clung to him, her cries coming louder.

"'Tis happening again," she got out.

"Go with it," he ground out as he reached his own release and roared in triumph as they both found the heights of happiness together.

Hal collapsed and not wanting to crush Elinor, immediately rolled to his side, still inside her. He had coupled with more women than he could count yet, in this moment, he realized 'twas the first time he had ever made love.

With the woman he loved.

He wrapped his arms about her. "I love you," he said, over and over. "I plan to love you this way every day for the rest of our lives. I will never leave you unless called to the king's service and if that happens?" He kissed her tenderly. "Know that I will always come home to you. For where you are, that is where my home will always be."

Elinor's head rest against his beating heart. "I love you so much, Hal. Whatever happens, I hope you'll always remember that."

Hal barely heard her words as he drifted off to sleep.

ELINOR EXPERIENCED COMPLETE bliss as she lay in her beloved's arms. She had no words for the powerful emotions running through her.

Hal completed her. She never knew what had been missing from her life until he entered it. It was a revelation, one that she would hold on to once they parted. It had been selfish of her to allow him to make love to her, knowing they would never marry. Somehow, despite his trip to Whitley to locate her, Hal hadn't yet learned of her terrible crime.

But Elinor had knowledge of the death she had caused. Because of it, she could not allow a marriage to occur between them. Hal was a good, kind man. A respected knight of the realm. To wed an outlaw such as herself would be unthinkable. She knew how he valued his family and would not want to destroy their good name—or his.

It was time to leave. Elinor must disappear for good this time. Make her way across the English border into Scotland, as she had planned. Hal would never think to hunt for her there.

The decision would only grow harder the longer she remained next to him. She listened to his beating heart under her ear and savored the feel of his naked body next to hers. Gently, she raised her head and turned away from him.

"Don't go," he murmured. His fingers caught her wrist and pulled her back to him. One hand caressed the curve of her hip as his warm lips pressed against her neck.

Hal made love to her again, slow and sweet, bringing Elinor to a high that dazzled her. Nestled in his arms once more, he began to talk to her about all that he hadn't shared before, starting with his siblings.

"Alys and Ancel are twins. Alys is the elder by a minute and never lets anyone forget it. She is a healer, as Mother is. Kit worships the ground she trods upon. 'Tis the same between Ancel and Margery. They are true partners in every way and cherish one another."

He told her of the twins and how they came to marry their spouses. Where they lived and the names of their children. Hal had a fine way of describing things so that she could see each person he spoke of and the places they lived.

"I am closest to Edward. He is two years younger than I am and became my shadow as we grew up. We fostered together at Winterbourne, as pages and then squires. My parents are close friends with the earl and countess and their sons are as cousins to me."

Hal told her of how Edward found Rosalyne while on a secret mission to Canterbury for the king and how she was a painter who had created not only triptychs for churches but completed portraits of King Richard and Queen Anne. Elinor could tell Hal had great admiration for Rosalyne de Montfort and the children she'd borne his brother.

"What of your other sisters?" she asked, eager to hear about them.

"Nan is a year younger than Edward. She followed the two of us around and demanded to do anything we did. She can be most stubborn, so it was easier to let her attempt whatever we did, be it swimming in the lake or riding a horse. I remember the day she begged to learn how to shoot a bow and arrow." He chuckled. "I thought the task would be beyond her but she stuck with it, taking in everything I taught her. And now she's a finer bowman than any man at Kinwick."

"Truly? I have seen bows before. They are large and unwieldy."

"She had one specially crafted. 'Tis light in weight but her aim is true. In fact, Nan is now at Sandbourne with my cousin Elysande and her husband, Michael, teaching their soldiers everything she knows about archery."

Hal stroked her arm absently. Elinor relished the contact.

"As for the last of my sisters? Nan found Jessimond."

His words confused her. "Found her where?"

"In the forest."

"Was she lost?" asked Elinor.

"Nay. Abandoned. Nan roamed our family estate and knows it better than anyone, other than my father. She and Father came across a tiny babe in the woods and brought her home." Hal smiled. "My mother likes nothing better than to hold a babe in her arms. Though she and Father did everything they could to locate Jessimond's parents, they never did. So Jess became the youngest de Montfort."

"But you call her sister, even though she is not your flesh and blood?"

Hal gave her a look as if she'd gone mad. "Of course. I would die protecting Jessimond, as I would any family member. She's as much a de Montfort as I am. We all love her." He cupped her cheek. "'Twill be the same with you, love. My parents already call you their daughter. Everyone will shower you with love and believe me, my family is large and loves one another with a passion. In fact, you may feel smothered by all their affection and attention."

Elinor couldn't comprehend such a thing but she believed Hal wouldn't exaggerate. She only wished she could experience such an all-encompassing love from his large family. What joy all these de Montforts must take in one another.

He kissed her brow and released her from his embrace and then climbed out of bed. "We should dress. Lord Hardwin's men have been sent to look for you. I need to bring you back to Winterbourne so they know you are safe. From there, we will travel to Kinwick."

Hal began pulling on his clothes. Elinor followed suit. She had lost the opportunity to leave when he awakened. She would need to be ready when the time came to do so again. She must cover her tracks well and vanish without a trace.

They tidied the bed and left the hunting lodge. A horse awaited them outside. Hal ran his hand affectionately along its neck.

"This was a gift to me from Michael and Elysande since I had lost my own."

Hurt flashed in his eyes and then it was gone in an instant, so fast that if Elinor had not been looking at him, she might have missed it. He mounted the steed and lifted her up in front of him, enfolding her in his arms. She was glad to have his protection. Having never been on a horse before, she tried her best to calm her nerves and trust in Hal.

As they crossed the clearing and entered the woods, she asked,

"What happened to your horse, Hal? Did you lose it before I met you? Is that why you were on foot?"

His body tensed next to hers. "My horse was taken from me. My armor. My weapons. I suffered humiliation and was full of despair when I came to you."

As Hal guided the horse slowly through the dense forest, he told her of his service in the king's royal guard and the battle where he lost everything, even handing over his precious sword. His tone remained neutral but Elinor knew him well enough to understand how devastated he'd been.

If the king regained power, she supposed he would want loyal men surrounding him. That would include Hal returning to court, along with his bride. Elinor couldn't imagine living in the royal palace with hundreds of the nobility. She would have nothing in common with any of the women and she'd feel trapped within the walls. It was another reason they should never marry.

She placed her hand over his, rubbing her thumb against it, wanting to ease his troubles. How could she abandon him when he had lost so much already? Mayhap, she could stay with him a bit longer. Try to bring some happiness into his life before she left.

He pulled her even closer into him, nuzzling her neck. A frisson of pleasure trickled through her at the gesture. Her body already wanted him again.

"You are still a knight, Hal," she reassured him. "You did your duty to the king. Your honor is intact."

"My father says the same. Mayhap one day, I will believe him."

They rode the rest of the way to Winterbourne in silence. Elinor savored being in the arms of the man she loved. Once they left the forest, Hal urged his horse on. They galloped the rest of the way until they rode through the gates and arrived at the keep. She saw Lord Hardwin and his wife standing beside Merryn and a tall, broad shouldered man with bits of gray at the temples of his dark hair. He must be Hal's father for their resemblance was startling. Seeing him, Elinor knew what Hal would look like in the years to come.

Hal dismounted and swept her from the horse. Merryn immediately pulled her into a tight embrace.

"We were so worried about you, Elinor."

She gave in to the hug, her eyes closed, wishing Merryn could truly be the loving mother she never had.

Then she found herself in Geoffrey de Montfort's arms. Though a large man, he treated her gently and made Elinor feel as safe as his son did.

"I am Geoffrey," he told her. "Hal's father." His eyes searched hers. "We know some of your story, Elinor, and how difficult your life has been. Know that you are now with your family and safe. You will never lack for anything again," he said fiercely. "Nothing."

Elinor felt the waves of love and protection coming from him. It moved her to tears. She blinked them back.

He released her. "I also hear that you are a fine falconer. My man, Joseph, is getting on up in years. Mayhap, you would consider eventually replacing him?" he asked hopefully.

How she wished she could. Become the Kinwick falconer. Marry into this loving family. Have children of her own.

Elinor felt like a traitor as she said, "I would be interested in meeting with Joseph and seeing his raptors."

"All in good time," Lord Hardwin interjected. "Would you like to come in and have something to eat and drink?"

Hal spoke up. "We have another two hours or so of daylight. I would rather take Elinor home, my lord."

"An excellent idea," Geoffrey seconded. He grasped Lord Hardwin's elbows. "You and Johamma take care. We will see you soon."

"For the wedding?" Lady Johamma asked, a twinkle in her eyes.

"The sooner, the better," Hal replied. "I am not known for my patience." He tossed a heated look Elinor's way.

"We will send word to everyone in the morning," Merryn said. "I hope within two weeks all will have arrived so they can witness the ceremony."

Hal returned Elinor to the saddle and swung up behind her. "Two weeks until we are husband and wife," he whispered in her ear.

As they rode away from Winterbourne, Elinor wondered how far away she could be two weeks from now.

# CHAPTER 23

ELINOR AWOKE TO her third morning at Kinwick. She hadn't been alone the entire time since they'd arrived. Her head told her she must find a way to vanish so that Hal could not track her but her heart wished to stay in the middle of everything. She promised herself today she would find a way to leave. How and where remained a mystery so she would keep her eyes peeled.

The previous two days she'd kept busy with Merryn and Jessimond. They'd shown her their herb garden and the room where they ground and stored the herbs. Merryn offered to teach Elinor about the ones she used in healing others, both at the castle and on the estate. She had accompanied them to the rolling meadow to gather flowers and herbs. A carpet of green grass announced spring's arrival and they had collected enough to fill the six baskets they'd taken with them. Elinor loved the view of the castle from the meadow, towering against the blue sky as white clouds rolled by.

Merryn had also taken her throughout the keep, showing her every room from the larder to the solar. Now that Edward and Rosalyne and their two children had left for Shallowheart, Merryn suggested that she and Hal use the chambers they had vacated.

"You will have ample room and find privacy in them," she had told Elinor. "Being newly wed, you will appreciate having somewhere to go that can be your own space to share time alone."

"Were Geoffrey's parents still alive when you came to live at Kinwick?" she asked. "Or did you immediately use the solar?"

A shadow flickered across Merryn's face. "His parents were the earl and countess when Geoffrey and I wed. We were given a large chamber of our own." Merryn paused. "I might as well share this with you, Elinor. It's not a secret but it is not something we speak of often."

The noblewoman took her arm. "Come to the solar with me."

Once there, Merryn poured wine for them and they sat in two large, comfortable chairs.

"Geoffrey and I wed but did not live together as man and wife for some time," Merryn began. "The details are not important. Know only that Geoffrey was taken by an enemy the day after our wedding and held hostage. When he returned after several years, we both had changed in many ways. I had given birth to Alys and Ancel during his absence. Geoffrey's father had died. I had run Kinwick on my own with some help from Raynor Le Roux, Geoffrey's cousin and close friend. You will meet him and Beatrice soon."

She paused, sipping her wine. "It took time for us to learn to accept who we had become, apart from each other. But once we did, we have treasured each day together and loved one another well. It's also why we insisted that our children would never face lengthy betrothals with people they did not even know. Geoffrey and I found love again and held on to it. We have nurtured it, much as you would tend a garden." Merryn smiled. "You might even say we have given our love the time and patience that you put in with your falcons. My point is that we have fashioned love as the center of our family. We want each of our children to find love for themselves so that they might experience the joy that we know every day together."

Merryn reached over and squeezed Elinor's knee. "We are so pleased that Hal has found you."

Elinor sensed her cheeks heating from guilt, knowing she wouldn't remain at Kinwick much longer.

Merryn's soft laughter filled the room. "No need to blush, my dear. I've seen Hal sneaking into your room at night. There's nothing wrong with sharing passion with your mate. Besides, you will be wed soon. Hopefully, you will be blessed with children sooner than later. Hal has been a wonderful uncle to his nieces and nephews and he will make a fine father."

Elinor pushed aside the covers and the remembered conversation from her mind. Hal had already left her bed a few hours ago. He had joined her both nights, loving her thoroughly before leaving to allow both of them to get some much needed rest.

A knock sounded at the door. "Come," she called.

Jessimond entered the room. The girl would be ten and two soon and looked nothing like either adopted parent. Both Geoffrey and Merryn were quite tall, while Jessimond would never come close to their height. Geoffrey possessed the same dark hair that Hal did, while Merryn had chestnut hair and sapphire blue eyes, much like Hal's. Their youngest child sported thick, golden-blond hair that cascaded in waves and she had the most unusual eyes Elinor had ever seen, a deep violet in color. Where her parents were genial, Jessimond was reserved without being shy.

Despite the physical differences, Jessimond was treated as kindly as Hal by her parents and everyone they'd come across at Kinwick. It was obvious both her family and all the servants harbored a deep affection for the girl. Elinor wished she could tell Jessimond how lucky she was to have been embraced by this family.

"Do you need help getting ready for mass?" asked Jessimond eagerly.

"I would like that."

Elinor allowed the young girl to brush out her hair and braid it for her. She slipped on a chemise and cotehardie that Merryn had brought her. They had belonged to Nan before she outgrew them. Elinor had worn the feminine clothes to mass and to dine in each day out of respect for her hosts but had slipped into her own clothes at other times.

Jessimond took her hand and escorted her to the Kinwick chapel, where Hal joined them. Elinor had actually enjoyed the ritual of mass the past two days. While coming and going, she had also met several people, men and women who tended the fields of the estate or worked as servants throughout the castle grounds. What surprised her most was how friendly and happy everyone seemed. She had never experienced that at Whitley, even when she was a child. She knew it was because of Geoffrey and Merryn. They cared for their people as much as they did their own family members.

Once mass ended, they returned to the keep. Elinor joined Geoffrey and Merryn on the dais.

Geoffrey gave her a friendly smile. "Merryn has monopolized your time the past two days but I would like to take you with me today. I think it's time you met Joseph and his raptors."

Excitement grew within her since she hadn't been around any falcons for weeks. Elinor tried to tamp it down, knowing she would never stay long enough to work with the Kinwick birds.

"Thank you. I would enjoy seeing them."

"We can go together after we break our fast. I'll return you in time for the noon meal and then I believe Hal wants to take you about the estate."

Hal slipped his hand into hers under the table. "I'll show you our land today. Once we are wed, we can visit each of the cottages so you can get to know all the workers on the estate. Mother said you have shown an interest in herbs. I know she would appreciate you accompanying her when she visits the tenants and sees to their needs."

Elinor found it hard to swallow the bread she chewed. Everyone at Kinwick was so kind. The de Montforts had opened their arms to her and wrapped her in love. She forced down the bread and her growing bitterness with a bit of ale. She was glad she would not be around to see their disappointment after she fled.

Geoffrey escorted her from the great hall once they completed the small meal.

"We could ride but Hal tells me that you haven't had the opportunity to learn how to do so. I know that is something he wants to teach you. Although you are always welcome to ride with him, it's a useful skill to have in the country. We'll find you a gentle horse that has a tough mouth and have you riding by the time you're Elinor de Montfort."

*Elinor de Montfort . . .*

They left the keep and descended the long staircase that led down to the inner bailey.

"We can reach Joseph's cottage by foot. If you tire, let me know and we can stop and rest."

"I am feeling strong again, my lord, after getting such good meals in me. Your cook certainly has a way with food."

Geoffrey laughed. "The old king stopped here on summer progress a few times over the years. He was so taken with Cook's tarts that he threatened to steal her from me. I kept a watchful eye to insure that she remained at Kinwick."

"I can see why. The apple ones she baked for last night's meal are the most delicious things I've ever put in my mouth."

"You must tell her that, Elinor," he urged. As they walked on, he said, "I know you grew up isolated from others, with only Jasper to interact with you. I have found it is important to always let others know how much you appreciate and care for them, whether they are your servants or workers or blood kin. That includes taking time to recognize what they have done, no matter how small. Most of the nobility take something as simple as an apple tart for granted but I believe in letting Cook know how her efforts are valued. It brings her joy knowing she did her job well and will cause her to strive to do even better in the future."

"I can tell Kinwick is a happy place. I am sure 'tis because of that thoughtfulness which is shared."

"We hope you will be happy here. Merryn and I can see how happy you have made Hal. I will warn you, though, that the first wave of relatives will hit today. You may be overwhelmed by them but they all have your best interest—and Hal's—at heart."

As they continued on the way, he told her some about his niece, Elysande, and her husband, Michael, a former knight of his, who would arrive sometime today, along with Nan. Geoffrey suggested that Elysande might help her select a horse to ride since she was so knowledgeable about them. His other niece, Avelyn, and her husband,

Kenric, would arrive by the noon meal tomorrow, as would Geoffrey's cousin, Raynor, and his wife, Beatrice.

"After that, Alys and Kit are supposed to be here in another two days' time, the same as Ancel and Margery, followed by my sister, Mary, and her husband. Last will be my son, Edward, and his wife, Rosalyne, who recently left Kinwick to live at Shallowheart, their new home. They are still settling into their responsibilities as its baron and baroness but will appear in plenty of time to see you and Hal wed. And of course, Hardie and Johamma will come from Winterbourne."

"There are so many names to remember. I hope I will not be too confused." Elinor doubted she would meet any of these relatives because she planned to get away from Kinwick before they began to arrive.

"Merryn's brother and wife live at Wellbury, the estate adjoining ours. Hugh and Milla will probably visit over the next several days, as well. Hopefully, you can learn each couple when they arrive. Be glad they are not all descending upon us at the same time," he teased.

After a half-hour's walk, Geoffrey said, "We are approaching Joseph's place, which is set away from our other cottages. He prefers solitude in order to train the birds. I will introduce you to him and then let you take it from there."

They came upon a lean man with a white beard and hair to match. He sat on a stump next to a broad perch and wore a leather gauntlet on his right hand. A large mews stood next to the perch, leading Elinor to believe Kinwick must have several raptors.

"Greetings, Joseph," called Geoffrey as they drew near. "I have brought my soon to be daughter-in-law with me. She is a falconer." He turned to her. "Elinor, this is Joseph. He has been Kinwick's falconer since my father's time as earl."

"I am pleased to meet you, Joseph," she said politely, though the falconer studied her through narrowed eyes, his doubt obvious as he rose to his feet.

"My lady."

"Please. Call me Elinor."

"You dress the part, though you have no gauntlet."

"Might I borrow an old one of yours?" she asked sweetly, doing her best to charm him.

Joseph grunted and walked to his cottage. He disappeared inside and returned a few moments later, tossing her the glove. Elinor slipped it on. It was a bit loose but she could manage with it.

"So, Lord Geoffrey claims you are a falconer."

The nobleman had sat on the stump and watched them with interest.

"I am," she said with pride.

"For how long?"

"Ten and six years."

The falconer snorted and then began peppering her with questions.

"What are babes called?"

"Eyases."

"When should they fly?"

"Usually the forty-second day, though my last pair, Bess and Tris, did so earlier."

"What kind of falcons did you train?"

"Raptors, Joseph. All good falconers refer to them this way," she said with a grin. After a moment, she said, "Peregrines. The best kind of hawk."

He nodded in approval. "Go on."

"Peregrines have strong hunting abilities and are one of the easiest falcons to train, as well as the swiftest bird of all. They have an advantage in that their natural flying style of circling allows game to be flushed easily. They enjoy the high diving stoop that ends with their quarry being taken."

"And how do the raptors accomplish this?" he prodded.

"First and foremost, by their speed. A peregrine can capture flying birds or game with a knockout blow using their clenched talons."

"Hmm. What else do you know?"

Elinor went on to discuss why females were preferred over males and detailed how she manned the hawks, hooded them, and the various ways she trained them to the lure.

"Do you blind them?"

"Never," she said emphatically. "Jasper, the falconer who taught me all I know, did so when I first came to him. I convinced him of a better way. He gave me a male to test my ideas. When I met with success, he allowed me to continue with the females we trained."

Joseph nodded in approval. "You speak as one with knowledge—but handling raptors is another story."

"I agree. Call your birds. Let me work with them."

The falconer did as Elinor asked and she put two of them through their paces for over an hour. By the time she finished, Geoffrey de Montfort wore a huge grin on his face while she saw new respect for her reflected in Joseph's brown eyes.

"And all that was with an ill-fitting gauntlet," he marveled. The falconer turned to Geoffrey. "Who is Lady Elinor to wed?"

"Hal."

Joseph waved a dismissive hand. "Sir Hal will never appreciate the skill and experience she has. I, on the other hand, am not married and would love to take her to wife." The old man slapped his knee as he cackled at his own joke and then looked to her. "I welcome you anytime, my lady, whether you merely visit my raptors or wish to help me train them. I am not getting any younger. One day soon, Kinwick will need a new falconer. You are most suited to be it. You have a true gift and relate to raptors better than anyone I've met."

"Thank you, Joseph. That is a generous compliment," Elinor said.

Geoffrey stood. "Thank you for your time, Joseph. Elinor and I need to return to the keep. Lord Michael and Lady Elysande are expected soon. I want to be there to greet them when they arrive."

The falconer nodded. "Another fine lady who knows horses better than a man." He winked at Elinor. "You and Lady Elysande will get along well. You're both adept at something only men usually pursue. Give her and Lord Michael my best."

"I shall," Elinor promised.

Geoffrey escorted her back to the keep. When they entered the bailey, Elinor saw a flurry of activity. Dozens of horses stood near the keep and more arrived as she and Geoffrey drew near. Many of the riders were soldiers in armor but others were women and children.

"I see Elysande and Michael have arrived on schedule. But we have others who have come early." He scanned the crowd. "Raynor and Beatrice are here. Avelyn and Kenric. My sister and her husband. Even Hugh and Milla are here." He shook his head, trying to hide a grin. "I don't envy you, Elinor."

Though overwhelmed as every eye turned expectantly in her direction, Elinor knew in the chaos of this many people at Kinwick that she would have a chance to depart unseen.

If only her heart wasn't so heavy.

# CHAPTER 24

ELINOR ONLY THOUGHT it would be easy to make her escape from Kinwick with so many de Montforts and relatives underfoot.

How wrong she had been.

Every moment of the next three days found her in the company of anywhere from one to a dozen people. She had met everyone in the bailey after her trip to visit Joseph and the entire group had dined in the great hall and spent all afternoon telling stories of the past. Many featured the escapades of Hal, which Elinor enjoyed immensely. It gave her insight into the small child who had become a boy and then a man in this large, loving family.

After the evening meal, she had stayed awhile and then pled a headache.

"I'd have an aching head, too, if all these relatives were thrust upon me," Nan said, giving her a sympathetic look.

Elinor liked Nan quite a bit. Hal's sister had the black hair of her father and her mother's sparkling blue eyes and seemed at ease in the company of men and women alike. If Elinor had lingered at Kinwick, she believed they would have become good friends.

Escaping to her chamber upstairs, she only had seconds alone before Merryn and Alys showed up, satchels in hand, filled with herbs to soothe her head and help her sleep. Alys and Kit had joined the family shortly before the evening meal. Seeing Alys was like a glimpse into the past of what Merryn must have looked like at the same age. Even now, the two women were almost identical except for a few wrinkles that distinguished Merryn as the older of the two.

Both of them fussed over her, while Alys remained in a chair by the bed all night in case Elinor needed anything. Hal had been unable to come to her bed since Jessimond had joined her, giving her chamber up for their many guests. Elinor's attempt to leave at night and gain a solid head start went by the wayside.

The following days had been filled with activities of all kinds. Elinor never found herself alone for a moment. Lady Mary and her daughter, Avelyn, had taken charge of what Elinor would wear for her wedding. Discovering she had no clothes other than a discarded cotehardie from Nan's chest, they set about creating a new wardrobe for Elinor, as well as a gown for her to wear to her upcoming wedding. They raided Merryn's store of materials and brought back bolts in various colors which all of the females investigated with interest. Each expressed her opinions of the different gowns Lady Mary and Avelyn could make up for her.

Nan came to her defense, insisting they also create a few tunics and pairs of pants.

"Above all, Elinor is a falconer. She cannot traipse about training hawks unless she is properly attired."

So tunics and pants were added into the mix of her new wardrobe.

Elysande and a group took Elinor to the stables so that Elinor could see a new horse from the Sandbourne stables that Elysande had ridden to Kinwick. When Elinor confessed she had never learned to ride, Elysande began inspecting the horses in each stall, trying to decide which one to use in order to give Elinor riding lessons.

During her search, Hal pulled Elinor away from the others and led her around the corner. He gave her a lingering kiss and her body hummed as he stroked her back side, cupping her buttocks.

"We are never alone," he complained good-naturedly. "I would have to have an enormous amount of relatives who truly like each other and want to spend time together, especially with you."

He kissed her again, pressing the full length of his body against hers. Her arms went round his neck.

"Hah! I knew you two would be up to no good."

They pulled apart. Elinor saw Kenric and Kit standing nearby with knowing looks in their eyes, both with arms crossed over their massive chests.

"I'll bet Hal's frustrated having to spend lonely nights apart from you, Elinor," Kenric teased.

"That will end as soon as we can be rid of all of you," retorted Hal. He gave her one more swift kiss and released her but Elinor saw the heat in his eyes remained.

"I promise you this, Elinor," Kit said. "Now that you've found a good man to love, your life will be richer and more complete than you ever imagined. I cherish each day with Alys." He waggled his brows. "And the nights even more."

"There you are," Elysande said. Nan and Jessimond trailed after her. "I think I've found the perfect mount for you, Elinor." She glared at the men. "Go on, all of you. I plan to spend the rest of the afternoon with Elinor, teaching her how to ride."

"Oh, she already knows how to ride some mounts," Kenric quipped. Laughing, he and Kit left the stables with Hal's sisters in tow.

"You, too, Hal," Elysande ordered.

"Surely, I can watch your lessons," he pleaded. "I barely have seen Elinor since everyone arrived."

"Nay," Elysande said firmly. "I don't want Elinor to be self-conscious in any way. Especially with the two of you shooting each other heated glances. She needs to focus on the task at hand. Be gone!"

Elinor had participated in two riding lessons with Elysande and admired her way with the horses and her deft hand in teaching. She hoped she could use what she'd learned in the future. Even if she'd become skilled enough to take a horse from the Kinwick stables to use in her escape, she would never have stolen from Geoffrey and Merryn in that way.

Beatrice had spent some time with her, as well. Elinor loved being around the dark-haired woman with a sweet smile and voice like an angel. Beatrice played a few songs on her lute each time the entire group gathered but she drew Elinor aside to play a new tune.

"I hope you like this one," Beatrice said. "I wrote it for you and Hal. I haven't put words to it yet. I wanted to see if you liked the melody before I did so."

Elinor's eyes misted when the final strains echoed. "You have moved me to tears," she told the noblewoman.

"Then I will fashion words for it. I'll sing it at the wedding feast if it pleases you."

"It will. Very much," Elinor assure her, giving a hard shove to the guilt that crept up.

Finally, Rosalyne had pulled her aside, handing Elinor a goblet filled with wine. They sat in a far corner of the great hall, away from the noisy conversations and constant laughter.

"I know what you are going through," Rosalyne shared. "I, too, am an only child. My parents died when I was but a babe and my uncle raised me in Canterbury. Though the city was large, our cottage was small and our life simple. Much, I gather, as yours has been up until now."

She looked around and smiled. "And then I married Edward and inherited all of these wonderful de Montforts and their kin and friends. It took time for me to learn each of their names and where they lived. Who had married whom and which children belonged to which parents." Rosalyne smiled. "But 'twas the most wonderful thing that ever happened to me. For when I fell in love with Edward and married him, I also fell in love with his family and married them, as well."

She took Elinor's hand. "These de Montforts love in a unique way, not only their wedded wife or husband but anyone who marries into or is born in their family. I realize how overwhelmed you must be by all of this, Elinor, but I am so pleased that you and Hal found one another." She squeezed Elinor's hand. "And that I have a new sister. I feel so blessed."

Elinor began to weep, great sobs coming from her. Every female de Montfort gathered around her, with Merryn shooing a concerned Hal and all the men away.

Merryn sat next to her and placed an arm around her. "Cry it out,

Elinor. 'Twill do you good."

"But... I'm... I'm not sure why I am even weeping," she sputtered.

Merryn stroked her hair. "You are merely overcome by all that has happened to you in recent weeks." She looked around. "And meeting all these new relatives."

Elinor nodded. "You're right. I am moved by all of the love in this room."

Peace descended over her. At that moment, she believed her future already decided. She could not leave these people and spurn what they offered her. In less than two days, she would become Elinor de Montfort. Elinor Swan would no longer exist. She would give up wearing her boyish clothes, though she still might sneak down and visit Joseph's raptors every now and then. She would dress as her station required and be known as the daughter-in-law of the Earl and Countess of Kinwick. No one would think to look for her here. No one knew she'd come south, much less to Kinwick. No one from Whitley knew she was to marry Hal.

Elinor Swan would cease to exist. As Elinor de Montfort, she would have the protection of the de Montfort name and all the men who would swear to keep her safe from harm.

Joy filled her. She *could* marry Hal and never look back—only forward.

"I would like to dance," she proclaimed, brushing the tears from her cheeks. "I never have and think it's about time I learned."

All the women around her smiled. Merryn ordered the trestle tables moved to the walls and for minstrels to come at once. Hal fought to make his way to her.

"Are you all right?" he asked, concern written on his brow.

"Never more right than now," she replied. "Unless, of course, the times I am in your arms with you inside me."

He rewarded her with a kiss that went on and on. In the distance, Elinor heard whoops but ignored them.

Then music began and Hal swept her to the center of the great hall.

"You will dance like you never have before, my love," he promised, a wicked gleam in his eyes.

She gave him a flirtatious smile. "Since I've never danced at all, my lord, I look forward to learning something new."

Hal yanked her to him and whispered in her ear, "And I look forward to our wedding night. We will dance in the sheets until dawn and beyond."

ELINOR AWOKE. NO nightmares had come to disrupt her sleep, as they had ever since she'd escaped from Whitley.

*It was her wedding day.*

The last of the de Montfort family had reached Kinwick last night. Ancel, the oldest brother and Alys' twin, had come with his wife, Margery, and their two children, Cyrus and Miranda. At five, Cyrus reminded Elinor of what Hal would have been like at the same age. Along with them came Cecily, Raynor's oldest child, with her husband, William, and their two sweet little ones. Being around so many babes made Elinor wonder what kind of mother she would be. The thought of giving birth made her nervous but she knew how eager Hal was for children. She vowed to be a better mother than the one who'd given birth to her. Her children would have a loving mother and father and never be neglected in any way.

As Elinor listened to the soft breaths of Jessimond next to her, she tried to remember how many children each married de Montfort had and what their names were. She believed she could finally remember who everyone was, even Merryn's brother and his wife, who had visited each day and would attend today's wedding.

A knock at the door caused her to spring from the bed. When Elinor opened it, a line of women stood outside with buckets of water. Merryn ordered them in and they began to fill a tub that two men at the rear brought and placed on the floor. As hot water steamed from it, Merryn poured in a vial and stirred the water with her hand. The sweet smell of lavender filled the air.

Then all the female de Montfort relatives seem to descend from nowhere. Elinor gave herself over to their ministrations. She was bathed and dried. Dressed in a smock of blue and a sideless surcoat of gold and embroidered with the same blue while Nan slid a blue garter up each leg to secure her hose. Jessimond slipped a new pair of shoes on her feet, so feminine and unlike the boots she wore each day. Alys brushed her hair until it dried and then shone. Nan handed her a small mirror.

Elinor's cheeks were full of color. Her eyes sparkled. It was the first time she'd ever seen her own image.

"She wears the look of a woman in love," Beatrice commented.

"And you should know," Elysande replied. She glanced around the room. "All of us who are married know, for we are fortunate enough to have made love matches. As you will today, Elinor."

Merryn came and stood before her. "I wore this circlet when Geoffrey and I wed. Would you care to wear it?"

Elinor's throat grew thick and she found it impossible to reply. She nodded and Merryn placed it on the crown of her head and helped her rise to her feet.

"I think you make a lovely bride," Margery told her. "Hal will think an angel has come from Heaven itself when he sees you."

"Tilda, let the others know we are ready," Merryn told a hovering servant. "Ladies, if you will proceed to the chapel, we will be with you shortly."

Everyone but Merryn filed out the door. She gave Elinor one last look and embraced her gently.

"I don't want to wrinkle you. But you do look lovely. As lovely as any de Montfort bride has ever been."

Geoffrey appeared in the doorway, looking handsome and distinguished. Elinor thought to the future and how Hal might look much the same come their own daughter's wedding day.

"Are you ready?" He offered her his arm.

Merryn kissed Elinor's cheek and then her husband's. The three left the bedchamber and proceeded to the chapel. Kinwick stood empty since everyone awaited them at the chapel but Elinor inhaled the scent of cooked goose and venison as they passed the great hall. Merryn had asked what she wanted served at the wedding feast and Elinor had discussed the menu with Cook. She had told the old woman that whatever Cook wanted to serve, they would all be happy to eat since her every creation was a delight. The servant's eyes had crinkled as she laughed heartily, happy at the compliment received from Elinor.

Merryn gave a wave and headed toward the chapel as minstrels assembled before them. The band of men began to play a merry tune as they started out. Geoffrey and Elinor fell in step behind them. As the music played, her heart beat quickly in anticipation.

In minutes, she would become Elinor de Montfort. Tonight, she and Hal would come together as man and wife. She blinked away the tears of happiness that misted her eyes as they passed the large circle of wedding guests that surrounded the doors of the chapel.

Geoffrey led her to a waiting Hal, who looked beyond handsome in midnight blue, his blue eyes vivid as he watched her glide toward him. Geoffrey handed her off to his son and Hal entwined his fingers through hers as they came to stand before the door of the church. Father Dannet, the Kinwick priest, met them there.

Since Elinor had never attended a wedding, she did not know what to expect. The priest asked them several questions, including if they were of age and if they had parental consent. That took Elinor aback for a moment. She hated that even the mention of her parents intruded on this happy day.

Father Dannet asked more questions before he gave a short homily. Elinor tamped down her impatience, wanting to speak her vows and bind herself to Hal forever.

Finally, it came time for them to pledge their love in front of those gathered. The priest had them face one another, their hands joined. Elinor trembled, her nerves getting the better of her, but Hal stood tall and confident.

"Sir Hal de Montfort, will thou have this woman to be thy wedded wife, to live together after God's ordinance in the holy estate of matrimony? Wilt thou love her, comfort her, honor and keep her, in sickness and in health; and forsaking all others, keep thee only unto her, so long as ye both shall live?"

Hal's voice rang out. "I will." His eyes held all the love in the world—and it was for her.

"Lady Elinor Swan, will thou . . ."

The priest's words became lost in the thunderous noise of many horses approaching. Everyone turned to see who arrived since all wedding guests had been accounted for.

As the first riders rounded the corner, cold fear tightened about her heart. The Swan family banner appeared.

*They had come for her, just as they had in her nightmares.*

# CHAPTER 25

Hal did not recognize the banner the rider carried but he noticed how tightly Elinor gripped his hands. Then Lord Nigel Swan came into view and dismounted from his horse.

Why would the Baron of Nelham choose to come to his cousin's wedding, especially when he had totally rejected her?

Suddenly, Elinor yanked her hands from his. Pain filled her eyes. "I cannot marry you. Forgive me, Hal. 'Tis not meant to be."

Terror laced with panic spread through him. He could not lose Elinor. Not now. Not after all they had been through.

The gathered crowd had parted so that the baron now stood before them. Beside him, he held the hand of a young boy and girl. Hal assumed these were the motherless children he'd spoken of when Hal had confronted the man at Whitley.

Elinor stepped toward the nobleman. "I know why you are here, Cousin Nigel. I promise to go with you quietly. Please, say nothing. I don't want anyone to know."

Confusion wrinkled the baron's brow. "Why would you go anywhere with me, Cousin Elinor? I have come here to right a wrong."

"I know," she hissed. "I understand the wrong must be righted but I beg you. Do not say anything in front of these good people. Please."

Lord Nigel raised the hands of the children. "First, I come to introduce you to Dumphey, my son, who will become the baron one day. And this is Helewyse, my girl. I wanted you to meet them, as you should have long before now. They are here to witness their father correct his sins. If I am to be a good example to my children, then I must start by making amends with you, Elinor."

"Amends?" she echoed.

Hal brought a protective arm about her shoulders and took one of her hands, which had turned ice cold. She didn't seem to notice as she gaped at Lord Nigel.

"Aye, Cousin. I can never undo the damage done to you by your father but I vow from this day forth to set things right between us."

He freed his hands and gestured to a soldier who'd come to stand behind him. The man handed over a large, leather pouch, which the baron gave to Hal. He took the bag, wondering what it contained.

Lord Nigel continued. "I have given your intended the bridal price Sir Hal should have received from the Swan family. I know your father never would have paid one because he cared so little for you. Frankly, I had no intention of paying one until this man came to see me."

The baron drew in a deep breath and exhaled slowly. "After his visit, I wallowed in pity for weeks because I'd lost my wife—yet my thoughts kept turning to you, Cousin. How we'd been forbidden to even mention your name for years. How you'd been sent away and had nothing—and yet this good knight somehow found you deep within that forest and wanted to marry you. He chastised me for not doing the right thing when I became Baron of Nelham. I could have restored you to our family and given you your due respect. I was remiss. For that, I apologize."

The nobleman locked eyes with Elinor. "I can never make it up to you, I fear. I only hope that one day you will find it in your heart to forgive me." He looked about. "I promise not to intrude further, as I see we have interrupted your wedding to Sir Hal. I did want to show my support of you by letting you know 'tis your family who provides your dowry to the de Montforts. My children have seen that I am a flawed man. I have made mistakes, Cousin, but I am trying to rectify this one."

Lord Nigel stepped toward Elinor and kissed her cheek.

"Wait!" she cried as he turned to leave.

Hal gripped her shoulder but she ignored him.

"I must go with you, Nigel. I must atone for my sins." Elinor bowed her head. "I am the one who killed your wife, my lord. I murdered Lady Rohesia."

The color drained from the nobleman's face. "What?" he whispered, as the gathered crowd shifted restlessly.

Elinor shook Hal's hand from her. Her eyes met his. "I am sorry, Hal. This is why I cannot marry you. 'Tis why I ran away before. I did not want to damage your reputation or stain your family's good name because of my sins. I was selfish to think I could wed you and ignore what I've done but the time has come to pay for what I have done."

"But you did not kill Lady Rohesia, Elinor," Hal said calmly, defying the heart that raced inside him.

"I did!" she proclaimed. She looked in anguish to her cousin. "I did not mean to, Nigel. I swear I didn't. And I am so sorry I caused Lady Rohesia's death."

"But... but... they told me she fell," the nobleman said. "How could you have killed her?"

"I provoked her," Elinor insisted. "She had replaced me as Whitley's falconer. She told me she was sending me away to the north because I was such a wicked person. I told her she had no authority over me and left the solar."

Elinor began crying. "She ran after me. She said things. Awful, terrible things. She demanded I give her total obedience. I refused. She was so angry with me, Nigel. She said I had betrayed my family when, in truth, I had none. When she saw I refused to give in to her demands, she turned away in frustration and lost her footing on the hem of her gown. She fell. *I made her fall.*"

Tears glittered in Lord Nigel's eyes. Hal clenched Elinor's shoulders and spun her to face him. Her eyes had glazed over, as if she were in shock.

"A man in battle swings his sword and kills. 'Tis a deliberate action against an enemy. Did you push Lady Rohesia, Elinor? Did you knock her down those stairs? Did you force her to lose her balance, on purpose, and take her life?"

She shook her head. "Nay. I was at the bottom of the staircase. But—"

"There *is* no but, Elinor. Lady Rohesia had a tragic accident—*but you did not cause it*. She fell of her own accord. You could not have saved her. You did not kill her, sweetheart. You weren't the one who caused her bodily injury." He shook her, hard. "You are not a murderess, love. You are blameless."

Hal prayed he had gotten through to her. He looked to Lord Nigel for support. Color had returned to the baron's face.

"Elinor?"

Hal turned her to face her cousin. His arm went round her waist to support her quivering frame.

"You did not kill her, Elinor. I know how full of hate Rohesia could be. She was an unhappy woman, no matter what happiness I tried to bring her. 'Twas her anger which killed her, Elinor. Her rage. That alone caused her to fall. Not you. 'Twas an accident."

Lord Nigel drew close to her. "I do not blame you, Cousin." He kissed her forehead and stepped back.

Elinor went limp. Hal scooped her up into his arms and watched her eyelids flutter and then close.

Suddenly, his mother appeared at his elbow.

"She's only fainted, Hal. She will be fine. Take her into the chapel. Tilda!" Merryn called over her shoulder. "Bring my satchel."

---

ELINOR'S MOUTH FELT dry. She licked her lips, which seemed parched.

"She's awake," a voice said.

Opening her eyes, she saw she rested on the ground. Her eyes searched the place and discovered she was inside the Kinwick chapel. Then everything came rushing back to her. Nigel's arrival. The vows halted. Her cousin's heartfelt apology and gift of the bridal price.

And her confession to killing Rohesia Swan.

But no one blamed her. Not Hal. Not Nigel.

Warm lips pressed against her forehead.

*Hal . . .*

"Are you well?" he asked softly, his breath tickling her cheek.

Elinor pushed up using her elbows and saw her feet sitting in Merryn's lap.

"You fainted," the noblewoman said. "'Tis best to lie flat with your feet raised when that occurs." She smiled. "You had some shocking news."

Hal took Elinor's hand and tenderly kissed her fingers. "I am so sorry that you thought you were to blame. That you tried to run. I wish you would have told me what troubled you."

Elinor closed her eyes as he brushed the back of his fingers against her cheek, savoring his touch. She opened them and said, "When I learned from Merryn that you went to Whitley, I knew you would find out the truth about Lady Rohesia's death. As a knight, you are sworn to bring justice. I couldn't bear the thought of you being the one to retrieve me and escort me to the hangman's noose."

She wiped her eyes. "I've had nightmares of the Nelham soldiers riding in as they did today, ready to take me into custody and return me to Whitley. I hoped with my name changing and living far from Cousin Nigel, no one would ever find me at Kinwick."

Sitting up, she latched on to Hal's hands. "I planned to leave. I didn't want to bring shame to your family and cause you more unhappiness. I know how miserable you were after the Battle of Radcot Bridge." She sniffed. "But then all of your family arrived and they were so kind and friendly. They showed me unconditional love simply because we'd chosen to be together. I wanted that. I wanted you. I wanted to be a part of this marvelous family."

"And so you shall be," Hal promised. "Whenever you wish." He looked at her lovingly. "Nigel has stayed. He is very worried about you."

"Father Dannet and all your guests are waiting, too," Merryn added. "He is willing to continue the ceremony but only if you feel up to it."

Elation poured through Elinor. No guilt remained. She had the love of a man who would walk through fire for her. "Then what are we waiting for?"

Hal helped her to her feet. Her first two steps proved shaky, so he swept her into his arms and carried her through the oak doors and into the spring day. A blue sky and warm sunshine greeted them, along with cheers from all who had waited patiently. Elinor's eyes swept across those gathered, feeling the love flow from them to her and Hal. She caught sight of Nigel, who nodded graciously.

Hal set her back on her feet, his arm firm about her waist. He looked to Father Dannet. "We are ready to continue, Father. I believe we left off with my having declared my vows. 'Tis time for Elinor to do the same."

The priest continued with the nuptial mass as if no interruption had occurred. Elinor repeated the same vows Hal had sworn to as she looked into the eyes of the man she would forever love. Then Father Dannet asked for the ring. Edward produced one and the priest blessed it. He returned it to Hal, who lifted her hand.

Placing the ring on her thumb, he said, "With this ring I thee wed and with my body I thee honor." He moved it to her next finger and the next as he promised, "With all my worldly goods I thee endow."

Finally, he slipped the ring on her fourth finger. "In the name of the Father, and of the Son, and of the Holy Spirit. Amen."

Father Dannet motioned for them to follow him inside the chapel. Hal and Elinor did so, with their guests falling in behind them. After more prayers, a mass was said. The priest directed Hal to finalize the ceremony by kissing his bride.

Hal's arms went about Elinor and drew her close. He bent and told her, "This will be the first of thousands of kisses that we share, Wife. I will try to make each one better than the one before."

With that, his lips met hers.

# EPILOGUE

*Kinwick Castle—Late August 1388*

HAL WATCHED THE exercises in the training yard from the dais. His father and Gilbert had left half an hour before, putting him in charge. Scanning the pairs of men engage in combat, he stopped to watch Ronald and another squire square off. He smiled as Ronald dispatched his opponent quickly, thanks to incorporating suggestions Hal had given the lad during previous practices.

He jumped down and strolled through the yard, giving advice to some men and demonstrating to others. When he reached Ronald, he motioned to him. Ronald came quickly.

"You are improving every day," he told the squire, whose grin spread wide at the compliment. "You aren't favoring your right anymore."

"That was a hard lesson to learn, my lord," the boy said. "Being right-handed, I have always felt that side stronger. But thanks to you, I'm not only aware I do so, I've stopped preferring it. I treat each side and hand equally now."

"It shows. Keep up the good work."

Ronald returned to his sparring partner. Both picked up a mace and went at it again.

"You're good with the men, Hal."

He turned and saw Gilbert had joined him. "Thank you, Gilbert. I appreciate your kind words. You have been in charge of the men's training since before I was born, so your opinion means a great deal to me."

The captain of Kinwick's guard nodded in acknowledgement. "Lord Geoffrey wishes to see you. He's in the solar."

"I'll go at once."

Hal set off for the keep, thinking his father wished to speak with him about the trip planned to the hunting lodge that was set to begin tomorrow. That lodge held a special place in Hal's heart since he'd found Elinor and made love to her there for the first time.

Thoughts of his wife brought a glow to his insides. Elinor now carried their babe in her belly. By January of next year, they would be parents to a boy or girl. Or even twins. Who knew? His mother had birthed Alys and Ancel, while Alys had produced Philippa and Wyatt. Mayhap he and Elinor would also welcome two bundles of joy at the same time.

Hal crossed the bailey and entered the keep. He headed straight to the solar and knocked. His father's deep voice bid him enter. As Hal opened the door, he saw Geoffrey de Montfort sitting at the table, pouring over a missive.

Henry Bolingbroke, the Earl of Derby, stood next to him.

Hal had not seen the king's cousin since that day at Radcot Bridge, when he'd been forced to give up everything he had to the nobleman. Derby looked up and gave him a genuine smile, which made him appear even younger than his one and twenty years.

"Sir Hal, 'tis good to see you again."

Hal bowed his head quickly. "And you, too, my lord."

Derby burst out laughing. "Oh, I doubt that. The last time we saw one another was not pleasant for you." A shadow crossed his face. "I regret my actions that day."

"Nay, my lord," Hal assured the earl. "You were on the winning side at Radcot. You had an army full of supporters. I had . . . well, I had me." He shrugged nonchalantly, not showing the hurt he still felt at the memory.

"I am sorry we were on opposites sides that day."

"Then return to the side of right and good," Hal tossed out.

Geoffrey de Montfort cleared his throat. "Lord Henry has brought news, Hal. Have a seat. Both of you."

Hal took a place next to his father, while Derby sat across from them.

"You know the Lords Appellant have controlled the government in the king's place for some months," Derby began. "We have failed in our task."

"How?" Hal asked.

"Three weeks ago, the Scots won a resounding victory at Otterburn. The Earl of Douglas led a raid that crossed the border into England, trying to take advantage of the division between Neville and Northumberland, who'd just taken over defending the border. Though we outnumbered them three to one, the Scots took the day—and both of Northumberland's sons."

"Has Douglas continued to press deeper into England?" Hal asked.

"Douglas is dead," Derby said, his voice flat. "But that hasn't stopped the Scots. The Lords Appellant are being blamed for the entire debacle. The north is frightened. The rumbling has begun. By this time next year, I guarantee you that my cousin will be back on his throne and in full control."

"And where will you be, my lord?" Hal challenged.

"If Richard will have me, back in his service and good graces," responded Derby smoothly. "Nottingham, more than likely, will join me in this defection. If anything, the king still has a fondness for me. I'm sure Nottingham and I will be rewarded and the three remaining Lords Appellant removed from office."

"So why are you at Kinwick?" Hal asked, puzzled.

Derby rose and walked to the corner. He retrieved a sword propped there and brought it to Hal.

"To return this to you."

The earl extended the weapon to Hal, who took it in disbelief.

"I thought I would never see this again."

"'Tis yours. It was always yours. I determined to return your sword to you the moment you handed it over to me. I know it was a hard thing to do, Hal. You were a brave man that day, in front of all those soldiers. You hold my admiration and my respect."

Derby offered his hand and Hal clasped it.

"Mayhap, we will cross paths again in London," the earl said. "Until then." He bowed to Geoffrey and left the room.

Hal turned to his father. "If the border wars are heating up, then you will be required to send men." A sick feeling washed over him. He knew he would have to go to war again—and most likely miss the birth of his first child.

Geoffrey nodded. "I will. Derby and I spoke of it. The call will go out soon. The Lords Appellant cannot leave unanswered what the Scots have begun." He rose and placed a hand on Hal's shoulder. "But you will not be part of the soldiers I send."

Anger flickered inside him. "You cannot show favoritism toward me, Father. I am one of your best knights. I must go and lead the Kinwick men."

"Nay. My captain of the guard never leaves Kinwick. He stays behind to ensure the protection of my castle and lands."

It took a moment for Hal to understand the meaning behind his father's words. "I . . . am to be your captain?" Astonishment filled him. "What about Gilbert?"

"Gilbert and I agree the time has come for you to take his place, Hal."

Elation poured through him. "I am most honored, Father. I never expected such recognition."

Geoffrey smiled. "I always expected this day would come. I planned for years for you to become Kinwick's captain. The time is now right."

"I hope Gilbert will choose to assist me in the yard."

"Nay. He specifically requested not to do so. He doesn't want the men's attention or loyalty divided between the two of you." Geoffrey chuckled. "Gilbert is retiring to a cottage I have given him. With Tilda."

"Tilda? *Our* Tilda?"

"Aye. It seems they have carried on with one another for years and none of us suspected a thing. Tilda will leave our service to care for her husband. Of course, that means another wedding."

"How is Mother taking this? Tilda has been by her side for many years."

"Merryn will be fine. She will depend more on Elinor to help her run Kinwick, though, whenever she is not working with Joseph and the raptors."

"Elinor would be delighted to have a larger role," Hal confirmed. "I will find her now and tell her." He grinned. "And let her know she is now bedding the captain of the guard."

He hugged Geoffrey tightly. "Thank you for having confidence in me, Father."

Hal left the solar, feeling as if he walked on air as he held his sword in his hand. He saw Elinor down the corridor from their chamber. Before he could call out to her, she paused and brought both hands to her belly. Cold fear gripped him. Margery had lost a babe several months after she conceived. Ancel told Hal he still felt sorrow from the loss of their little one.

Racing down the hall, he reached his wife. His sword clanged to the ground. Elinor looked up and gave him a brilliant smile.

She grabbed his hand and rested it against her belly, both her hands atop his one. "Wait," she commanded.

Hal looked in her eyes, confused. Then something bumped his hand. Once. Twice. He beamed from ear to ear.

"'Tis the babe?" he asked.

Elinor nodded. "I have felt small twinges until just now. This was a kick. I'm certain of it. Oh, Hal, I am so glad you are here to share this moment with me."

He stared in wonder at her rounded belly. Another nudge pushed at his hand. Hal bent and cradled her belly with his hands. "Greetings, little one. We cannot wait for your arrival."

Rising, he captured her hand and brought it palm up to his lips and pressed a fervent kiss to the center. Elinor's gaze met his, full of desire.

"Shall we celebrate feeling the babe move?" she asked, her lips twitching in amusement.

He retrieved the sword to show her. "We have many things to rejoice in. Our babe. The Earl of Derby returning my sword." Hal paused as her eyes grew wide. "And I have just learned that my father has appointed me his new captain of the guard."

Elinor squealed in excitement and threw her arms about his neck, pulling him down for a slow kiss.

She finally broke the kiss and said seductively, "I believe I mentioned a celebration, Husband?"

Hal swept her off her feet and stepped through their chamber door. He kicked it shut with his foot and took her to their bed.

"I like the way you think, Wife." He placed her on the bed and began removing her shoes. "I plan to work my way from the crown of your head to your tiniest toe. By the time I finish, hours from now, you will be loved completely."

"Completely?"

"Thoroughly."

"Thoroughly?" she echoed.

Hal nodded.

"Then you better get started," Elinor told him.

So he did.

*Knights of Honor Series* by Alexa Aston
Word of Honor
Marked by Honor
Code of Honor
Journey to Honor
Heart of Honor
Bold in Honor
Love and Honor
Gift of Honor

## About the Author

As a child, Alexa Aston gathered her neighborhood friends together and made up stories for them to act out, her first venture into creating memorable characters. Following her passion for history and love of learning, she became a teacher who began writing on the side to maintain her sanity in a sea of teenage hormones.

Alexa's historical romances use history as a backdrop to place her characters in extraordinary circumstances, where their intense desire for one another grows into the treasured gift of love.

She is the author of *The Knights of Honor*, a medieval romance series that takes place in 14th century England during the reign of Edward III and centers on the de Montfort family. Each romance focuses on the code of chivalry that bound knights of this era.

A native Texan, Alexa lives with her husband in a Dallas suburb, where she eats her fair share of dark chocolate and plots out stories while she walks every morning. She enjoys reading, watching movies and sports, and can't get enough of *Fixer Upper* or *Game of Thrones*. Alexa also writes romantic suspense, western historicals, and standalone medieval novels as Lauren Linwood.

Alexa loves to hear from her readers. You can connect with her through FB, Twitter, and her website: alexaaston.com.

Facebook: facebook.com/authoralexaaston

Twitter: twitter.com/AlexaAston

BookBub Follow: bookbub.com/authors/alexa-aston

Newsletter sign-up: madmimi.com/signups/422152/join

Amazon Page: amazon.com/author/alexaaston

Made in the USA
Middletown, DE
04 August 2018